CW00673884

WARHAMMER
AGE of SIGMAR

Lady of SORROWS

C L Werner

BLACK LIBRARY

A BLACK LIBRARY PUBLICATION

First published in 2020.
This edition published in Great Britain in 2021 by
Black Library,
Games Workshop Ltd.,
Willow Road,
Nottingham,
NG7 2WS, UK.

10 9 8 7 6 5 4 3 2 1

Produced by Games Workshop in Nottingham.
Cover illustration by Alexander Mokhov.

Lady of Sorrows © Copyright Games Workshop Limited 2021. Lady
of Sorrows, GW, Games Workshop, Black Library, Warhammer,
Warhammer Age of Sigmar, Stormcast Eternals, and all associated
logos, illustrations, images, names, creatures, races, vehicles,
locations, weapons, characters, and the distinctive likenesses
thereof, are either ® or TM, and/or © Games Workshop Limited,
variably registered around the world.
All Rights Reserved.

A CIP record for this book is available from the British Library.

ISBN 13: 978-1-78999-264-9

No part of this publication may be reproduced, stored in a retrieval
system, or transmitted in any form or by any means, electronic,
mechanical, photocopying, recording or otherwise, without the
prior permission of the publishers.

This is a work of fiction. All the characters and events portrayed
in this book are fictional, and any resemblance to real people or
incidents is purely coincidental.

See Black Library on the internet at

blacklibrary.com

Find out more about Games Workshop
and the worlds of Warhammer at

games-workshop.com

Printed and bound by CPI Group (UK) Ltd, Croydon, CR0 4YY

Kevin Ross, for all our assorted misdeeds

From the maelstrom of a sundered world, the
Eight Realms were born. The formless and the divine
exploded into life.

Strange new worlds appeared in the firmament, each one
gilded with spirits, gods and men. Noblest of the gods was
Sigmar. For years beyond reckoning he illuminated the realms,
wreathed in light and majesty as he carved out his reign. His
strength was the power of thunder. His wisdom was infinite.
Mortal and immortal alike kneeled before his lofty throne.
Great empires rose and, for a while, treachery was banished.
Sigmar claimed the land and sky as his own and ruled over a
glorious age of myth.

But cruelty is tenacious. As had been foreseen, the great
alliance of gods and men tore itself apart. Myth and legend
crumbled into Chaos. Darkness flooded the realms. Torture,
slavery and fear replaced the glory that came before. Sigmar
turned his back on the mortal kingdoms, disgusted by their
fate. He fixed his gaze instead on the remains of the world he
had lost long ago, brooding over its charred core, searching
endlessly for a sign of hope. And then, in the dark heat of
his rage, he caught a glimpse of something magnificent. He
pictured a weapon born of the heavens. A beacon powerful
enough to pierce the endless night. An army hewn from
everything he had lost.

Sigmar set his artisans to work and for long ages they toiled,
striving to harness the power of the stars. As Sigmar's great
work neared completion, he turned back to the realms and saw
that the dominion of Chaos was almost complete. The hour
for vengeance had come. Finally, with lightning blazing across
his brow, he stepped forth to unleash his creations.

The Age of Sigmar had begun.

...and so it came to pass that the bane of Belvegrod was passed on unto those who would reclaim the Drowned City. From the restless grave did the Lady of Sorrows strike, marshalling her spectral hosts until they were as grains of sand upon the shore. Up from their accursed tombs did they rise, to visit death and despair against the living – remorseless as the clutch of death, relentless as the fury of darkness.

Neither prayer nor deed could defy the curse set down. Ever and again would the Lady of Sorrows turn her wrath against the inheritors of Belvegrod. Her victims piled like cordwood in the streets, the weeping of mourners rolling across the waters like a roaring storm. Still her hosts would come, ceaseless and indefatigable, striking out against the living who dared defy her vengeance. Unto the tenth generation and beyond, still there could be no slaughter sufficient to satisfy her wrath. Upon each generation would her hate be spent that all should share in misery and weep for those borne away by the haunters of night.

Never should there come an end to the lamentations of the living. Never should peace descend upon Belvegrod. Never should the cycle of death be concluded until the curse be broken.

CHAPTER ONE

The Belvegrod lighthouse was a relic of another age. It stood atop
a great spire of rock that stretched away from the jagged cliff face
like the prow of a ship. A sheer drop of two hundred feet from the
edge before the murky depths of Graveswater, and still another
two hundred feet from the summit of the cliff to the pinnacle
of the lighthouse. Colossal in scale, the tower might have been
raised by gargants such was its enormity. It was the tremendous
scope of its construction as much as its place atop the cliff that
was credited with the structure's survival. It was the only part of
Belvegrod that had withstood the cataclysm that drowned the rest
of the city centuries ago.

Kvetka always felt a sense of awe when she looked up at the
lighthouse. Hundreds of legends were told about it by her people,
passed down from parent to child over countless generations. The
descendants of those who'd fled Belvegrod's destruction spoke of
the last Keeper of the Light, standing fast at his post as the waters
rolled over the city. First his voice had been raised in prayers

to Sigmar for deliverance, but as the catastrophe grew worse he began to curse the God-King with the obscenest oaths. Finally, the Keeper's mind broke and his mad laughter crackled across the desolation, chilling the refugees as they fled the rising tide.

Though it was claimed by the Azyrites that the lighthouse had been cleansed of any malevolent gheists, Kvetka's people knew better. A place as old as the tower was not so easily parted from its past. The Keeper's mad spirit still walked in the night, climbing the steps to his eternal post. The only sure way to escape his spectral attentions was to carry a hoop of wolfbloom inside the left shoe or the left glove. A gheist was always drawn to the sinister side of a person, but the spurs of the wolfbloom would turn it away.

Kvetka flexed her gloved fingers and winced as the sharp spurs scraped her skin. 'You don't really believe in that,' she told herself. Certainly the Azyrites disdained what they considered heathen superstition. They took no safeguards against the Keeper's gheist and none of them had run afoul of his spirit. The Reclaimed had an answer for that, of course. Her people said the gheist only showed itself to those who belonged in Belvegrod, not to outsiders.

The Azyrites made it easy to dislike them. They were a proud and haughty people, arrogant in their customs and manners. They weren't of Shyish and never failed to seize a moment when they could remind the Reclaimed of that fact. Their eyes had beheld the wonders of Azyrheim and the Celestial Realm and for them there was no other standard of quality. They had no time for the traditions and sensitivities of others, still less for trying to understand.

'Careful, Kvetka, or you will start sounding like Ivor,' she chided herself. She pulled her cloak a bit tighter about her shoulders to fight the chill wafting up the cliff from Graveswater. She looked back down the winding trail to the city below.

No, Kvetka corrected herself, not a city but rather two towns. Two settlements that were as distinct from one another as a duardin and an orruk. The Twinned Towns, they were called by travellers, but only because of their proximity to one another. Both had been raised upon the ruins of the old city when the flood was drawn away by the magic of Sigmar's Stormcasts. A part of Belvegrod was exposed, expanding the island on which the lighthouse stood.

The colonists from Azyr, following in the wake of Sigmar's knights, established the town of Westreach. They used the old ruins as a quarry, razing what had been to build homes such as they'd known in their own realm. The Reclaimed settled the other half of the island, creating the town of Eastdale. They didn't tear down the ruins but rather sought to restore them, to recover something of the glories of their ancestors.

Left to their own, the two peoples kept themselves apart. The townmasters made an effort to foster a sense of comradeship between the communities, but the gulf between them was too wide to bridge. The Azyrites were determined to change everything into a semblance of their own realm. They refused to understand the Reclaimed and their determination to recover the legacy of their own past.

Only at the Belvegrod lighthouse did the two communities regularly interact. Here the wise came together to conduct their studies, seeking to unlock the mysteries of past, present... and future.

The future. Kvetka shivered when she considered what that meant for the Twinned Towns. They existed under a baleful curse that infected them all with misery and despair. Each night, phantoms from the ruins came to prowl and prey upon the living. There was hardly a family in either settlement that hadn't lost someone to the undead. Yet even that was nothing beside the doom that hovered over them all. The Twinned Towns were plagued as no other place by the nighthaunts. Once a generation a great host of the fiends would lay siege to them, driving the people before them like a tidal wave. Commanded by the remorseless Lady of Sorrows, the spectres would sweep over the communities, killing all they caught. For hundreds of years the pattern had been repeated. Each time, the people were driven to the very brink of destruction, but miraculously escaped annihilation. The phantom hosts would falter in the end, receding back into the mists to regather their strength, to await the hour when the Lady of Sorrows would call them once more from their graves.

The future. Was there any for the Twinned Towns aside from this cursed cycle of death and destruction? The answer to that question was what those gathered in the lighthouse sought so keenly. Hope for their people.

Kvetka quickened her step as the path plateaued and she drew closer to the base of the lighthouse. Four guards stood outside the massive iron doors set into the tower's granite walls. Two wore the gilded armour of Westreach, their breastplates sculpted into the sharp beaks of gryphons. The other two wore the studded hauberks of Eastdale, charms and talismans hanging about their necks. The Azyrite guards moved to bar her path, but the Reclaimed soldiers gave them a sharp look and they desisted. Kvetka thanked the men from her town and walked past the guard post. The iron doors loomed before her. As she reached for them, they were suddenly drawn back.

Standing in the doorway was a man she'd hoped to avoid. The Azyrite had a dusky complexion, with eyes like pools of frost. His pure white hair was cut close to his skull, little more than fuzz. His face was sharp and vulturine, devoid of warmth and compassion. Those were qualities that many of Sigmar's warrior priests made an effort to cultivate, but not Mahyar. His was a harsh and uncompromising kind of faith – a faith in which all were found wanting.

Especially if their blood was that of Shyish rather than Azyr.

Mahyar gave her a cold look. 'Ivor has been waiting for you,' the priest stated, his voice as pleasant as a drawn dagger.

Even among the Reclaimed, there were few who cared to cross words with Mahyar. Kvetka was one of those few.

'Hierophant Ivor,' she dared to correct the priest. 'His rank is due the same respect as yours, *Elder* Mahyar.'

Fire boiled up in the priest's eyes. 'Save your sharp tongue for Ivor. He is the one who believes your presence here has some value.' Mahyar stepped aside and gestured to the great winding stair that circled the tower's central column. 'They're in the observatory.'

Kvetka gave him a puzzled look. 'Will you not be attending the augury?'

'Once I have rendered my prayers to Sigmar and requested his wisdom in interpreting the import of these divinations, I shall return for the augury,' Mahyar replied superciliously.

'Oh,' Kvetka said. 'I won't delay you then. It would be a tragedy if your insight was absent. I don't know how we should accomplish anything without your guidance.' A puckish smile was on her face when she turned and made her way to the spiral stair. It was probably too much to ask that Sigmar cause one of his own priests to get lost on the way back to Westreach, but she couldn't help wishing for such a happy occurrence. There were many admirable people in the Sigmarite temple, clergy who strove to treat Azyrite and Reclaimed alike with dignity and consideration. There were also pompous zealots like Mahyar, people so certain of their own rectitude that they treated anyone different with intolerance and contempt.

Yes, Kvetka supposed it was too much to wish Mahyar would break his leg on the way down from the lighthouse, but she made that wish just the same.

* * *

15

Perhaps Kvetka would stumble and break a leg on her way up the lighthouse. It was an uncharitable thing for a priest to wish harm upon someone for anything as petty as the irritation Kvetka always provoked in him, but Mahyar couldn't help the feeling. He'd have to wear a hair shirt under his vestments on the morrow as penance for his resentment of the scholar. There was a difference between upholding the conventions of Sigmar's temple and baser, personal enmity. He wasn't so arrogant as to excuse himself for what he knew was a failing of his own character.

Over the years he'd let Kvetka's impertinence get to him. She took a wicked delight in challenging his authority, never allowing an opportunity to defy him escape. Mahyar was too honest to abuse his position and retaliate. He'd seen for himself that Kvetka's animosity was directed at him alone. She was respectful enough to other priests, and made all the proper observations to the God-King. No, it was a personal dislike between them, the cause of which Mahyar couldn't remember. It no longer mattered. Their mutual hostility didn't need a reason to endure.

Mahyar paused when he reached the guard post outside the tower. He craned his neck back and saw that the immense perspicillum was slowly extending out from the spire of the lighthouse. He indulged in a brief smile. Ivor was always urging haste, frantic that everything and everyone should be assembled as quickly as possible, yet every time the result was the same. Everything would be in readiness and everyone would wait. Try as he might, Ivor couldn't hurry the astrological conjunctions that governed the science of divination.

The priest's footsteps echoed through the lighthouse as he ascended the spiral stairway. The many libraries, studies and laboratories inside the tower were empty now. Everyone was up in the observatory, waiting for the stars to fall into alignment. It was an eerie feeling, to know that he was the only person among all those chambers and corridors. It was a solitude far different from the cell of contemplation in the temple. There, even in isolation, he knew there were other people around. Here, he was alone. That primal, irrational part of his brain magnified every stray sound that reached his ears. Though he would never say it, Mahyar could understand why the Reclaimed imagined the Keeper's gheist haunting the tower. The faint sound of water dripping in some distant room became creeping footsteps. A draught from some crack in the wall became the touch of spectral fingers. Such superstition was rightly condemned, but Mahyar appreciated why it persisted.

A third of the way up the tower voices drifted down to Mahyar. Sometimes he could pick out an isolated word, distinguish an individual voice, but overall it was as intelligible as a cataract's rumble. Still, it was enough to fend off that sense of loneliness as he climbed the stair.

At the top of the stairs, a set of gilded doors opened onto the observatory. In times past, the great light had resided here, throwing its rays across Graveswater to guide ships to Belvegrod's port. The old assemblage for the light, a fabulous mechanism crafted by duardin engineers in a bygone age, still dominated the round room. The light itself, however, had been removed, its role taken over by two lesser beacons constructed by the people of Westreach and Eastdale. Instead, the revolving platform that had once served the light now acted as the base for the perspicillum.

The telescope was immense in its proportions, with a framework of shining bronze inlaid with runes of gold and silver. Within its cylindrical body were concentric rings of the same material, each stamped with their own layers of runes. Mahyar could read enough of the duardin characters to know that many related to vision and distance, perception and understanding. He also knew that the lenses within the perspicillum weren't fashioned from glass, but rather the shed scales of stardrakes polished and cut until they were as thin as parchment and as transparent as water. These panes were then set into round sigmarite frames, the celestial metal binding the lenses so securely that even falling down the steps of the tower couldn't dislodge them.

For all that he put his own trust in omens from his god, Mahyar couldn't help but respect the exacting craftsmanship that had gone into constructing the perspicillum.

The priest turned his attention away from the telescope to the room around it. Scholars sat about the desks, quills in hand, ink and parchment ready before them. He briefly watched Kvetka as she tested the keenness of her quill. Unsatisfied, she began sharpening it with a knife she took from her belt. He frowned when he saw her tap the blade against the edge of her desk three times before returning it to its sheath. If there was any activity the Reclaimed conducted that didn't have some superstition attached to it, he'd yet to discover it.

The desks of the scholars dominated the left half of the observatory. The right half had been surrendered to charts and diagrams, each exactingly represented on a sheet of vellum that was fastened to an ebony frame. The men and women who walked among the stands and consulted the drawings were a mixed group. Most of the wizards from both of the Twinned Towns were here, from grey-headed masters to eager young apprentices. None among those who studied the arcane arts in Westreach and Eastdale would miss one of these auguries if they could help it. They weren't alone, however. Mixed in among the wizards were priests of Sigmar, their white robes providing a marked contrast to the colourful raiment of the mages. The priests were here to offer guidance and support, to invoke Sigmar's favour for the divinations being conducted. At least, that was the more comforting aspect of their presence. Magic, even the most benign kind, could be a capricious servant. There were times when the power invoked by a wizard became uncontrollable and would wreak havoc on the bodies and souls of those it afflicted. Though the lighthouse was defended by innumerable wards and arcane barriers, there was always the threat of a spell running amok or a daemon manifesting itself. If such happened, it was the role of the priests to subdue both cause and effect, to prevent anything conjured within the tower from escaping into the towns below.

'I began to think you wouldn't make it back, brother.' The words were spoken by a tall, emaciated man with a dreamy expression. He wore a golden hammer on a chain around his neck and upon his shorn scalp the same symbol had been branded. His raiment was cut in the same fashion as one of Sigmar's prelates, but where the priests' robes were white, his were a bright blue. His hands clenched a staff topped by a golden icon shaped after the twin-tailed comet of Sigmar.

'Bairam, it is good to see you.' Mahyar felt like a fool as soon as the words left his tongue. The man in the blue robes was an augur, a holy man who'd surrendered his sight in order to focus completely upon the spiritual rather than the physical world. His eyes were completely white, as lifeless as a boiled egg.

'You understand if I cannot return the sentiment,' Bairam chuckled at Mahyar's discomfort. There was no malice in his levity, but rather assurance that he didn't resent the error. For all that he was blind, he had a remarkable sense for reading the emotions of those around him. Bairam called it his second sight, an ability to perceive the nature of people he encountered. He could evaluate the health of a person merely by standing in the same room with them and few were the liars who could deceive him for more than the most fleeting of moments.

'I confess I'm surprised to find you here,' Mahyar said as he helped guide Bairam across the observatory; the augur might be able to perceive a living presence after his strange fashion, but he wasn't so capable when it came to desks and lecterns. 'It is usually your custom to ignore these divinations.'

Bairam nodded. 'Indeed,' he said. 'Many times these rituals reveal nothing of consequence. But today, when I sat before Sigmar's altar in adoration, I was gripped by a compulsion to come here.' His fingers tightened on Mahyar's arm. 'Tonight,' he pronounced, 'they *will* learn something of consequence.'

Mahyar had heard such assurances from wizards and scholars at every one of these rituals. Never had he given their words any importance. When Bairam said it, however, it gave him a feeling of foreboding. He looked aside at the perspicillum and the two duardin engineers who were operating it. The great telescope now extended twenty feet through the hatch in the observatory's domed roof. The ceiling was rotating along with the platform, angling so that it was in the proper alignment.

What was it, Mahyar wondered, that they were going to find tonight?

Kvetka felt the shudder that rolled through the lighthouse as the perspicillum was brought into position and locked into place by the duardin. She glanced up at the narrow band of sky exposed by the open ceiling. The stars were dim and ghostly, their rays as wholesome as an open grave. She turned her eyes towards the Azyrite scholar seated at the desk beside her. Envy swelled in her chest. The man's ancestors had come from another realm, from a place where the sky was beautiful and bright, not menacing and ghoulish. Even if he himself had never seen it, he'd have heard stories passed down through his family, stories about the land they'd come from.

She looked back to the giant telescope. She wasn't about to let anything as petty as unreasoning jealousy distract her now. Let the Azyrites have their stories. Deny it as hard as they wanted, they were people of Shyish now. No more for them the ease and security of Sigmar's realm. They must endure the horrors of Nagash's haunted dominion just like the Reclaimed. They would never make these lands like those they'd left behind, however hard they tried. The sooner the Azyrites understood that, the better things would be for them all.

Ivor walked towards the perspicillum. He was an old man with a long silver beard and pale skin, dressed in golden robes. Most learned of the wizards of Eastdale, he'd ascended to the position of hierophant and governor of the lighthouse by careful politicking as much as for his arcane skills. Ivor knew how to appease his detractors and under his leadership a new co-operation had been reached between the wizards and the Temple of Sigmar, though the gap between Reclaimed and Azyrite was less easily bridged.

'Comrades and colleagues,' Ivor called out when he stood at the perspicillum. Kvetka thought he must have worked some minor spell to project his voice, for his words sounded as though he were standing right next to her.

Now that all eyes were turned towards him, Ivor continued. 'The time is upon us once more. The constellations favour our endeavours.' He pointed his finger up at the ceiling. 'Our vision shall be cast out across the realm. We shall stare upon the edge of Shyish! The perspicillum will reveal to us that place where the grains of tomorrow drain away into the infinite.' He turned his pointing finger upon his audience, making no distinction between wizard, priest or scholar. 'A last warning, my friends. To hunt the future is to pursue the ultimate unknown. What is revealed to us may be the seed of hope or the blight of despair. Those unprepared for the latter would do well to leave now.'

There was a stir among the crowd as a few of the scholars left their desks and removed themselves. Kvetka felt a pang of sympathy. Those who left were young, and this was their first time sitting at one of the divination rites. She could remember her own initiation, twenty years ago, and how overwhelmed she had been by everything. She'd been tempted to walk out too. Only pride had kept her in her chair, an unwillingness to belittle herself in front of Azyrites.

'Do not begrudge them their reticence,' Ivor said. For just a moment Kvetka saw him focus on the augur Bairam and a worried look came onto the wizard's face. 'Perhaps after we read the portents, we will wish that we too had absented ourselves.'

The hierophant said no more. Turning to the duardin, he gave them a brief nod. One engineer worked a flywheel at the back of the perspicillum, the other threw a series of levers along the telescope's side. A low, ghostly moan rattled through the observatory. A grey light erupted from an angled tube at the back of the device. Upon the smoothed dome of the ceiling the light flickered, hazy and indistinct. Ivor now joined the duardin in their labours, helping them adjust the machinery.

From a grey haze, the image being projected upon the ceiling now resolved itself into clarity. Kvetka watched as a rippling wave slowly undulated across the dome: not a liquid tide, but a gritty stream of grains. They were looking upon the sifting gravesands that gathered on the edge of Shyish. Each mote of substance was the crystallisation of a lost tomorrow, all the days and hours stripped away from the dead.

The gathered wizards were intent upon the projected image. Kvetka could feel the atmosphere in the observatory change as they drew on their magic. Each of them reached out to the distant gravesands, seeking to draw meaning from the sifting grains. As some fragment of wisdom was drawn out of the cascade, the gleaning wizard would call out the impression that was conveyed. Random words, shards of a greater whole, but the scholars dutifully copied every word that they distilled from the babble.

Kvetka had a talent for this part of the rite. Over the years she'd honed her concentration like a razor, able to focus upon one thing and ignore all others. Ivor himself was always impressed by her method and had often bemoaned the fact that so few scholars were able to emulate her ability. If they could, then each could record a different wizard and nothing would be lost during the ritual.

Tonight, Kvetka's focus was on Gajevic, a thin, bookish wizard from Eastdale. Even if he was a wizard, she was still puzzled that Ivor had asked her to pay attention to such an unremarkable man. He was timid, awkward and always furtively looking for some avenue of escape when forced into any kind of social interaction; there was nothing that impressed Kvetka as important about Gajevic.

Clearly, however, something had impressed Bairam. Kvetka could see the Sigmarite augur faced towards Gajevic, his blind eyes staring emptily at the wizard. That, she was now certain, was why Ivor had requested she pay close attention to Gajevic: some premonition Bairam had that was related to him.

'Crypt' was the first word Kvetka wrote down. It was far from the last. Over the course of an hour there were many others. Alone they had no meaning. Later, like pieces of a puzzle, they would try to fit them together into some coherent revelation.

Four sheets of parchment were filled with Gajevic's words. The ink on Kvetka's quill changed in hue as time passed, from black to blue and then to a fiery orange. It was vital the sequence of the words be known if there was to be any meaning gleaned from them, a purpose the changeling ink fulfilled.

It was as Kvetka was starting on a fifth sheet of parchment that Gajevic's voice rose in a scream. There was no need for anyone to write down the words he shouted.

'The Lady of Sorrows!' Gajevic cried, before collapsing to the floor. In the same instant, the projected image on the ceiling lost its focus. Ivor and the duardin tried to restore the projection while several of the watching priests moved to examine Gajevic. The hierophant and the engineers failed to bring back the perspicillum's picture of the gravesands, but the priests were able to rouse Gajevic from his stupor.

'What happened? Is the ritual over?' Gajevic asked as he was helped back to his feet.

It was the stern warrior priest Mahyar who answered the wizard. 'You screamed,' he said. His eyes took on a steely glint and Kvetka could see his fingers curling about the knife on his belt. 'You invoked something profane before you collapsed.'

Gajevic gaped at Mahyar, utterly oblivious to the menace in his tone or the knife that could be drawn in the next heartbeat. 'I screamed?' He ran his hands through his hair, as though he could knead the answer into his brain. 'What does it mean?'

Kvetka rose from behind her desk. 'We must study what the wizards have gleaned from the gravesands,' she declared. Her voice was loud enough to carry across the observatory, but her eyes were fixed on Mahyar. 'Then, perhaps, we'll know what it means.'

Mahyar returned her scrutiny with a scowl, but his fingers drifted away from the knife. He walked over to join Bairam. For the moment, at least, the warrior priest appeared satisfied.

'All of you, gather your notes,' Ivor called to the scholars. 'Bring them together and we will try to arrange them as they were spoken.' He looked over to Kvetka. 'Make a copy of what you have recorded. Denote each word in the order you wrote it down. We may want to refer back to the original.'

'Yes, excellency,' Kvetka replied. She didn't question the request, though she'd never heard it made before. The usual practice was to cross out words as their place in the sequence was determined, yet Ivor wanted her original retained for consultation.

There was something else that was unusual. Deciphering the

divination was a process that could take hours, if not days. Once they were satisfied the perspicillum hadn't drawn some daemon back from the edge of the realm, the priests would make their departure.

This time, however, the priests made no move to leave. When Kvetka glanced over to where Mahyar was standing, he had an expectant look on his face. He was waiting for something.

Waiting. Mahyar was a zealous man, pious and sincere in his faith. There was nothing he wouldn't do if he felt it to be Sigmar's will. Yet the supreme test of faith for him was waiting. Inactivity. Enforced idleness. As the hours crawled by he imagined the damned in the lowest underworlds, tortured by their misdeeds.

'Patience is the noblest virtue,' Bairam said, his eerie senses picking up on Mahyar's mood.

'I was born in a hut slapped together from the rubble of a hovel,' Mahyar stated. 'There isn't a speck of noble blood in my veins.'

Bairam chuckled at the retort. 'Believe then that your perseverance isn't without purpose.' He waved his hand vaguely to where the scholars were cobbling together the results of the ritual. 'You know that I surrendered my sight so that I might perceive the God-King's will clearly. You've witnessed the veracity of my premonitions before. I tell you, never has an omen been borne to me with such intensity as the one that compelled me to attend tonight's ritual. A revelation of great importance is before us.'

Mahyar looked towards the wizard Gajevic and considered the words he'd screamed. 'Perhaps it would've been better if it was all for nothing.'

'Perhaps,' Bairam conceded, 'but would it be better to prepare for a calamity before it strikes, or sit in blissful ignorance until its force cannot be escaped? The wheel of fate turns, with or without our consent. If there is a chance, however remote, to end this cycle of despair, would that not be worth knowing? The Twinned Towns will always exist at the edge of annihilation so long as the Lady of Sorrows threatens us, so long as her spectres prey upon our people and bleed the vitality from our community.'

Agitation among the scholars drew Mahyar's attention. He saw a few of them rush into the observatory with stacks of books. They'd been consulting a wide array of scrolls and tomes, both sacred texts brought down from Azyr by the first colonists and eldritch volumes salvaged from Belvegrod's dim past. The Azyrites preferred to rely upon the enlightened wisdom found in their books while the Reclaimed perused the superstitious dread of their ancestors – different interpretations that could seldom be reconciled. Mahyar knew the resulting debates could last for months as each faction argued some trifling nuance that favoured their own resources.

Ivor, however, was unwilling to allow the usual deliberations. He kept referring to one set of notes as a framework upon which everything else had to be built. Mahyar was irked to find this record the hierophant put so much value on had been written down by Kvetka.

'My friends, the arguing of details is pointless,' Ivor declared, trying to appease the arguing factions. He held up Kvetka's notes. 'We understand the pattern. We know what is before us.'

'What is before us is doom,' one of the Azyrite scholars moaned. 'The revelation means doom to our people. The Lady of Sorrows is coming with her legions...'

'She has come against us before with her armies,' Mahyar interrupted. 'By the grace and glory of Sigmar, we've defied her efforts to wipe us out.'

'It's been twenty years since she attacked our towns,' another scholar stated.

'Then we're about due to suffer her attentions again,' Mahyar said. 'Take courage,' he advised the frightened scholar. 'Courage is the best armour against the nighthaunts. We've beaten back the undead before. If we remain stalwart, we shall do so again.'

Kvetka stood up from her desk. She pounced on Mahyar's last word as if it were the choicest of morsels. 'What if there never had to be another "again"? What if we could ensure our towns need never fear the Lady of Sorrows?'

Ivor nodded as she spoke. He stepped to her side and lifted up the combined text she'd been compiling. 'That is the revelation we have drawn from the gravesands. A way to break the malignant curse that threatens our communities. A way to fight back rather than meekly awaiting the next attack.'

Mahyar weighed the hierophant's words. 'How would we do this?' he asked. 'How would we strike against an enemy that's already dead?'

'By mounting an expedition against the one who calls the dead from their tombs,' Kvetka said. 'By moving against the Lady of Sorrows herself.'

'Madness,' one of the other scholars objected.

'Necessity,' Ivor corrected him. 'We have a chance to fulfil prophecy. To break the endless cycle of destruction that has cursed our towns for so long. At last we can live in peace.'

'The old texts agree,' Kvetka said. 'They speak of a chosen one, a hero of two realms, who will be the key to breaking the curse.'

'Who is this hero?' Mahyar wanted to know.

It was Ivor who answered. The old wizard tapped the notes he held. 'There is such a hero even now in the Twinned Towns. A man of two realms who has attained such renown as to be spoken of even in your temple.'

Mahyar snapped his fingers. Instantly he knew who Ivor meant. 'Jahangir! His father was from Westreach, but his mother was of Eastdale.'

'One of the only men celebrated by both Azyrites and Reclaimed,' Bairam agreed. 'An expedition drawn from both towns could only be led by such a man. Only he can fulfil the prophecy.'

'Yes, but to succeed he must first seek out the Veiled Oracle,' Kvetka said. 'Among the Reclaimed, her powers are well known of old. She is an ancient seeress who dwells in a tower several days' march from the Sea of Tears. Only the mystic knows the secret to entering the fortress of the Lady of Sorrows.'

The wizard Gajevic gave another name to the place. Even spoken in a whisper, it crept into the ear of everyone in the observatory. 'The crypt-court of Lady Olynder.'

CHAPTER TWO

A cold wind whipped across Graveswater and sent its icy fingers crawling through the streets of Westreach. Jahangir could feel its sting even through the fur cloak he wore over his armour, like cold lips dancing across the back of his neck, hungry and eager for the warm life within his body.

Jahangir raised his fist and motioned for his patrol to stop. He slowly looked around, peering into the shadows. No one in the Twinned Towns ignored that uncanny creeping of their skin or the cold chill that dripped down their spines. It was more than imagination that haunted the island, more than tricks of light and dark that struck fear in the night.

The blue glow of the small lantern tied to Jahangir's shoulder revealed the desolate ruins his soldiers were investigating. Crusted in the dried slime left by ages beneath the sea, the walls looked more like ancient fossils than anything carved by men. Gaps in the shapeless hulks showed where doors and windows had been before they rotted away. Many of the roofs and upper floors had collapsed, their rubble protruding from broken walls in jumbled heaps of debris. Some of the streets that stretched between the buildings were closed by piles of detritus from the decay of some lofty spire or narrow tower. Others were unobstructed, leering from the darkness like the open maws of lurking beasts.

'Do you see something, commander?' one of the soldiers following behind Jahangir asked as he continued to study the shadows.

'No, Omid,' Jahangir replied. 'There's nothing to be *seen*.'

The emphasis he put upon the last word brought an uneasy nod from Omid. The soldiers of the Tombwatch knew only too clearly that the forces menacing their settlement weren't always things that could be seen with the eye.

Jahangir took a step forwards out into the plaza before them. He had one hand clenched about the grip of his sword. The scabbard was made of griffon-bone and carved with potent prayers and appeals to Sigmar. It acted to endow the blade inside with a dweomer inimical to the restless dead. But the enchantment was fleeting and it would take many hours inside the scabbard to be replenished. So it was that the Tombwatch didn't draw their weapons until the fray was upon them.

'Stay here,' Jahangir told his patrol. He knew it was an order that wasn't to their liking. Some of them resented the commander's insistence on always putting himself at the forefront, feeling he took too many risks upon himself instead of letting one of them do it for him. He knew other officers would be content to do so, but Jahangir had never overcome a peculiar conceit as he rose through the ranks: he would not order someone to do something he wasn't ready to do himself.

The cold feeling increased as Jahangir advanced. He glanced back at his patrol: twenty soldiers in the mail shirts and basset helms of Westreach, each armed with sword or spear. Behind them were ten recruits arrayed in leather jupons and carrying baskets with extra weapons and rounded shields adorned with the image of Ghal Maraz. The sword-bearers would provide support in any fight, equipping the soldiers with new blades when the enchantment expended on the ones they had. If a sword-bearer proved sufficiently valiant, there would be promotion for them within the Tombwatch. It was Jahangir's experience that no amount of training could prepare someone for the menace of the ruins. Only actually being brought into the danger would gauge someone's worth, whether they would stand their ground or flee when the nighthaunts rose from their tombs.

Tombs. Jahangir was sickened by the very word. The burial practices of the Twinned Towns didn't allow for such places. They couldn't. In Shyish the threat of the dead returning from their graves was too great to risk. The people of Westreach cast their dead into Burial Bay, wrapping the bodies in long shrouds on which were written prayers for Sigmar's protection. Each body was fastened to the long chain that stretched across the bay, held fast so that even if unnatural life did rouse the corpse, the undead wouldn't menace the living. For the people of Eastdale there was an even more sinister ritual. Their dead were cremated upon a great stone called Mournbane. When the fire was spent, the ashes were gathered and brewed into a tea which the family of the deceased would drink. In this way, tradition held, the spirit of the dead would be spread among the living and there would be nothing of either body or soul to be resurrected by even the Great Necromancer himself.

The customs of Azyrite and Reclaimed were much different from those of old Belvegrod. Jahangir judged that the ancestors of the Reclaimed had been obsessed with death. Certainly Nagash had been the most important of their gods, his effigy to be found in every ruin, his name carved into the mantle of every doorway. Beneath each house and temple, tombs were built. With no cemetery outside the city, the Belvegrodians kept their dead with them. The older the family, the greater the nest of catacombs under their home. As the Twinned Towns expanded and built upon the ruins, the spirits of the dead stirred from their forgotten graves to prey upon the settlers. When that happened, it fell to the Tombwatch to follow these spectres back to their lairs and put an end to their evil.

Jahangir only wished it were so simple. Trying to follow a spectral creature through the darkened ruins was more easily said than done. The nighthaunts were transparent in strong light, but almost invisible in the shadowy ruins. They could pass through walls and sink through floors, glide over holes in the ground that would swallow their more substantial pursuers. Most times the lairs of these undead could only be found by a process of elimination – narrowing the search area based upon the pattern of their attacks. That, of course, meant waiting until there were enough victims of the malignant spirits to establish such a pattern.

Jahangir felt guilt over each innocent life lost to the nighthaunts. Anything that could be done to stop the attacks felt like an obligation to him, no matter the risk. So it was that he continued to walk away from his patrol. He was offering himself as bait. His warm blood, his vibrant life force, would be a beacon to the undead. If one was near, it would come for him once the temptation grew strong enough. When it finally struck, Jahangir would need to stave it off until the rest of the patrol could reach him, and in those desperate moments his survival would depend on his speed. The success of the Tombwatch's mission rested on his nerve.

Forwards. With the patrol halted behind him, Jahangir could hear each of his footfalls echoing through the ruins. He watched the darkness, wary for any wisp of motion, the faint outline of a shrouded form slinking towards him. His ears were sharp for the noise of rubble being disturbed, of some rotten door being moved by a spectral presence. Each step he took, he wondered if the haunted catacombs lay somewhere just below his foot. The patrol's objective could be that close and none of them would know it.

The lights carried by the soldiers no longer offered Jahangir any illumination. Only the lamp strapped to his own shoulder penetrated the darkness that closed around him. His senses were vigilant for the least provocation, the faintest warning that the enemy was stealing towards him.

It was neither sight nor sound that made Jahangir whip around and draw his blade. Some inner cry of warning made him act, some instinct carried to him by his mother's blood. As the enchanted steel left its sheath, a nimbus of golden light crackled around the weapon. In the glow of this light, the grisly thing that was rushing for the commander was revealed.

'Chainrasp,' Jahangir hissed as the thing flew at him. It was only a partial manifestation of a human form. The withered arms, torso and head of the entity were cloaked in a tattered black shroud, but it had nothing below the level of its ribs and simply drifted above the ground like mist. The thing, even its dark mantle, was insubstantial, and as Jahangir looked at the creature he could see through it. The most solid aspect of its composition were the long chains locked about its torso that dragged across the street as it moved.

Discovered by its intended prey, the chainrasp uttered a pitiable moan. The sound dripped with despair, sorrow so malignant that for a heartbeat Jahangir felt like throwing down his weapon and letting the spectre overwhelm him. He shook off the suicidal impulse and brought his sword slashing at the undead. The edge raked across the chainrasp's bony hand. What remained of its face curled back in bewilderment when it saw its fingers severed as the blade passed through them. They evaporated into ashy smoke.

'Company, advance!' Jahangir shouted, calling his patrol into action. He swung his sword once more, but made no effort to strike his foe. Now that the chainrasp knew the blade could hurt it, it showed greater caution in its efforts to reach him. Jahangir knew it was only a momentary respite. A minute, perhaps less, and the sword's magic would become too weak to harm the spectre.

A minute... and how far had Jahangir walked? Too far for the patrol to cover in that amount of time?

The chainrasp drew away from Jahangir. It turned its hooded head and stared at the rushing soldiers. The creature still had enough of a mind to realise it had been tricked. It spun away and tried to slip back into the shadows.

'No you don't!' Jahangir threw himself into the spectre's path. The sword licked out once again, intercepting the chainrasp before it could reach the darkness of a dilapidated house. It drew back, its bony jaws opening wide as it moaned once more.

'I don't want to hear about it,' Jahangir growled. He moved towards the entity, threatening it with sweeps of his sword. The chainrasp gave ground before him, backing away to keep beyond the reach of the enchanted steel.

Jahangir's difficulty was twofold. He had to keep the chainrasp from either reaching him or getting away, but at the same time he couldn't strike it down with his sword. He needed to keep the spirit engaged until the patrol reached him, to press it so closely that it wasn't able to simply sink into the ground or fade into a wall. While the golden aura of his sword shone upon it, the night-haunt was unable to evaporate into the shadows.

But that aura was quickly fading. Each thrust and swing at the chainrasp was a little less vibrant than the one before, and Jahangir knew it wouldn't be long before his blade lost all of its potency. He could see the smouldering eyes in the skeletal head blaze with hungry eagerness when the spectre made the same discovery. It didn't try to escape now, but instead hovered just beyond the reach of his sword. Waiting for the moment when it would be free to strike.

Jahangir made one last slash to fend off the chainrasp's feint. The aura of his sword was reduced to a mere glint now. If his foe chose, it could escape easily. Instead, the spectre gave a hungry moan and flew at him. The commander flung up his sword, but the now mundane steel simply passed through the apparition. He could feel the chill of the bony claws as they reached for him.

A blinding flash of light exploded across the plaza. The chainrasp whipped away, its shrouded figure bathed in white flames. Splotches of ectoplasm dripped from the burning spectre as it fled through the darkened ruins, a piteous wail echoing through the desolation.

Jahangir sheathed his sword and struggled to draw his breath. His chest felt cold from where the chainrasp's spectral talons had brushed his armour. He could see the streaks of decay left by its hands. But for the protective wards affixed to his breastplate, he knew the creature would have done far worse to him. The magic invoked by Sigmar's priests had slowed the fiend just long enough for the patrol to reach him.

A strongly built woman carrying a spear rushed towards Jahangir. She had a clay flask in one hand, its stopper hanging against its side by a little chain. 'Commander, are you all right?'

Jahangir nodded and pointed to the flask. 'It didn't touch me. Thanks to you, Soraya.' He frowned as he looked at the flaming spots of ectoplasm on the ground. 'I didn't want to use the sacred salts until we were ready.'

'Do you think the patrol would have gone ahead if we lost you?' Soraya countered. Jahangir could only bow to her logic. There was no chance the patrol would have continued the hunt. They'd have retrieved his body and returned to Westreach.

The other soldiers gathered around Jahangir and one of the

sword-bearers brought him another sword. He removed his old one from his belt and secured its replacement, then gave his troops a stern look.

'We've employed the sacred salts sooner than I'd have liked,' he said, gesturing to the smouldering patches of ectoplasm that formed a trail leading deeper into the ruins. 'We'll have to track this spectre quickly before it is completely consumed by the flame. There'll be no room for caution now. Not if we're to find the lair and vanquish the rest of these nighthaunts.'

Omid stepped forwards, one hand gripping the hilt of his sword. 'We're with you, commander. Tell us what to do and it will be done.'

Jahangir gave the soldier a steady look, then turned his eyes to Soraya and the others. 'Pray for Sigmar's favour,' he told them. 'If the chainrasp makes it back to its tomb, there's no chance of taking the rest of the nighthaunts unawares. If it burns up before reaching its lair we'll have to do this whole thing all over again.

'It's a lot to ask,' Jahangir continued, 'but all of you know what will happen if we don't go ahead. Another night of these fiends stalking the streets of Westreach in search of prey.' He held the gaze of each of his troops.

'We're not going to let that happen,' Jahangir vowed.

The splotches of burning ectoplasm led to the decayed wreck of an ancient temple. Jahangir could hear a few whispered prayers when his patrol entered the crumbling edifice. Morbid sculptures leered down at them from the walls, the mantle of dried sea scum that caked them giving the illusion they were real bodies in the last stages of decay.

Ahead of them was an altar of black basalt and behind it a ghastly statue carved from alabaster. Both were devoid of the patina that covered everything else. Jahangir doubted if the most fecund growth would dare to grow on such things regardless of how many centuries they were drowned beneath the sea. The altar had a spiral pattern cut into its surface and deep grooves that branched away to either side before ending in curved, funnel-like openings. Jahangir had seen their like before: blood gutters to bear away the vitality of those sacrificed in this temple – sacrificed to the dread god whose deathly image had been cut from a block of alabaster. The fleshless head and the tall crown it wore were all too familiar to the inhabitants of the Twinned Towns, its depiction repeated throughout the ruins of Belvegrod. Nagash, the God of Death. The Lord of Undeath.

'This is bad,' Omid whispered. He pointed to the splotches of ectoplasm. 'The trail leads to those stairs. That means a crypt under the temple.'

Jahangir understood only too well Omid's anxiety when he looked to the scum-covered steps that descended into the temple's floor. Those Belvegrodians without family to tend them, or those taken as a sacrifice to Nagash and his Mortarchs, became the property of the temples and were consigned to niches in maze-like crypts.

'A family catacomb might yield half a dozen restless spirits,' Jahangir said. 'But here, where the dead were abandoned and the living were butchered...'

Soraya stared up at the forbidding idol. Her eyes were wide with alarm. 'Do we go back? We know this is the place now. We could return tomorrow.'

Jahangir shook his head. 'The risk is too great. The nighthaunts know we've found this place. The most cognisant of them will relocate somewhere else. They'll scatter and we might never find them all.' It was the worst possibility for the Tombwatch, to have a nest of wraiths disperse, especially with the numbers that might be infesting the temple's crypt.

The commander turned to face his patrol. 'Sword-bearers, I need two of you to set down your gear and run back to the watch-house. You need to report what we've found and where we've gone. If we fail, others have to take up the hunt.' He gestured to two of his soldiers. 'Give them your lamps,' he ordered.

Once the two messengers were on their way, Jahangir dispersed the weapons from the discarded baskets. Each soldier took an extra sword while the recruits shared the remaining blades between them. Jahangir suspected they'd not have far to carry the extra weight.

'Sigmar guide and protect us,' Jahangir prayed at the head of the steps. Then he followed the splotches of burning ectoplasm into the gloom beneath the temple.

The steps led down to a vast vault. Niches lined the walls of the crypt on every side, each covered in a residue of what had once been a coffin: brittle fragments of wood, the corroded remnants of metal plates and handles, the splintered shards of ancient bones. Jahangir could see into a dozen and more of the stone ledges by the white flicker that shone from a large pool of fire. The chain-rasp Soraya had struck with the sacred salts had made it this far, but no farther. He advanced warily towards the spectre's smouldering remains. Standing over the puddle of ectoplasm, he peered at the walls. Interspersed among the niches were archways that led into more vaults.

'Eight more chambers branching off just from this one,' Jahangir said. 'Who knows how many more open off from the others.' He could feel the tang of the supernatural in the air, the uncanny sensation that crawled across his skin. 'The nighthaunts are here,' he warned the patrol.

Soraya took her spear and poked one of the ledges with the butt of the shaft. Dust from dried scum and decayed wood billowed up as she prodded the debris. Bones crumbled into powder when she touched them. She pulled back and whipped her spear around, ready to snatch away the carved sheath that capped the head of her weapon.

'Where are they?' Omid muttered, his eyes roving from one archway to the next.

'Near,' Jahangir replied, tersely. He too watched the archways. The quiet was far from comforting. The most debased nighthaunts were on the level of beasts, unthinking entities that simply lashed out at the living without any strategy or planning. Others retained a degree of intelligence, twisted reflections of their minds when they were alive. These were the truly dangerous ones, lurking and biding their time until the moment was right. These higher wraiths would dominate the baser spirits and force them to submit to their will. As ghastly as a sudden rush of dozens of nighthaunts would be, Jahangir knew this silence meant even greater danger.

'We'll look to that one,' Jahangir decided, and motioned his patrol towards the archway on their right. 'Sword-bearers at the centre. Omid, take five watchmen as a rearguard.' Once they adjusted their formation, Jahangir led them into the farther vault.

Here too all was silence. The smell was even mustier than that of the chamber outside. The coffins on the ledges that lined the walls were in better condition, probably a result of the stale air and lack of circulation. Jahangir led his troops in a brief inspection. Soraya tested another of the coffins, trying to provoke some kind of reaction. The casket collapsed under her efforts, but no irate phantom rose to challenge the desecration.

'Perhaps they've already fled,' Soraya suggested.

Jahangir shook his head. 'They're here,' he said. 'We'll find them.' He glanced at the dozens of coffins set into the vault's walls. 'Or they'll find us.'

The patrol withdrew from the annex and back into the main crypt. The fire from the sacred salts was growing weak now; only a few faint flickers of white shivered across the pool of ectoplasm, the smaller splotches already extinguished and rapidly vanishing. Jahangir had a sense of foreboding when he saw the fire fading. He thought about withdrawing his patrol. Then he thought about how many innocents would become victims of the nighthaunts if they scattered to new lairs.

'The next annex,' Jahangir ordered, and waved his arm at the archway just past the one they'd left.

Using the same wariness as before, the Tombwatch entered the vault. Soraya again tested one of the coffins, leaning away as it collapsed under her touch. The soldiers waited, tense for any kind of reaction.

'Looks like they aren't home after all,' Omid muttered. His words were frivolous but there was a haunted unease in his voice.

Jahangir waited a few moments more. He *knew* there was something close. Something malignant and hostile that was aware of their every move. Again, the question was whether they would find it, or if it would find them.

'Back to the crypt,' Jahangir ordered and motioned his patrol to withdraw.

The first of the watchmen was just within the archway when he suddenly screamed. The man twitched and writhed like a brine-toad in a skillet. From where he stood Jahangir could see the soldier's body withering, drying up as his essence was drained away. Phantom claws seized him from either side of the archway, spectral hands emerging from the solid stone.

'The enemy is upon us!' Jahangir shouted. 'Stay back from the walls!' He turned to Omid and pointed at the bottle hanging from the man's belt. 'Splash the floor so they can't come up from beneath us!'

Omid quickly ripped the cork from the bottle and began spattering the ground with liquid: holy water drawn from the font within

Sigmar's temple, a mixture from the rivers of Azyr and the seas of Shyish. It was too weak to do any harm to the nighthaunts, but it could repel them. For a little while.

'They're coming out of the walls!' Soraya shouted. She ripped the cover from the head of her spear. The metal tip blazed with golden light, illuminating the ghastly shapes that were drifting out of the walls on every side. More chainrasps like the one they'd followed to the temple. The chorus of groans that sounded from the apparitions scratched across the mind of every mortal who heard them, seeking to coax the living into joining the dead.

'Sigmar is our armour and our shield!' Jahangir shouted as he drew his sword. 'You are warriors of Westreach! Your lives do not belong to you, but to those you protect!'

Some of the sword-bearers and even a few soldiers had started to waver, to break ranks and move towards the nighthaunts. Their commander's speech snapped the despair that had seized them. They quickly fell back into formation. The watchmen drew their blades or uncapped their spears while the recruits set down the weapon baskets and raised their shields.

A wailing more baleful than anything Jahangir had ever heard before echoed through the chamber. He saw a creature drift down from the ceiling above. Unlike the chainrasps, it was no shadowy apparition, but glowed with a silvery light. Its body was lean and withered, dried down to a husk, but even in such condition there was a monstrous intensity in the eyes that blazed from the depths of its skull. Jahangir knew this was no mindless gheist; it was a being driven by a malignant intelligence. He could see the emblem that was displayed on its wispy robes. In life, this thing had been a priestess of Nagash.

The banshee raised its emaciated arms and gave voice to another of its terrifying howls. At its cry, the chainrasps flew at the Tombwatch. Scores of vengeful phantoms surrounded Jahangir's patrol.

Enchanted swords struck at the nighthaunts, tearing through their shrouded forms. Spears impaled the creatures, their wispy shapes hanging off the tips like old rags. In only a matter of heartbeats, the soldiers vanquished dozens of the apparitions.

The graveyard howl rang out again as the banshee summoned more chainrasps from their tombs. From wall and ceiling, the spectral creatures emerged, their hungry moans rattling through the vault. Wherever Omid had failed to splash the holy water, shrouded entities boiled up from the floor, their bony claws outstretched.

'Sigmar stands with the brave!' Jahangir yelled to his patrol. 'Faith and courage!' He whipped his sword through the skull of a chainrasp and saw its shape disintegrate into smoke. Instantly he had to thrust downwards at a phantom seeping up from the floor. It evaporated under his blade before it could fully emerge from the flagstones, but the golden glow around his weapon dwindled to a dim flicker. Jahangir threw it aside and grabbed the second blade he bore. He ripped it from its scabbard just as another spectre flew at him. He sent its head tumbling away from its shoulders and watched as its body faded into nothingness.

'Commander! Help!'

Jahangir turned towards the cry, but it was already too late. One of his soldiers, unluckier than him, was caught by the chainrasps as he tried to switch weapons, dragged away from his comrades by spectral claws. Sprawled across the floor, he was set upon by a mob of hungry phantoms, bathing him in shadow as they drained his vitality.

'Close ranks!' Jahangir commanded. 'Sword-bearers, watch for gaps!' Two of the recruits closed the spot left by the dead soldier, using their shields to fend off the spectres. Soon Soraya, the dweomer of her spear spent, moved to support them with a sword from one of the baskets. The wards on the shields, like those on their armour, could provide only momentary protection from the undead if the creatures were determined to reach their prey.

Jahangir darted a look up at the banshee. So long as the undead priestess was dominating them, the chainrasps would be unrelenting. The silvery manifestation howled again, drawing still more nighthaunts to replace those vanquished by the Tombwatch. What need did the spectral general have to enter the fray when it could call hundreds, perhaps thousands of phantoms from the catacombs?

Another scream. Another soldier lost to the undead horde. Then a sword-bearer was pulled from their midst, caught by two chainrasps that drifted down from the ceiling.

'Commander! They're too many!' Omid cried. 'We can't hold them back!'

'Close ranks!' Jahangir snarled again, as he dispatched another of the skull-faced apparitions. 'We will hold them! We will prevail!'

The banshee shifted its position and stared down at Jahangir, its fleshless face grinning as though amused by his bold claims. It had every reason to be amused when it howled again and more chainrasps flooded into the vault. Barring a miracle, Jahangir didn't think there was anything that could turn the battle.

White flame suddenly spread across the chainrasps near the archway, and dire moans became slobbering wails. Some tried to seep back into the walls and became caught partway in the stone as their essence took on a semblance of solidity. Others rushed deeper into the vault, spreading the flames that licked across their shrouds to other phantoms. The rest lunged at Jahangir's surrounded force in a last, spiteful effort. The white fire that so eagerly engulfed the undead found no purchase on living flesh, and the chainrasps were soon dispatched by enchanted swords.

The banshee wailed and howled. No longer did it gloat over its certain victory. Its cries brought more phantoms into the vault, but many passed through the walls only to meet one of the already burning chainrasps. They too were soon alight.

'Where'd that fire come from?' Soraya shouted, shocked by the sudden turn the fray had taken.

Jahangir laughed. 'The nighthaunts aren't the only ones being reinforced!' In through the archway surged another group of soldiers. Their armour marked them as belonging to the Tombwatch, but their pale skin and dark hair showed them to be Reclaimed from Eastdale rather than Azyrites from Westreach. What they were doing so far from their own area, Jahangir didn't question. It was enough that they *were* here.

The Reclaimed shared some of the methods and tools used by the Azyrites, such as the sacred salts that wrought such havoc on the chainrasps. Other weapons were peculiar to their ancient customs and traditions. Bowmen sent shafts of bat-thorn into the burning phantoms, causing them to lose their cohesion and drift into plumes of vapour. Axemen charged in, their weapons clattering from all the charms and talismans tied to them. These too did their part to disperse the chainrasps, splitting them into smoky shreds.

The tide was turning, but the fight wasn't over. The banshee turned towards the archway. As terrifying as its cries had been, the entity now produced a scream more horrifying than anything that had come before. Six of the newly arrived soldiers fell instantly, their bodies pale and lifeless before they struck the floor. The survivors shouted in despair, their hands hurriedly reaching for talismans strung about their necks even as their widened eyes watched their comrades die.

'Loose!' Jahangir ordered the soldiers, trying to snap them from the horror that gripped them. 'Shoot her! Get her to come down to us!' As he yelled the command, his hand closed about the Sigmarite charm he carried. He didn't know if it would be any more effective against the banshee's cries than the talismans of the Reclaimed, but it helped him fend off his own fear to think there was at least a chance of resisting its deadly wail.

Before the banshee could scream again, a lone bowman took aim at it. He loosed the bat-thorn shaft, but an arrow that could finish a weakened chainrasp wasn't so effective against the undead priestess. Jahangir saw the shaft pass harmlessly through the creature. The banshee was less certain of its immunity now and darted down from its place near the ceiling. It opened its mouth for another murderous shriek.

'You've killed enough tonight!' Jahangir roared. He lunged through the ranks of his own men and past burning chainrasps. The banshee spun around just as he brought his sword slashing down at its head. The last motes of golden light were extinguished as he struck, but there was still enough magic in the blow to cause the priestess to fade into nothingness.

The instant Jahangir struck down the banshee, the horde of chainrasps disintegrated. The weakest spirits were simply extinguished, vanishing as they joined their leader in oblivion. Others were gripped by confusion, incapable even of defending themselves as the Tombwatch surged forwards to dispatch them.

Jahangir turned to claim a new sword and join the rest of the Tombwatch in vanquishing the lingering phantoms. As he did, the bowman who'd tried to shoot the banshee walked over. He was a tall man, his face dominated by a thick black moustache. Around his neck he wore the gold pectoral that marked him as a captain.

'I am in your debt,' the man shouted, touching his lips with his fingers in the manner used by the Reclaimed to prove their sincerity. He spun around as the dark shade of a chainrasp went flying past him, its essence already evaporating into scattered wisps. When he was certain it was vanquished, he turned back to Jahangir. 'My arrow didn't strike true. If you hadn't intervened, I'd be dead.'

Jahangir took quick stock of the crypt, but the wraith that had flown past the archer appeared to be the last of its ilk. He turned his attention to the bowman. 'It is my patrol that is in your debt,' Jahangir answered, copying the captain's gesture. 'Had you and your warriors not arrived when you did, my command would've been overwhelmed. We are fortunate you came when you did.'

The captain shook his head. 'It wasn't entirely chance. We were looking for you, Commander Jahangir. We met one of the recruits you were sending back to the watch-house. He told us where you'd gone.'

'Whatever your reasons, you have the gratitude of myself and my men,' Jahangir insisted.

As though to contest Jahangir's words, sounds of argument broke out in the vault. The last chainrasps had been dispatched and now the Azyrites of Jahangir's patrol were facing the Reclaimed. The cause of dissension was clear when Jahangir saw Omid quarrelling with one of the bowmen.

'Bat-thorn arrows,' Omid sneered, plucking one of the missiles from the floor. 'I'd like to see these work on something that wasn't already weakened by holy water.'

The bowman was a short, wiry man with a crooked nose and gimlet eyes. 'I'd like to see an Azyrite try to pull up his boots without pestering Sigmar for help. The God-King has no time for those who don't help themselves.'

The moustached captain snarled at the bowman. 'Ratimir! Compose yourself. We didn't come here to fight with Azyrites.'

Ratimir scowled and backed away. 'I'm sorry, Captain Venteslav.'

Omid scowled as well, but his distaste was directed at the captain. He stopped just short of putting that distaste into words.

Jahangir gave him a warning look to make sure things stayed that way.

'I'll apologise for my soldiers,' Jahangir told Venteslav. 'When someone faces certain death, they're bound to be on edge. A bit of rest will set them right.'

Venteslav frowned. 'I'm afraid that is impossible. At least for you.' He drew a folded piece of parchment from a pouch on his belt. 'Orders. From the townmasters. They want you to go to the lighthouse.' He looked over at the surviving elements of Jahangir's patrol. 'Your people can go back to their watch-house and rest, but you'll have to come with us.'

'As though we'd abandon the commander to a bunch of...' Omid's outburst faltered when Jahangir looked over at him.

'You just volunteered to be my escort,' Jahangir informed Omid. He turned his attention to Soraya. 'I'll want you along as well in case I have to send word back to the watch-house.'

'Commander, I can...' Again, a look from Jahangir made Omid choke back his words.

Soraya took one of the few remaining swords from the baskets and strapped it to her belt. 'Whatever needs to be done, it'll be done,' she said. The look in her eyes when she stared at the Reclaimed wasn't as hostile as Omid's, but it was far from friendly. Any gratitude was now tempered by what appeared to be the arrest of her commander.

'The rest of you head back to the watch-house,' Jahangir told his troops. 'See that our dead are properly attended.' He turned to Venteslav. 'Do you want them to see to your casualties?'

Venteslav waved some of his soldiers forward to collect the bodies. 'It is a considerate offer, but we'll see to them ourselves. If a stranger is the first to handle a corpse, they might frighten the spirit out. And I think we've all had enough of bodiless spectres tonight.'

Jahangir simply nodded, deciding not to argue the merits of the superstition. Though his mother had taught him much, it seemed there was always some other tradition the Reclaimed held that he didn't know about. He was a man of two worlds, or at least so it felt to him at times like this. He knew something of each, but not enough of either to feel like he fully belonged. It was a condition that had vexed him sorely growing up and something that no amount of brooding would resolve. Instead he decided to focus on the mysterious purpose that had brought Venteslav down into the ruins bordering Westreach.

'Lead the way, captain,' Jahangir said. 'I'm anxious to learn what's so important that they want me at the lighthouse.'

CHAPTER THREE

Jahangir's escort brought him to the great lecture hall deep within the Belvegrod lighthouse. A rounded indoor amphitheatre with ranks of great pillars rising up from the floor to support the vaulted ceiling, the chamber reminded him of an arena more than any sort of place for debate and discussion. Then again, he supposed that words and ideas could cut every bit as keenly as swords.

A small group was gathered in the hall, most of them seated on the benches that ringed the amphitheatre. Jahangir recognised Lector Rasoul from the Temple of Sigmar and Lord Heshmat, the townmaster of Westreach. He spotted several of his town's most celebrated scholars and wizards. Not all of those in attendance were Azyrites, however, for there were many Reclaimed, but the only people from Eastdale he could name were the boyar Tihomir and the renowned historian Stanimira.

The gathering was focused upon Hierophant Ivor and the small group of people standing with him near a lectern at the centre of the room. Jahangir was surprised to see the augur Bairam among the master of the lighthouse's entourage. For the first time he realised that whatever had caused this meeting, it was much bigger than himself.

'Commander, we have been eagerly waiting for you,' Ivor said when he noticed Jahangir's entry into the hall. The wizard punctuated his greeting with a curt bow.

Jahangir returned Ivor's courtesy. 'Your summons was fortunate,' he said, indicating Venteslav. 'If not for the intervention of the soldiers you dispatched, my patrol might have been wiped out.'

Ivor's expression became grim. 'It was more than good fortune. We had warning of the danger that threatened you.' He glanced over at Bairam.

'Dark forces stalk you,' the augur said, his blind eyes turned towards Jahangir. 'A premonition of your peril made it imperative to bring you here at once.'

'I've led many patrols into the ruins,' Jahangir reminded Bairam and Ivor. 'We were just unlucky this night to find a nest of nighthaunts stronger than we were prepared to face.'

A middle-aged woman with the fair complexion and dark hair of Eastdale stepped forwards. 'It was more than bad luck. You've been marked, commander. It was no happenstance that you were beset by such a force of undead. They were waiting for you.'

Ivor nodded and added further explanation. 'What Kvetka says is true. The nighthaunts laid a trap for you. It was not some disturbance of their graves that made them rise in such force tonight. It was a malignant will compelling them to seek you out and destroy you.' He hesitated and swept his eyes over the people gathered on the benches. 'Commands dispensed by the Mortarch of Grief.'

Faces blanched when Ivor invoked the fearsome entity. Jahangir felt a shiver course through him. Lady Olynder, dread servant of Nagash himself. He tried to reject the idea that such a malignant power had taken personal interest in him. 'Why would the Lady of Sorrows bother to destroy me?'

'Because you have the power to destroy her,' Kvetka answered. 'Or at least destroy the curse she has set against the Twinned Towns.' She stepped towards him and held out a sheaf of parchment on which random words had been written. 'We looked into the gravesands tonight and had a glimpse of things yet to pass.'

A thin wizard, younger and much less imposing than Ivor, joined Kvetka. 'I watched the gravesands fall and gave names to the images that sifted through the grains.'

'Gajevic saw a hero,' Kvetka said, 'a man of two worlds who would lead the way. Who would unlock the curse Lady Olynder has cast upon our towns.'

'That man is you, Jahangir,' Bairam declared, 'a hero who is respected in both Westreach and Eastdale, a leader who can unite both our peoples in a common cause.'

Jahangir stood dumbfounded. He wasn't certain which troubled him more, the thought of Lady Olynder seeking to destroy him or this idea that he was some mighty hero fated to deliver the Twinned Towns from an ancient curse.

'I'm not who you think I am,' Jahangir protested. He looked up at the gathered notables on the benches. 'I am only a commander in the Tombwatch. I'm no mighty leader, no great hero.' He turned back towards Ivor. 'You must've made some mistake.'

'There was no mistake,' Ivor replied. He held his finger up to emphasise his point. 'The attack upon you – foreseen by Bairam – proves it. The Lady of Sorrows sets her terrible slaves against you. She seeks your destruction. She does not do so without purpose.'

'You've been chosen,' Kvetka added. 'Marked by fate as the key to breaking Lady Olynder's curse.'

Jahangir could only shake his head. 'I don't know anything about prophecies and divinations. I'm a simple soldier trying to protect my people. That's what I know.'

'You brave the ruins every night to defend our towns from the undead that haunt old Belvegrod,' Ivor said, 'but what is the menace they pose when compared to the armies Lady Olynder sets upon us? Each generation her spirit hosts swell with the souls of those killed in her last attack. Each time her processions sweep into our towns it becomes harder to defeat them. Unless her curse is broken, one day the Twinned Towns must fall to the Lady of Sorrows.'

All eyes were upon Jahangir while he digested the hierophant's speech. He felt the weight of their gaze, the hope they were placing upon him, the responsibility of defending the Twinned Towns from the Mortarch of Grief herself. He knew the pain inflicted upon their communities by the Lady of Sorrows, the endless cycle of death and misery. Was he equal to such a task? Who was he, after all, to be called a hero?

Kvetka seemed to see the doubt that gnawed at him. Her eyes were sympathetic when she spoke. 'It is for Sigmar to decide who's special – who is marked for greatness. You're unique among our people, someone to whom both those of Westreach and Eastdale will look upon with respect and admiration. One whom everyone can place their trust in. You're the one seen in the portents. There is no one else.'

'What must I do?' Jahangir finally said.

'Our divinations have revealed to us a plan,' Kvetka told him. 'You must lead an expedition to seek out the Veiled Oracle, the great seeress the Reclaimed venerated through the long years before the Stormcasts came to establish the Twinned Towns. She knows the secret ways into Lady Olynder's crypt-fortress.'

From where he sat on the benches, Lord Heshmat spoke up. 'Every resource Westreach can offer you is at your disposal.'

The boyar Tihomir gave his counterpart an ugly look before calling down to Jahangir. 'Whatever Eastdale can provide for your quest, you have only to ask it of us. A hundred soldiers... they are yours. Animals? Supplies? These too are yours.'

'If what you require is beyond the capabilities of Eastdale, I am certain Westreach won't let you down,' Lord Heshmat insisted.

Before the two townmasters could fall to arguing, Lector Rasoul intervened. 'The temple stands with you, Jahangir. You will have warrior priests and gryph-hounds, sacred salts and protective talismans – any weapon that will help you against the foul undead.'

'The Belvegrod lighthouse will also assist you,' Ivor said. He gestured at the walls around him. 'We have gathered the wisdom of two realms within these halls. That knowledge is at your disposal. Secrets arcane and mundane.'

'I fear we can hardly march across Shyish with a library in our packs,' Jahangir pointed out.

Ivor smiled at the retort. 'No, but you can take with you those who have consulted these tomes and carry their knowledge.' He tapped his fingers against the side of his head.

Jahangir frowned. 'I will welcome the help, but anyone you send with me must be not only wise but able to endure the rigours of travel.'

'Do not fear,' Ivor said. 'I know I am too old to make such a journey.' He waved his hand at Kvetka and Gajevic. 'It will need a younger generation to follow where you would lead them. I will select those who I believe can help you *and* do so without slowing the pace of your march.'

'Whatever help you can give will be most welcome,' Jahangir assured the hierophant. He turned back towards the townmasters. 'I will need a hundred soldiers.'

'You will have two hundred,' Tihomir declared before Heshmat could say anything.

Jahangir nodded towards Venteslav. 'I would like Venteslav as my adjutant.' He raised his hand to stifle any protest from the townmasters. 'I am sure there are many fine officers you could suggest, but I haven't seen them in battle against the undead.' He gave Venteslav an appreciative nod. 'I've seen you fighting the nighthaunts and have an idea of your mettle. I know I can count on you.'

'You do me an honour,' Venteslav said. 'I will do my utmost to be worthy of your trust.'

'Is there anything else you know you will need?' Ivor wanted to know.

Jahangir thought for a moment, trying to remember all he knew about the Veiled Oracle. 'They say the oracle dwells in a citadel within the Barrowbogs. I'll need a guide who knows that region.'

'I will make your need known to the traders visiting Westreach,' Heshmat said.

'And I'll see if there's anyone in Eastdale who's suitable,' Tihomir declared.

'We have to find someone,' Jahangir told the assembly. 'Maps and descriptions in books have their limitations. If this expedition is to have any chance at success, I need someone who has seen the lands beyond the Sea of Tears and Graveswater. Someone who knows the dangers we must avoid.'

'There's one danger you cannot avoid,' Bairam warned, his empty eyes facing Jahangir. 'Between you and your destiny, the spectre of Lady Olynder stands. Prevail or perish, you have been chosen to stand against the Lady of Sorrows. But in this contest, know that you do not stand alone. We are with you. Our prayers are with you. And through our prayers, Sigmar himself is with you.'

Jahangir followed Venteslav through the winding streets of Eastdale. Only six hours had passed since the meeting in the

Belvegrod lighthouse and he was keenly aware of how little sleep he'd managed to steal in that time. He sympathised when he watched Soraya try to stifle a yawn. He could have left her in the watch-house but he knew she'd take it as a slight if he failed to include her in this venture. Omid wouldn't care, but she would.

Eastdale was a marked contrast to the well-defined and planned layout of Westreach. Because the Reclaimed had restored the old ruins, the settlement was forced to follow the ancient plan of Belvegrod. If 'plan' was even a suitable word for it. The old city had evolved over many centuries of habitation, expanding beyond the limitations of its original design. Once-broad avenues became cramped as new structures were built. Linear roads became winding paths as they were diverted to accommodate more and more buildings. To walk these streets wasn't to see the promise of a new tomorrow but rather the echo of a lost past.

All around them Jahangir could see the mark of long-held superstition. From his mother, he knew some of the importance of what he saw. Signs were always laid out on the east side of streets because it was believed that restless gheists could only ever turn to the west in their wanderings. From each lamp post a clove of garlic was hung, the bulb cut crosswise so that precisely one quarter of the bulb was removed. The paw of a white cat, preserved in wax, was nailed over a cellar door to fend off infestations of morgue-mice. A bundle of broken sticks sitting in a clay jar could be seen at each intersection so that a traveller caught abroad at night might cast them into the street if the undead were stalking his trail.

Jahangir understood the meaning of these old practices. The bundles of sticks, for instance, came from the belief that a gheist would be compelled to stop and count each one before it could continue chasing its prey. He had seen for himself that more than a few of these traditions were only empty superstition without any veracity to them. Yet the people as a whole were slow to cast aside teachings passed down from parent to child.

Venteslav drew Jahangir's attention to a large inn that dominated the street into which they'd turned. 'The man we're looking for is there,' he said.

'Are you certain he'll still be there?' Soraya stifled another yawn with the back of her hand.

'I've got three of my soldiers watching the place,' Venteslav answered. 'They're under orders not to let him leave.' A brief smile flashed on his dour visage. 'Besides, the man we want enjoys his wine. Our problem won't be catching him, it'll be keeping him coherent enough to understand what we want him for.'

'That could be a blessing,' Jahangir said as they marched towards the inn. 'The more he understands what is needed of him, the less likely he is to agree.'

Venteslav brushed a hand across the shackles hanging from his belt. 'He'll agree to come.'

'Let's try to persuade him first.' Jahangir shook his head. 'However noble our mission, it'd be unwise to depend on a guide who was coerced into accompanying us. The perils beyond the Sea of Tears are numerous enough without a doubtful guide leading the way.'

'Is there time to persuade him?' Soraya asked. 'They made a strong case that we were ambushed beneath the temple. If the Lady of Sorrows is hunting you, any delay has to be avoided.'

'We'll gain nothing with a guide we can't trust,' Jahangir said. 'If I have drawn the attention of Lady Olynder, she can send her nighthaunts against me out there just as easily as she can here. No, I have to be certain I can depend on this guide.' He darted a reproving look at Venteslav. 'And if he has to be dragged from Eastdale in chains it won't bolster my confidence in his loyalty.'

With his position made clear, Jahangir continued towards the inn. It was a rambling, stone-walled structure, the lower floor built from the dull grey rock that had been common in Belvegrod. The upper floors were of much more recent construction, made from the shiny black mournwood that grew all around the shores of Graveswater and the Sea of Tears. Jahangir could see the little skull-like effigies that were carved into the wood above each window and doorway, tiny representations of Nagash that the Reclaimed believed would scare off restless spirits.

The inn's common room was filled with low tables and long benches. A counter ran along one wall. Kegs of mead stood behind the bar as well as tall shelves with pitchers of wine. Two young women tended the bar, supplying patrons with leather jacks and wooden cups filled with their drink of choice. Jahangir was surprised to see a cask of duardin ale perched discreetly in one corner, but it seemed the innkeeper was eager to please a varied clientele. Of course, that proclivity didn't extend so far as to encourage Azyrites. A quick glance at the offerings confirmed to Jahangir he was in Eastdale – nowhere did he see so much as a hint of the foamy beer favoured by the inhabitants of Westreach.

'That's Oysian.' Venteslav drew Jahangir's attention to one of the tables. Gathered on its benches was a group of men dressed in heavy fur cloaks. Only their hands and faces were uncovered, exposing skin that was like polished ebony in colour and faces that had a lean and hawkish cast to them. Even with a fire blazing in the hearth just beyond their table, they were rubbing their hands together for warmth.

'Shadoom?' Jahangir asked. He'd only ever seen a few of them before. They lived in a distant land where, so they claimed, it never snowed and the summers were hot enough to make dragons sweat. They rarely made the journey as far north as the Twinned Towns, but when they did they brought fantastic goods that were coveted by all the wealthiest families.

Venteslav nodded. 'Their caravan crossed the Drowned City three days ago. They've already sold their wares but are waiting for a good omen before starting back. Which is fortunate for us.'

'How is it fortunate?' Soraya asked. 'Surely we don't need to go to the lands of the Shadoom to find the Veiled Oracle?'

'You'll see,' Venteslav promised. He strode towards the table and greeted the traders with a few words in their own language. The speech was so rapid, Jahangir couldn't even be sure there was any distinction between individual words. Finally, one of the fur-cloaked traders stood up and smiled.

'Commander Jahangir,' the man said, beaming, his voice so deep that it sounded like he was pulling it up from the soles of his feet. 'I am Oysian Loi Trewin.' He glanced over at his companions and chuckled. 'You might call me "war chief". Among my people there's little distinction between what is gained by combat and what is gained by commerce.'

Jahangir bowed his head to the trader. 'Has Captain Venteslav explained to you what we need?'

Oysian laughed again. 'You wish to buy my guide.'

'I wish to *hire* your guide,' Jahangir corrected him. The difference didn't appear to register with Oysian.

'I am agreed to sell him to you,' Oysian said. 'He would be of little worth when we returned home. I don't think even the necromancers would find a use for him.' He looked aside at his companions and for a moment there was a sly look on his face. 'We paid forty gold dinars for him. I would say fifty pieces of gold and he is yours.'

'They enjoy haggling,' Venteslav whispered to Jahangir. 'For them, haggling is like crossing swords in a fight. It helps them gauge someone's bravery and skill.'

'I've no time to entertain the Shadoom customs,' Jahangir stated. He met Oysian's gaze. 'Fifty gold pieces.' He sealed the bargain with the one gesture he was familiar with, spitting in his palm and clapping his hands together. Oysian replied in kind, just a hint of disappointment in his eyes. The other traders whispered and laughed among themselves, clearly amused Jahangir had given up so easily.

Jahangir tried his best to ignore the mockery, but there was an edge to his voice when he asked Oysian to turn over the guide. All he could see gathered around the table were Shadoom.

Indignation flashed in Oysian's eyes. 'Not here,' he growled. 'Do you think we would eat and drink in the company of *that*?' He waved his hand at the ceiling. 'Up there. He keeps to his room. Away from us.'

'I have Ratimir watching the door,' Venteslav explained. 'Just in case their guide didn't know the sort of contract he'd made when he joined Oysian but has since figured it out.'

'You think he'd try to sneak off?' Soraya gave the Shadoom a hard look. 'Maybe we're buying something they don't have any more.'

Jahangir started towards the stairs at the back of the room. 'There's a quick way to find out.' The others joined him as they climbed to the upper floor. A narrow hallway opened before them, flanked on either side by iron-banded doors. Ratimir stood outside one of those doors. He saluted Venteslav when he saw the captain.

'Anything?' Venteslav asked.

'He hasn't tried to leave, but I've heard him moving around in there,' Ratimir reported. 'Oysian said he prefers to keep late hours.'

Jahangir stepped between the two Reclaimed soldiers. 'We don't have time to indulge this man's preferences any more than we have time to haggle with the Shadoom.' He rapped on the door. A faintly unpleasant odour impressed itself on him. He could hear the sound of frantic activity inside. Thinking of what Soraya had said, he didn't wait any longer. Putting his shoulder to the door, he forced it open.

The smell struck Jahangir almost like a physical blow. The cause was at once obvious. Two chickens and part of a pig were strung up near the window, basking in the sunlight. The window was cracked open and swarms of flies buzzed around the hanging meat, drawn by the stench of decay.

A small chest stood in one corner of the room. The opposite corner had a bed, low to the floor after the traditions of the Reclaimed so that nocturnal haunts could find no hiding place beneath it. A table and a chair completed the furnishings. If one discounted the bones that littered the floor. These, Jahangir could see, had been viciously gnawed and cracked open to get at the marrow. His first thought was a large dog. Only there was no dog in the room. There was no one except the man he'd come here to find.

The man stood just behind the bed, a vicious spiked mace gripped in both hands. Partly covered by his bed sheets was the carcass of a cat. The animal had been dead long enough to have turned rotten and there were spots where the fur had been peeled back to expose the necrotic flesh. To Jahangir's disgust, he could see bite marks.

'Cryptborn,' Soraya hissed. With one hand she made the sign of Sigmar; with the other she drew her sword.

A grimace formed on the man's face when he heard Soraya speak, lips pulling back to expose yellow, fang-like teeth. The gesture didn't improve his gangrel appearance. His skin had a pasty, light grey colour and a texture that evoked the slimy belly of a toad. His build was hunched and wiry, and his features had a feral cast to them with a sloping forehead and a broad, pushed-in nose. His eyes were beady with a reddish hue. The clothes he wore were shaggy hides and uncured skins.

Jahangir moved between Soraya and the man. *Cryptborn*, she'd named him, one of the foul ghoul-blooded creatures that lurked at the very periphery of civilisation. The lowest kind of being that could still be called human.

'Zorgrath?' Jahangir addressed the man. For an answer there was a barely perceptible nod. 'The towns of Westreach and Eastdale intend to hire you as a guide.' He pointed at the floor. 'We've already bought out your contract from the Shadoom.'

The grimace softened slightly and Zorgrath lowered the mace. 'You bought me away from Oysian and his brothers?'

'I think they had some peculiar ideas about your agreement,' Jahangir informed him.

The cryptborn laughed, a brittle grating sound like the scratch of nails on a coffin lid. 'I think so too.' He gazed intently at Jahangir. 'You will forgive me if I don't express any gratitude.'

'It should be enough that you're free,' Venteslav snapped.

'Free?' Zorgrath laughed again. 'I think not. You merely want me in your debt so that I can repay the favour.'

'Commander, forget about this grave-robbing dreg.' Soraya waved her hand at the rotting carcasses. 'You can't trust a thing like him.'

'You can trust me not to steal your rations on the trail,' Zorgrath grinned. One hand dropped from the mace to whip back the sheet and reveal exactly how little was left of the cat. 'I find my own. Of course, I prefer to let them ripen a bit.' He savoured the revulsion he provoked.

Jahangir took a step forward and threw the sheet back over the gnawed carcass. 'We need someone who can guide an expedition across the Barrowbogs.'

What little brow there was on Zorgrath's forehead knotted in thought when he heard Jahangir speak. 'The Barrowbogs are a treacherous place. What do you want there?'

'You'll be told only after you accept the job,' Jahangir stated. 'The townmasters are willing to pay you one hundred in gold for your services.'

Zorgrath nodded and licked his teeth. The offer was clearly enticing. Still, he had an uncertain look in his eyes. 'The Barrow-bogs are a dangerous place. Spirits haunt those lands, things that even in life had no kinship to humans. They don't welcome visitors. This journey isn't one to take lightly. Not for the faint-hearted or the unprepared.'

'The Twinned Towns have put everything at our disposal,' Jahangir explained. 'I've been given two hundred warriors for the journey. Wizards and warrior priests. The best weapons and armour our communities can provide. The only resource I don't have is time. Will you join us?'

The cryptborn looked around at the room he was in, at the carcasses hanging in the window. He glanced down at his rough attire and ran his hand across the uncured hides. 'One hundred gold and your towns provide me with new gear.' He turned and gave Soraya a toothy smile. 'I may eat like an animal, but I don't like looking like one.'

Jahangir nodded. He motioned Ratimir forwards. 'You'll see that our new guide has everything he needs. Whatever the cost, defer it to the townmasters.'

The Reclaimed soldier started to smile, but a curt order from Venteslav curbed his enthusiasm. 'Whatever *he* needs,' the captain emphasised. 'If I see so much as a new boot buckle on you, I promise there'll be a reckoning.'

Two days after his meeting in the Belvegrod lighthouse everything was ready. As Jahangir looked out across the great company that had been put under his command, the weight of his responsibility once more bore down upon him. *Hero*. The word was as sacred as the names of Sigmar and all his pantheon. Who was he to bear it? But then, who was he to reject it?

The townmasters had been as good as their promises. Two hundred soldiers from Westreach and Eastdale had been provided, all of them arrayed in the best armour and bearing the best weapons. The baggage train numbered a hundred animals, a mix of the sure-footed demi-gryphs and the robust marshmares. There were an equal number of teamsters, cooks, smiths and craftsmen – any sort of specialist the expedition might require.

'An impressive force, general,' Venteslav commented. The Reclaimed captain stood close to Jahangir while they watched the expedition assemble in the ruins outside Westreach. The wide plaza and crumbling streets were filled with more activity than they'd seen in decades. Nearby, the broad avenue of the Mournmarch stretched towards the island's outer wall and the limit of the lands claimed by the Twinned Towns.

'Much more than a mere patrol of Tombwatch,' Jahangir agreed. He was still uncomfortable with his new rank, but it had been decided that so important a mission couldn't be led by a commander.

'Looking for our guide?' Venteslav asked when he noticed how intently Jahangir was studying the formation. 'I've got Ratimir and Soraya keeping tabs on him. Between the two of them, he won't slip away. Ratimir knows he's got money now and Soraya... that's a good soldier you've got there. I think she'd walk up to a morghast and poke it in the eye socket if she was ordered to.'

'Soraya appreciates the certainty of commands,' Jahangir said. 'She likes having something she can depend on. Her past is, well, not what could be called stable. I think the Tombwatch is the first thing she ever had in her life that she could be sure of.' He shook his head and pointed at the assembled forces.

'I don't think our towns have mustered a force this big since... since the last time a procession of nighthaunts swarmed into

Westreach.' Jahangir pointed at a group of people dressed not in armour but in cloaks and robes. 'Wizards. Wizards and scholars. A fair number of priests too. I'm a military man, Venteslav. How am I supposed to issue commands to those kinds of people? I've only the vaguest notion of how magic works, much less what it can be depended upon to accomplish.'

Venteslav tapped an iron coin fastened to his sleeve when Jahangir mentioned wizards. 'Magic is something you want to eat with a long spoon,' he said. 'It's reckless to depend on spells to achieve anything. You can let wizards make the path easier, but you don't want to be in the position where your plans need magic to work.'

'But isn't that the entire purpose of this expedition?' Jahangir asked. 'We seek out the Veiled Oracle. We are depending on the oracle's magic not simply to make the path easier, but to show us where it is.'

'Sometimes you've got to have faith,' Venteslav responded. He nodded towards one of the warrior priests as the man moved among the troops. 'The word's got around, you know. About what they saw in their divinations up at the lighthouse. You're the chosen one. Everyone on this expedition believes in you. They have faith you'll deliver us all from the Lady of Sorrows and fulfil the prophecy.'

Jahangir slowly turned away. 'I'd say they were wrong,' he told Venteslav in a whisper. 'Except it seems Lady Olynder thinks I can break this curse too.' He sighed and looked past his troops to the rooftops of Westreach rising in the distance. The stone slate roofs, so different from those of Eastdale, seemed to wave at him in farewell. He wondered if he'd ever see them again. If he'd walk the streets of his town again.

'Right or wrong, we have to go,' Jahangir said. 'Because I am the chosen one, and if I stay here, Lady Olynder will come for me. I won't put the Twinned Towns at risk for my sake.'

'We'll win,' Venteslav assured him. 'You've heard the prophecy. You've been chosen by fate to lead the way and break the curse. You're the one who will finally end this nightmare.' He waved his hand at the assembled troops. 'Think how many more lives were lost when last Lady Olynder attacked. Even if it costs all of us, it will be a small price to pay if no future generation has to suffer her malice.'

Jahangir nodded. 'A lot depends upon us,' he said. 'Let us pray to Sigmar that I am equal to everything that is expected of me.'

CHAPTER FOUR

Jahangir's expedition advanced down the Mournmarch. The wide road was flanked on either side by tall bronze poles from which hung iron lanterns. Each lantern was engraved with prayers to Sigmar and had been blessed in one of the temples before being placed. Lamplighters used special candles to illuminate the road, enough of the divine light of Azyr shining from them as to keep the nighthaunts away. At least, unless a powerful will forced the phantoms to overcome their hesitance.

The Mournmarch was the only overland route to the island, but today there was no traffic along it. All travellers had been diverted to clear the way for Jahangir's force. A few hardy souls braved the ruins to cheer the soldiers on as they passed, but for the most part the expedition was alone.

'Have you ever been past the wall?' Jahangir asked Venteslav.

The captain tugged on his moustache for a moment. 'I was on a boat once. A friend started paddling out into the Sea of Tears. That was enough for me.'

'I've been on shore,' Jahangir said. 'Years ago, before I received my commission in the Tombwatch.' He glanced back over his shoulder at the quickly dwindling rooftops of Westreach. 'It's different. You can feel it through your whole being. A kind of haze surrounds you, like you're being concealed. Hidden from the sight of Sigmar.'

'Be careful talking like that,' Venteslav warned. 'Chosen one or not, the warrior priests don't like to hear anyone claiming there are limitations to the God-King's power.'

'It isn't blasphemy to recognise the threat,' Jahangir pointed out. 'The farther we get from the Twinned Towns, the more the power of Nagash holds sway. Our enemy is one of his Mortarchs. Faith in Sigmar won't lessen the danger.' He gestured to the massive wall on the shore of the island. 'Once we're out there, we're completely in enemy territory.'

The expedition continued its march. The ruins fell away now, leaving a great swathe of open ground where buildings had been cleared away. When the wall had first been built the settlers tore down the nearby structures and used the rubble to build the mighty barrier. The ramparts stood over a hundred feet above the road and stretched away to either side for a mile and more, following the irregular shoreline. Towers spaced along the battlements at intervals of fifty feet rose higher still, their flattened rooftops surrounded on each side by iron lanterns. Jahangir could see archers walking between the crenellations, their blue uniforms briefly visible between the grey battlements.

Between the towers that straddled the Mournmarch, the great gatehouse stood. The massive doors slowly shuddered open, their weight setting the ground quaking. Forty feet high and twenty feet thick, the giant portals were cast in steel. Across their surface were etched sacred orisons and holy icons of Sigmar's mighty warhammer, the fabled Ghal Maraz. Images of the blazing sun and its purifying rays were picked out in gold leaf, accommodating the Eastdale tradition that the undead feared daylight as keenly as they did the God-King. Jahangir could hear the rumble of the immense windlass within the gatehouse as it pulled the doors apart and opened the path for him.

'You would think nothing in the Mortal Realms could overwhelm these walls,' Venteslav muttered with awe in his voice.

'Yet they have,' Jahangir said. 'Once a generation the legions of Lady Olynder lay siege to these walls. In defiance of every effort, every prayer and spell set against them, the nighthaunts bypass our defences. They sweep across the island to ransack Westreach and send the people fleeing into Eastdale.'

Venteslav laid his fingers on the iron coin pinned to his tunic. 'We've beaten them back every time. By the grace of Sigmar, never have the nighthaunts been able to conquer all. Their strength is spent before they reach Eastdale and always they've been vanquished. The Lady of Sorrows slinks away to nurse her wounds and rebuild her legions.'

'The cycle has to be broken,' Jahangir swore. 'What kind of inheritance is it to leave to our children, this promise that one day the nighthaunts will come to threaten their world? No, there must be an end to it. If by taking the offensive, by moving the fight to the Mortarch's stronghold we can stop this chain of death and war...'

Jahangir's voice trailed off. The great gates were open now and he had an unobstructed view of what lay beyond. A wispy fog was rolling across the Sea of Tears, thin enough not to obscure anything but to bleed away any suggestion of colour. All was cast in shades of muted grey, as though Jahangir looked on a scene spun from dusty cobwebs.

The Mournmarch passed through the gates and arched downwards to join a wide bridge of black timber and cold-wrought iron. The bridge stretched away across the sluggish waters of the sea, lethargic waves limply splashing against the wooden pilings. Farther away from the island, Jahangir could see the first sharp turns the bridge made in its erratic course from the Twinned Towns to the mainland. The pilings had been raised only where there was nothing else to support the bridge. In other places, the bones of old Belvegrod had been put to use.

Jahangir walked with the first of his soldiers as they passed through the gate. He stared out across the dark waters of the sea. Black shapes reared up, sometimes just breaking the surface: the ruins of the Drowned City. The settlers who built the Twinned Towns had claimed only the smallest portion of what had been Belvegrod. The rest was out here, entombed in ages past beneath the Sea of Tears.

Great towers and spires poked up from the waves. Many were clustered together and so had been employed to anchor the bridge in place. Others, isolated and too distant to be of any use to the builders, stood with vacant windows and crumbling roofs – refuge for the carrion-shrikes and other birds that hunted for eels in these ghastly waters.

'Some of the oldest records we've recovered claim that Belvegrod was flooded by Lady Olynder.' Jahangir turned his head at the sound of Kvetka's voice. The scholar stood beside him, her eyes filled with trepidation. 'They say that her anger melted into her sorrow to create the deluge.' She gave Jahangir an apologetic smile. 'Of course, such stories are hotly argued. Some maintain that the Mortarch of Grief is a much more recent creation of Nagash and that even if her malignant spirit was active in such distant times she wouldn't have possessed the power to wreak such a cataclysm.'

'If wizards like Ivor and augurs like Bairam can send their vision into the future, perhaps a creature as powerful as Lady Olynder can send her evil into the past,' Jahangir said. He saw the scholar shudder at the grim suggestion. 'I don't say such things are possible – I leave the nuances of magic to those who've studied them – but I do know it is always dangerous to underestimate the ability of an enemy.'

'Or to underestimate your own ability,' Kvetka said. 'You shouldn't doubt the divination. All that was learned from the gravesands was carefully studied and discussed. There's no mistake, Jahangir. It is you who was chosen to defy the Lady of Sorrows. The man of two worlds. Do you know how rare your heritage is?'

Jahangir felt bitterness at the question. 'You ask me that? For you it is an academic question. For me, it has been my life. Part Azyrite, part Reclaimed. Belonging to both and neither. I've had to work twice as hard for everything I've achieved, and in doing so I've proved myself better than those who would have stood in my way.'

'A hard path is what forges a hero,' the scholar said.

'I'm not some legend stepping from one of your books.' Jahangir slapped his hand against his chest. 'I'm flesh and blood. Dreams and hurts all bound together by what I've seen and felt. I'm a man trying to save his people – all of his people – because through it all I still believe they're worth saving.'

Kvetka reached into the satchel she had slung over her shoulder. Inside were several books and scrolls. She started to draw one of them out. 'It is recorded that...'

Jahangir waved aside whatever she was going to say. 'If I'm the chosen one, as your divinations claim, then nothing you say matters. I'm fated to break the curse. If you're wrong about me, it doesn't matter. I still intend to see the quest through. Come what may.' He pointed back to where the other scholars and wizards were just approaching the gates. 'Go back and stay with your people. If there's any danger waiting for us, it will strike the vanguard first. There's room up here only for the best warriors. You will forgive me, but I think you'd agree that your studies don't include mastery of sword and spear.'

He could tell that the last comment stung Kvetka's pride. It was a simple statement of fact, but one Jahangir thought the scholar had only appreciated in a distant, academic fashion. She and perhaps the others from the lighthouse were so convinced of this prophecy that they'd failed to truly appreciate the danger of what they were doing. The expedition was striking out for the mainland, into the haunted lands where the power of Nagash ruled. This was no longer theory to be debated and discussed, but grim and pitiless reality.

Jahangir watched Kvetka push her way back through the ranks of his soldiers.

'I rather think you upset her,' Venteslav commented. He'd kept silent during the exchange.

'She's so confident she knows what's ahead of us that she's forgotten an old Shyishan saying,' Jahangir said. There was a distant look in his eyes when he quoted it for Venteslav, his memory slipping back to his boyhood. When his father had been away with the Tombwatch, his mother had taught him the traditions of the Reclaimed.

'Only the past is unchanging,' Jahangir recited. 'Only the dead know the measure of their days.'

The expedition was stretched out across a half mile of bridge, advancing with a cautious creep that felt to Jahangir both agonisingly slow and recklessly fast. On every side the cold Sea of Tears surrounded them now. The wall that protected the Twinned Towns was lost in the foggy distance, only the distorted glow of its lanterns giving any perspective on how far they'd marched.

Despite the admonishments of their officers and the warrior priests, the soldiers couldn't help but look over the sides of the bridge and peer down at the Drowned City. Old Belvegrod stared back at them with murky streets and buildings coated in slime. The small, sickly fish that swam these haunted waters would flit into view, darting out from empty windows and crumbled doorways. Stalks of witherweed, one of the few plants stubborn enough to defy the slime, erupted from cracks in the walls, their wide leaves swaying in the current.

Jahangir didn't know what impression the Drowned City made upon his warriors, but he hoped it was in some harmony with his own grim perspective. The doom that had taken Belvegrod was the same annihilation Lady Olynder would eventually bring to the Twinned Towns unless she was stopped. That realisation bolstered his own determination. He was confident it would do the same for his troops.

'I feel like a worm crawling across a coffin,' Venteslav said. He had a sprig of wolfbloom in one fist as he walked beside Jahangir. 'The old remedy against ill sendings,' he explained when he saw Jahangir looking at the dried weed.

'Just don't let any of the troops start scattering rice across the bridge,' Jahangir said. 'We'll need every grain for eating.'

'It wouldn't do any good anyway,' Venteslav replied. 'It's when a spirit is following you that it has to stop and count rice. When you're walking towards it the phantom's not bound by such rules.'

Jahangir gave a closer look to the soldiers with them in the vanguard: twenty Azyrites to the left and an equal number of Reclaimed to the right. Both groups appeared interested in what the officers were discussing. Jahangir felt the burden of being the man in the middle. The one who had to lead both factions.

'Some traditions have more than a little truth to them,' Jahangir told Venteslav. 'It is wrong to dismiss them out of hand.' Surreptitiously he watched the soldiers around them and tried to modulate his tone so all could hear him. 'Still, there are some which I've yet to see confirmed. Many times my patrols in the Tombwatch have scattered rice or sand to try and distract a nighthaunt. I've never seen such a tactic delay the undead. But I have seen a talisman of wolfbloom that struck sparks from the claws of chainrasps that tried to grasp the one who wore it. I've heard spirits wail in fright when an old rhyme was invoked.' His hand fell to the sword hanging from his belt. 'The best way to deal with evil spirits remains a blade of blessed steel and a heart full of courage. Fear is the nectar the nighthaunts covet. Deny them that sustenance and you're halfway to defeating them. Faith and customs can't help if you're already cowering inside your own skin.'

Venteslav nodded. He too had noted the attention the soldiers were paying to their conversation. 'I think that little speech put some heart into them,' he said in a lowered tone. 'Your people and mine.'

'*Our* people,' Jahangir said. 'If this quest is to have any chance of success, the difference between Eastdale and Westreach has to be cast aside. Only together can we march against the enemy. Otherwise she will pick us off bit by bit.'

'You expect her to attack,' Venteslav stated. 'When?'

'When we're least prepared,' Jahangir answered. 'When we least expect it.' He clenched his fingers about the pommel of his sword. 'I'm sure of one thing. That was a deliberate trap your patrol rescued mine from. Anything as remorseless as Lady Olynder won't stop because the first effort was balked. She'll try again, and in conditions that favour her.'

Jahangir looked out across the bleak Sea of Tears and the scattered rooftops that rose from the waves. A dark mass behind the fog to the south might be the shore. At least the bridge was angling off in that direction. If so, he estimated that their march was almost at the midway point. Equidistant from the island and the mainland.

As Jahangir stared over the submerged ruins, motes of glowing light flitting over the water caught his attention. If not for their colouring and the unease they provoked, he might have thought they were simple flameflies. A feeling of mounting dread gripped him as he saw more of the glowing specks speeding above the waves.

'Venteslav, alert the rest of the column,' Jahangir told the captain. 'Tell them to be ready for an attack.'

Venteslav started to question the order, but one look at Jahangir's face must have swayed him. He turned and hurried back along the bridge to warn the others and ready them to repel enemies.

'Close formation,' Jahangir commanded the soldiers in the vanguard. 'We'll make a stand at the next bend.' The gravity in his voice brooked no hesitation. Azyrites and Reclaimed came together, locking their shields to form an armoured wedge as they quick-marched to the turn twenty yards ahead of them.

Jahangir followed the soldiers, but he kept his eyes on the ghostly wisps. There were more of them now. Individually none were any larger than his fingernail, but they were sweeping together in glowing streams that spiralled across the Sea of Tears. Each current of light coruscated above the Drowned City, becoming larger and more vibrant as more motes flowed into them. They converged upon the steeple of a sunken temple, its bell tower caked in dried scum, the bell itself corroded into a shapeless form. The rest of the structure was just a black mass beneath the waves.

The converging streams melded into a spectral flare, almost blinding in its intensity. The coldness that radiated from that luminance smashed into Jahangir like a physical blow, numbing his flesh and filling his mind with dark thoughts of dejection and despair. He saw again his parents, who had forsaken the customs of their people for love – and who'd ultimately let that love turn to bitterness and resentment because of their son. Because neither could decide how he should be raised, to which people he should belong. The flare responded to his grim memories, becoming more and more distinct. Within the light, a figure took shape, great and terrible. It was cast in the image of a woman, her withered form draped in billowing gossamer, her face shrouded by a flowing veil. Though her eyes were hidden, Jahangir could feel the intensity of their gaze: a dreary enmity, both malevolent and weary, a remorseless hate that time hadn't dulled even if the purpose behind it had faded away. From beneath the veil, tears of crimson leaked and dripped down her pallid raiment, shining like rubies through the misty fog.

Lady Olynder. The Mortarch of Grief herself made manifest. No more did she leave the destruction of Jahangir to minions. She had come to ensure his death.

For several minutes there was only silence from the expedition. A terrified awe seized the warriors and wizards who followed Jahangir that none were able to violate even as they choked back the screams that grew in their throats. Courage, that most delicate of armour, had been sundered. Prepared to fight the undead legions, the expedition was shocked to confront the Lady of Sorrows herself at the very border of the Twinned Towns.

'Sigmar!' Jahangir shouted, his cry piercing the stillness like a blade. It took all of his heart to strip away the numbness that filled him, the dark impulses that plucked at his mind and urged him to self-destruction. Never had it taken such monumental effort for so simple an act. Merely focusing his mind upon the God-King was a feat of endurance that sent a shudder through him. As he shouted to the heavens and invoked his god, he felt the Mortarch's pitiless hate like a thousand scarabs boring into his flesh. Others, less resolute than himself, were unequal to the test. A splash sounded from behind him and Jahangir looked back in horror to see a soldier sinking into the sluggish water. Another lunged for the edge of the bridge, breaking free of the companions who tried to restrain him. His wail of misery echoed through the air as he plunged into the Sea of Tears.

'Sigmar!' Jahangir cried again, filling the name with all the defiance he could muster.

'Sigmar!' The shout was taken up, voices calling out from all along the bridge. Jahangir's effort had broken the awful spell, freeing others from Lady Olynder's mesmerising domination. Archers nocked arrows to their bows and sent a rain of missiles at the drowned steeple. Wizards gestured with wands and staves, pointing at the structure and the glowing apparition. Spheres of blazing fire, ribbons of crackling lightning, globs of molten rock – a dozen violent spells focused themselves on the horrible entity and sent destruction speeding towards her.

Away from Lady Olynder's figure, two lesser shapes now detached themselves, spectral handmaidens that spiralled away from their mistress. They circled her with a speed that staggered belief and from each a gibbous light emanated, surrounding the terrifying Mortarch. No shaft or spell pierced that phantasmal barrier. To Jahangir's eyes, it looked as though the enemy and the steeple folded into themselves, shifting in some impossible way. Formerly standing above the Sea of Tears, in a heartbeat both were unaccountably beneath the waves. More than merely an illusion, the violation of logic and reality saw the attacks directed at their enemy skip harmlessly across the sea.

Cries of disbelief, shouts of frustration and despair rose from Jahangir's force.

'Have faith in Sigmar! Take heart in the nobility of our cause!' he admonished his troops. 'Don't forget who you fight for, who you'd save from this evil.'

As he bellowed encouragement to his warriors, another sound echoed over the Sea of Tears. From deep below the surface the doleful notes of a ringing bell bubbled up, the noise reverberating through the bridge like an earthquake. Animals shrieked and broke loose from their handlers, the most frantic of them smashing through the stone barriers to plunge off the edge of the spans and into the murky depths. The sky darkened as the daylight recoiled and hid itself behind unseen clouds. A coldness wafted down upon the scene, turning breath into frost.

The impossible ringing that sounded from under the waves increased, joined by the tolling of dozens more bells. Every submerged temple and shrine added to the sepulchral music until it became a hellish clamour. Clappers long decayed to rust, the bells rang out in ghostly refrain.

Jahangir could see shapes now emerging from the Drowned City: tattered shrouds, black with decay, rippled around skeletal shapes that flew towards the surface. Darker than the shadows through which they swam, the nighthaunts were as obvious to his sight as though each were illuminated by its own candle. A fearful legion, conjured up from the household catacombs and temple vaults of old Belvegrod, summoned by the dread command of Lady Olynder.

'When they reach the surface, loose your arrows!' Jahangir ordered his men. Some of the archers cast their shafts early, the impetus of their shots lost as they hit the water. Most waited until the nighthaunts were above the waves. Volleys of arrows rained down from the bridge, each shaft etched with a prayer copied from the sacred *Liber Sigmar*, each arrowhead quenched in holy water after being forged. When they struck the spectral entities, the undead evaporated and collapsed in upon themselves, leaving only a slick of dark residue floating on the waves.

The wizards and priests added their magic to the fray. Shafts of golden light pierced the fog to immolate clutches of ascending phantoms, vanquishing them through divine wrath. Rays of fire seared into the shrouded apparitions, consuming them in arcane pyres. Jahangir saw other chainrasps writhing, caught by ribbons of electricity, smoke steaming away from their spectral essence.

Scores of the undead were destroyed as they reached the surface, yet they were only the smallest fragment of the legions being drawn from their watery tombs. Jahangir could see hundreds – thousands – more pouring upwards. Lady Olynder and the steeple from which she commanded her procession had materialised once again on the surface of the sea. At a gesture of her bony hand a great wave reared up and washed down across the bridge only a few yards from Jahangir and the vanguard. He felt the spray pelt him, each drop stinging his skin like frost. But it wasn't the wave that threatened the soldiers, rather that which it left behind on the bridge.

Drawn up from the Drowned City, a piteous sight met Jahangir's gaze. They were people, their faces gripped by despair, eyes frantic with terror. Men and women, elders and children, noble and common. A great crowd overwhelmed by fear, crushed beneath the oppression of cataclysm – Jahangir knew these were spirits called up from the last of Belvegrod's dead, those who'd tried to escape when the Sea of Tears flooded their homes. Tears welled in his eyes as he felt their anguish, the torment that even now enslaved them.

At the forefront of the spectral horde was the vision of a man in elegant armour riding a barded horse. His face was noble; his eyes shone with compassion. Jahangir sensed the rider's story. A hero of Belvegrod, he could have escaped the drowning city but he'd gone back. Gone back to lead others to safety. Again and again he'd returned, each time abandoned by more of his followers as fear overcame them until at last he returned alone. Alone to die in a last, futile effort.

Jahangir felt a poisonous sympathy for the hero's spectre. Tendrils of doubt wormed through his soul. He would fail and of what consequence would his efforts be then? Why risk himself for those unworthy of his bravery?

'No,' Jahangir hissed at the apparition. 'I'm *not* like you.'

The spectre's face, so fine and noble, vanished the moment he rejected it. In the blink of an eye the entire crowd on the bridge changed. Flesh became exposed bone, faces became grinning skulls, clothing became mouldering shrouds. The rider on its horse now appeared as a rotted corpse clad in black armour, its steed a decayed thing with smoke boiling off its hooves.

The knight glowered at Jahangir. Its fleshless jaws opened in a challenging wail and then its nightmarish steed was galloping forwards, intent upon riding him down.

Across the bridge the phantoms surged, led by their long-dead champion. The enchanted shields carried by the Azyrites caused many of the chainrasps to explode into drifting columns of mist. The Reclaimed brandished talismans and charms in their fists as they stabbed their spears into the nighthaunts, inflicting grievous wounds from which steaming ectoplasm flowed. Whether guarded by blessed shields or protected by ancient tradition, none of the warriors were able to stem the advance of the shrouded knight as it drove its steed towards Jahangir. Two men were smashed down by the smoking hooves as the phantom horse trampled them. Another was impaled upon the jagged lance the rider bore. His body writhed as the shaft transfixed him and the knight lifted him into the air. A cadaverous hue stole across his visage, but more horrible still was the lack of any mark of injury – the lance impaling him didn't pierce the man's flesh or armour, but struck instead at the soul within.

The same could not be said for the dying man's comrades. The shrouded knight shook its victim from side to side, using his body like a battering ram to clear a path as he barrelled through the ranks. In the resultant gap, lesser spirits swept forwards, flinging themselves on the soldiers before they could restore their formation.

On all sides the nighthaunts now converged upon the bridge. Where the defending wards were strong the least of the spectres were repelled. Others, more steeped in the dark energies of necromancy, spilled over the walls, spectral steam rising from them as they defied the protective spells. They were quickly set upon by the soldiers, brought low by blessed steel. Always, for each undead vanquished, another reached the bridge to take its place. Where the panicked beasts had broken through the walls, the situation was more dire. Here the bridge was inundated by the nighthaunts, even the least of them able to bypass the shattered wards. Wizards from the lighthouse and priests from the temple hurried to these places, trying to stem the onslaught by means of spell and prayer.

Jahangir could spare no further attention to the greater battle as the last of his vanguard were shoved aside by the shrouded knight. He felt the burn of the apparition's glowing eyes as it glared at him from its saddle. With a contemptuous gesture, it shook its lance and sent the body of the man impaled upon it sprawling at Jahangir's feet. The lance withdrawn, the warrior's tormented spirit fled. The corpse rapidly withered now, collapsing into dust in a matter of heartbeats.

Jahangir raised his sword in defiance and leapt at the rider. The enchanted blade hewed through the spectral lance, shearing across its haft and ripping down across the neck of the phantom steed. The severed length of the lance went spinning away, swiftly losing even the semblance of shape as it dissipated into mist. The horse reared as it was struck, its fleshless head nearly hewn from the skeletal body. It struck out with its smoking hooves, but Jahangir ducked beneath them and stabbed the point of his blade deep into the apparition's chest.

The undead horse wilted under Jahangir's thrust, its essence crashing down in a morass of steaming ectoplasm. Out from that destruction, the knight arose. It flew above Jahangir, the broken lance in its fingers bubbling away to be replaced by a sinister double-edged sword.

Again Jahangir felt malignance clawing at his mind, trying to destroy him from within. He felt utter contempt for this monster, a degree of loathing more powerful than anything he'd known. He was ashamed of the moment of pity he'd held for the spectre and the man who'd ridden back to rescue innocents from a doomed city. There'd been no chivalry in the knight's gesture. He'd ridden back not to save lives, but to increase his own prestige and renown. At the last, when he feared he wouldn't live to capitalise from his heroics, he'd abandoned those who looked to him for salvation. The streets of Belvegrod had been littered with the broken bodies of those he had trampled in a last desperate attempt to escape.

Into that extreme of loathing, again there was that whisper. An insidious insinuation that Jahangir and the undead knight were alike. What was Jahangir but a selfish man clinging to the image of a hero? A man arrogant enough in his pride to let others declare him chosen by fate to rescue them? As these questions wracked his brain his heart shuddered with despair. *Lay down your sword. Accept your doom.*

Narrowly did Jahangir recover his senses in time to parry the phantom blade as the shrouded knight hurtled down at him. The wraith recoiled, not expecting its enemy to meet the attack. Its ethereal weapon couldn't pass through Jahangir's blessed sword and the creature was flung back, drifting away like a puff of smoke.

'I am *not* like you,' Jahangir snarled at the apparition. He darted a glance across the Sea of Tears towards the steeple where Lady Olynder dominated her undead legions. He knew it was from her that his thoughts of doom and despair emanated, foisted upon his mind by her black magic. 'By the glory of Sigmar, I will *never* be like him!' he shouted defiantly.

'General! Look out!' The shout rose from one of the soldiers. He sprang ahead of Jahangir, putting himself between his commander and the undead champion. The spectral rider slashed him with its phantom sword.

'Fight me, damn you!' Jahangir snarled at the fiend. The valiant sacrifice of the soldier both enraged and shamed him. The man had died for his sake, and he still wasn't convinced he was worthy of such loyalty.

The shrouded knight rushed for Jahangir once more. It swung its blade at his helm, but he was able to duck beneath its sweep and bring his own sword raking across its side. The decayed armour split under the blow, spilling away in misty tatters to expose shattered ribs and the shrivelled residue of organs.

The phantom sword lashed out once again. This time Jahangir felt its cold touch, but it failed to pierce the armour he wore, failed to strike the soul within his flesh. Before the knight could attack again, the holy sword whipped up at the spectre's head. For an instant, Jahangir felt resistance. It was like stabbing into mud, the drag of something too shapeless to defy his strength. The knight's essence yielded, coils of spectral mist flying from the creature as Jahangir sawed through its vaporous skull. Fragments of the bisected head drifted away, losing cohesion as the malignant spirit that bound them was extinguished.

Jahangir turned from the vanquished wraith. Only a handful of the vanguard remained now, desperately striving to hold back the horde of chainrasps that howled across the bridge. The rest of the expedition was equally beset by the nighthaunts. Vengeful undead were everywhere, threatening to overwhelm the living defenders at any moment.

'Hold fast!' Jahangir shouted to his remaining soldiers, trying to inspire them against a seemingly unending foe. His troops closed ranks, concentrating around their commander. Even now there was a desperate look of hope in their eyes, a conviction that their hero would yet prevail. A few waved their weapons at the fragments of the shrouded knight, cheering Jahangir's triumph over his foe. Their confidence in him only added to the turmoil in Jahangir's mind.

'Slowly fall back,' Jahangir ordered. 'The archers on the other span will support us with their arrows.' He didn't know how much reality there was in such a claim, but at least it would give his men purpose and some promise of help.

Before Jahangir could take even a few steps, a shriek echoed across the Sea of Tears. The Lady of Sorrows flew away from the drowned steeple. For a second he dared to hope she was leaving the battlefield, but despair crashed down upon him when the Mortarch glided over the waves to the bridge. As she moved across the span, funeral roses erupted from the stones. For only an instant were they vibrant and alive, then they withered in the ghastly presence of Lady Olynder, dead petals scattering before her as she advanced.

The mental anguish that had assailed him before now gripped Jahangir with unimaginable intensity. Nor was he alone in feeling the psychic torment. Soldiers in the vanguard dropped their weapons and fell to their knees, tears flowing down their faces. The chainrasps rolled over the defeated men, tearing them to ribbons with their skeletal talons.

Jahangir struggled to resist Lady Olynder's baleful magic. He fixated on the divinations that had set him upon this course. 'I am the chosen one!' he shouted at the terrifying apparition. 'I have been fated to break your curse!'

The Mortarch's face was hidden behind the thick veil she wore. For the first time Jahangir realised that it wasn't part of a shroud, but the mouldering remnant of bridal splendour. The long white dress that flowed around her, for just an instant, assumed the appearance of its ancient finery. Her hands became soft and vibrant, alive with warmth and grace. He heard her voice echo in his mind, more wondrous and enticing than that of any living woman.

'Hope is the lie that prolongs folly...' Her words thrilled through his soul. 'The underworlds overflow with those who continued to cling to hope even as it betrayed them.'

Jahangir felt his convictions slipping away, withering in the melody of her words. A heartbeat, perhaps, and he would have submitted, but in that heartbeat he saw the last of his vanguard die. It wasn't fear for his own life that allowed him to break free, but fear for the lives he was responsible for.

'Hope isn't the traitor!' Jahangir shouted as he raised his sword. 'You are!'

Lady Olynder wailed, her beauty and bridal finery transformed once again into graveyard decay. He could feel her enmity smashing down on him, as ferocious as that of the most savage beast. The banshees that attended her shrieked, and with their cries the horde of chainrasps swept across the bridge. Jahangir struck out at the horde, but the spectres darted past him, avoiding his blows. They weren't seeking his life, but the lives of his followers.

'Fight me, damn you!' Jahangir raged. He started to pursue the chainrasps, but before he could reach them he was knocked off his feet. The whole bridge was shaking from side to side, bucking and jostling with such violence it was impossible for him to stand.

From where he lay, Jahangir could see members of the expedition being flung off the quaking span into the waters. The glow and crackle of spells invoked by the wizards did little to appease the elemental wrath that shook the whole of the bridge now. The nighthaunts, gliding several feet above it, moved freely and set themselves against the reeling mortals. The battle became a massacre.

'All hope is delusion,' Lady Olynder pronounced. Gone were the captivating, dulcet tones, replaced by a scratchy moan. Jahangir watched as she lifted the staff-like sceptre she held. He could feel the icy touch of sorcery as she unleashed her magic.

The tremor was magnified in its intensity. From where he was sprawled, Jahangir saw the ancient rooftops that supported the bridge become distorted. The old masonry appeared to spin into itself in a manner he could liken only to churning butter. The effect brought immediate results. Screams filled the air as the bridge crumbled away. Section by section, the spans fell into the Sea of Tears and dragged down all those who stood upon them, leaving only the ethereal nighthaunts hovering above the waves.

The section of bridge where Jahangir lay was spared the violence of Lady Olynder's spells. As the tremor subsided, he gazed in horror at the people struggling in the water – people he'd led to destruction. A moment, and then the hovering wraiths descended upon them. Drowning soldiers were grappled by the malignant spirits and dragged down into the gloomy depths.

'Is this the purpose for which you were chosen?' The bitter mockery of Lady Olynder slashed through Jahangir. He leapt to his feet and charged at her with his sword.

'Damn you!' he raged. The Mortarch's handmaidens started forwards to intercept him, but a gesture from Lady Olynder held them in place.

'I was damned long ago by a thing far greater than you, hero,' Lady Olynder said. She moved forwards, dead roses preceding her. Jahangir was battered by the despondent aura she exuded, his resolve shattered by his failure to save his troops. His grip on his sword faltered as the enormity of hopelessness washed over him.

'Shall I show you the purpose for which you were chosen?' Lady Olynder held forth her staff.

Jahangir could see that the head of the staff was made of glass. Within it, grains of sand fell, seeming to defy gravity no matter which way the staff was held. More, there was meaning in the pattern they formed. He thought of Ivor and the lighthouse and the divinations. He knew he was looking at the gravesands that sifted across the edge of Shyish and held within them all the patterns of tomorrow.

Jahangir's mind was unable to decipher the meaning of those patterns, but he felt an outside force helping him find sense in the sifting grains. He knew it was the power of Lady Olynder exerting itself, but he also knew there was no deception in that power. She had no reason to lie to him. No falsehood could annihilate his hope more completely than the future for which he'd been chosen. The full prophecy, not the cobbled-together fragments related to him by Ivor's fools.

An inarticulate shriek tore itself from Jahangir's throat. His sword fell from his hand as he turned and fled. Before him was the shattered edge of the bridge. Below him were the dark waves and the Drowned City. His mind cracking from the horrible revelation, Jahangir didn't hesitate. He leapt from the bridge and plunged into the black water. The depths beckoned him and the weight of his armour sped his journey into their embrace.

As his vision faded, Jahangir could see the glowing figure of Lady Olynder staring down at him from the bridge. Only in death did he understand how futile it had all been.

To think mortal blood could defy the Lady of Sorrows.

CHAPTER FIVE

Mahyar felt as though he'd swallowed half of the sea. The other half of it was dripping from his sodden clothing. He coughed up another mouthful of water and sank down on the slab of stone that protruded from the sandy beach. He looked aside at the figure sprawled on the ground nearby and shook his head.

The gods had a grim sense of humour.

It was a miracle that Mahyar hadn't drowned when the bridge collapsed. He'd lost his warhammer when he hit the water and only a frantic effort enabled him to break the straps that held his armoured breastplate before its weight could drag him deeper. He'd seen many sinking into the dark who weren't so fortunate, sucked down by the steel mail they wore. When he fought his way up to the surface, it was complete bedlam. Desperate people thrashed about in the waves trying to find anything that would buoy them and save them from drowning. Hovering above, silent as death itself, were the nighthaunts. When the undead tired of waiting, they swept down to claim those who'd survived the collapse.

Mahyar still didn't know why the spectres hadn't come for him. It seemed to him nothing short of miraculous, a boon from Sigmar himself. He started to swim for the shore, but hadn't gone far before he saw someone struggling to stay above the waves. His own reprieve made him feel obligated to try to save the person, reaching the spot just as the head slipped under the surface. He caught hold of the woman and pulled her back. She was insensible as he swam to the shore.

Only when they were both on the beach did Mahyar get a good look at her. The irony of it added a note of bitter humour to the catastrophe. The woman he'd rescued was Kvetka. If he'd known that before, maybe he'd have let her drown. Perhaps that was why she was the one – of all those in the expedition – he'd been drawn to save. A lesson in humility, in casting aside prejudice and submitting to the will of Sigmar. Trusting in the greater wisdom of the God-King.

Mahyar staggered to his feet and moved over to where Kvetka lay. He could see that she was still breathing, so that at least was a good sign. Her flesh was almost blue in colour, her body shivering under her soaked robes. He knew how keenly the cold air was afflicting himself, so he could only imagine how much worse it must be for the bookish scholar, someone who'd strengthened her knowledge to the exclusion of her physical stamina. The priest looked around the shoreline, seeking anything with which he might try to start a fire. All he saw was sand and rubble from the Drowned City. Whatever was farther inland remained hidden behind a veil of fog.

'Sigmar guide me,' Mahyar prayed. He looked for any pile of stones that might at least serve as a bulwark against the chill breeze rolling off the Sea of Tears. He sighted what looked like a promising spot, but when he stooped to pick up Kvetka he caught movement out of the corner of his eye. He turned towards the water, ready to confront whatever was coming towards the shore even if it meant defying it with nothing more than his bare hands.

A dark mass trudged its way through the sluggish water. At first all Mahyar could see was a mop of stringy hair. Then a face emerged: gaunt, strained, but with a far more robust colour than Kvetka's shivering form. He was thin and spare, wearing purple-coloured robes, and Mahyar was surprised to find that he recognised the man. Gajevic, the wizard whose divinations when deciphering the gravesands had helped set this chain of tragedy into motion. The warrior priest's suspicions were aroused to find that the timid conjuror had survived when so many others had been lost. His unease was further provoked when he noted that despite walking out from the sea, the wizard's body and clothes were completely dry.

Gajevic stopped and smiled when he reached the beach. It was an awkward, nervous expression. Meek and anxious. Mahyar might have been disarmed by that show of timidity if not for the lack of wetness in the wizard's garb.

'Then I'm not the only one who escaped,' Gajevic said, a note of relief in his voice.

'By the grace of Sigmar, some of us have survived,' Mahyar replied. He gave the wizard a suspicious look. 'Perhaps other gods saw fit to intervene as well.'

Gajevic cringed when Mahyar voiced the accusation. 'I... I am... no disciple... not one of... Nagash's slaves...' He stiffened and forced himself to meet Mahyar's gaze. 'The nighthaunts nearly took me on the bridge. I wouldn't have survived at all except I had a spell prepared.'

'Warned by your familiar spirits,' Mahyar growled. 'Advised what to expect and how to escape it.' His hands clenched and unclenched at his side, as though his fingers were wrapped around the wizard's throat.

'No!' Gajevic cried. 'I didn't know! How could I have known? Would I have been so callous as to risk...' He pointed to Kvetka. 'I saw you swimming above me as I walked below. It was my influence that made you swim to Kvetka and rescue her.'

Red rage flashed through Mahyar's vision. He was willing enough to accept the influence of Sigmar over the course of his fate, but to be manipulated by sorcery edged upon the blasphemous. Perhaps he would strangle the conjuror after all.

'More evidence you knew what would happen and were ready for it,' Mahyar said. 'You forget that I was there. I was in the Belvegrod lighthouse when the perspicillum was turned upon the gravesands. It was your observations that were attended with the most care during the divination. How easy for you to withhold some of what you saw. To turn a portent of doom into a promise of salvation.' He took a step towards Gajevic. 'You knew what would happen and were ready for it. What kind of spirits warned you? Gheists from your master Nagash? Truly there is no trusting a wizard.'

The wizard backed away, retreating into the waves. Water swirled around his waist. A look of absolute terror covered his face. Then he lunged at Mahyar, moving with such unexpected speed and recklessness that the warrior priest was caught unprepared. The scrawny wizard bowled him over, knocking him down in the surf. For an instant, Mahyar was utterly helpless, but Gajevic didn't seize the opportunity. He ran on, bolting up onto the shore until he was well away from the water. He stood there, shivering and panting as Mahyar recovered from his fall.

'That was your one chance, warlock,' Mahyar snarled. 'You will regret not taking advantage of it.' He charged towards Gajevic. The wizard raised his hand, holding his palm outwards in an arresting gesture. Mahyar's intention was to grab the conjuror by the throat. Instead he found himself frozen in place, unable to move so much as a muscle.

'You must listen,' Gajevic pleaded. 'I didn't know anything more than what the perspicillum revealed to me. The spell... I was ready...' A flush of embarrassment coloured his face. The explanation, when it came, was so simple that it completely disarmed Mahyar. 'I can't swim.'

'What?' Mahyar muttered. The arcane hold that had seized him was gone now, but so too was the impulse to strangle Gajevic.

'As soon as we set out on the bridge,' Gajevic explained. 'I thought I'd be all right, but all I could think about was falling into the water. Drowning in the Drowned City. My mind kept turning back to an incantation that would protect me. It was all I could think of... even when the attack came.' His head snapped around and he stared at Kvetka lying on the sand.

'She's alive,' Mahyar assured him.

Gajevic knelt beside her and carefully pressed his finger against her wet robe. 'The cold will take her,' he commented. He glanced over at Mahyar, as though really seeing him for the first time. 'You're in danger too.'

The wizard clapped his hands together. Mahyar could hear strange words sizzling across Gajevic's lips as he invoked some arcane formula. His conjuring was swift. In a few moments crackling flames billowed from the wizard's hands. He sat down beside Kvetka and motioned Mahyar to join him.

'My magic will warm you both,' Gajevic promised. It was true. Mahyar could feel the invigorating heat pouring into his chilled flesh. He watched steam rise from Kvetka's sodden robes. Her skin began to shift back to a healthier hue.

'If I'm to understand you, it was your magic that guided me to her,' Mahyar said, nodding at the still-insensible scholar. 'Was there anyone else? Were there any other survivors?'

Gajevic hung his head and shrugged. 'I don't know,' he confessed.

'In all the confusion… with the bridge crashing down… so many nighthaunts…'

'Jahangir…' Mahyar could scarcely keep his voice from breaking when he spoke the name. 'What about him? Did he survive?' The last question was asked with a desperate eagerness. Like the others, Mahyar had believed in the prophecy, that Jahangir had been chosen to break Lady Olynder's curse.

'I don't know,' Gajevic repeated, his voice a low whisper. 'When I last saw him, he was fighting one of the Mortarch's marshals. I lost sight of him after that.'

'I saw him after you did,' Mahyar said with a shudder. 'But when I saw him his foe wasn't a mere wraith.' His hand gripped the hammer icon that hung from his neck and he glanced back at the sea and the fog and the things that lay hidden behind that veil – the horror that had descended upon them all and cast their hopes into ruin.

'When I saw Jahangir,' Mahyar continued, 'he stood alone. Alone against the Lady of Sorrows.'

'There! A light!' Soraya almost slipped off the barrel when she pointed towards the shore. Only a frantic adjustment of her grip kept her from sliding off into the water. Ratimir made a grab for her arm to keep her steady, but in doing so threatened to plunge them all under the surface.

'Watch what you're doing!' Zorgrath snapped at them. 'It'd be a sorry thing to come so far only to sink ourselves now!'

The two soldiers glowered at the grey-skinned cryptborn. It was insult enough to be scolded by the ghoulish creature, but much worse when they knew he was right.

'A light,' Soraya repeated. 'I saw a light on shore.' Ratimir was facing towards her with his back to the shoreline. Zorgrath, while his other senses were keyed to a degree that was extraordinary, wasn't able to see small things at any great distance. The two men had to rely on her word that what she saw was there.

'Maybe there are other survivors...' Ratimir put the thought into words. His face curled up into a sour look and there was a guilty expression in his eyes.

Soraya knew her own face was equally dour. Their own survival hadn't come without a price. When the bridge collapsed, hundreds of people were hurled into the sea. The barrel they clung to had bobbed back to the surface as they floundered in the water. They'd reached it before anyone else. It was Ratimir who declared it wouldn't buoy more than the three of them. That, of course, hadn't stopped drowning men from trying to save themselves. They'd been forced to fight for their barrel. The faces of the doomed wretches they'd shoved away would always haunt Soraya.

'Does the light look warm or cold?' Zorgrath asked. 'If it seems cold, it is best to turn away. Jack-o-wisps prefer to lurk near still water, but some may have been drawn here by the Mortarch's presence.'

'It... looks warm,' Soraya ventured. 'At any rate, it doesn't resemble anything I've seen while patrolling with the Tombwatch.'

'Then we'll risk it,' Zorgrath decided, his sharp teeth exposed as he smiled at Soraya.

'I'm not going,' Ratimir protested. 'I've no desire to have my belly sucked out through my skin by a jack-o-wisp!'

Zorgrath turned his smile towards Ratimir. 'I assumed you wanted to go where the barrel goes. You can leave us here, if you prefer.'

Ratimir cast his gaze over the dark, sluggish waves. 'I'll stay,' he grumbled.

'Take heart, Rat,' Soraya told him. 'If we find it is jack-o-wisps, they'll probably only get one of us.' She regretted making the jest when she saw the cunning gleam that came into his eyes. A desperate man would seize the most desperate ideas.

With what seemed to Soraya agonising slowness the barrel drew nearer to shore. Relief flowed through her when she saw figures sitting around the light. Certainly not jack-o-wisps then. Whoever was out there, they were solid rather than spectral. Or were they? Closing in upon the shore she noted that the light came from a flickering flame, a flame that rose from the cupped hand of one of the figures.

'Back!' Soraya hissed at her companions. She tried to paddle the barrel away from the shore but Zorgrath resisted her efforts.

'Still yourself,' the guide told her. 'Whoever's over there, whatever they're doing, they're alive at least.' He gestured with his thumb to his squashed nose. 'Trust me, I know what dead and alive smell like and the difference between the two.'

Reassured by Zorgrath's insistence, they paddled to the beach. As soon as her feet could feel sand under them, Soraya pushed away from the barrel. For all that it had served her, she looked on it as though it were diseased. She knew her safety had been bought only at a horrible price.

Ratimir and Zorgrath followed her as she trudged through the waves. Soraya could see that there were three people on the beach: two sitting, the other stretched out across the sand. One of them stood up and turned towards her. He was a powerfully built man with the dusky skin of an Azyrite. The robes he wore were tattered, but she could make out the icon of Ghal Maraz embroidered across the chest. Seeing that eased her mind. She couldn't imagine a creature of Nagash wearing Sigmar's symbol.

The man who remained sitting was thin and pale and it was from his cupped hand that the fire burned. He took no hurt from the flame, though even at this distance Soraya could feel its heat. Her skin prickled as she recognised it as some sort of magic.

Unlike the Azyrite, this man's clothes were completely dry, not even slightly damp as near as she could tell.

'One of the wizards from the lighthouse,' Ratimir said, unease in his voice. When he said it, Soraya remembered where she'd seen these men before. They'd both been there when Jahangir was called to the lighthouse. That one was indeed a wizard, the other a warrior priest of Sigmar.

The third person, the one lying on the sand, was likewise familiar from that brief visit to the lighthouse. Like the wizard, she had the pale complexion of the Reclaimed. Soraya couldn't put a name to the woman, but thought she'd been some sort of scholar rather than a wizard. Whatever her vocation, she looked to be in worse shape than her companions.

'So we weren't the only ones who escaped?' the dusky priest called out. There was a note of challenge in his tone and his hands were balled into fists as he looked them over. He paid particular attention to Zorgrath. 'How is it you survived?'

'We were lucky enough to grab hold of that when the bridge fell,' Soraya said, pointing to the barrel as it floated on the waves. 'We were able to swim away when the nighthaunts dived down to prey on the drowning.'

'Have you seen anyone else?' the priest asked.

Soraya responded with a shake of her head. 'Your light has been the only sign of life we've seen.' That news obviously troubled the priest. Likely for more reasons than one. The same light that could lead survivors to them might also draw prowling undead.

'Speaking of your fire, I'm soaked to the bone,' Ratimir stated, wringing the hem of his tunic. Like Soraya, he'd cast off his armour while hanging onto the barrel when it seemed the extra weight would pull them down.

The warrior priest looked uncertain. 'It might be better...'

'There could be others out there,' Soraya cut him off. 'Lost like we were. They might yet find your light. If it saves someone, isn't that a risk worth taking?'

'I can sustain the spell until Kvetka recovers.' The wizard spoke for the first time. 'The others can warm themselves, Mahyar.'

Mahyar shook his head. Again his gaze turned to Zorgrath. 'It would be a mistake to trust too easily, Gajevic...'

The cryptborn barked with jackal-like laughter. 'You can't accuse me of leading your friends into a trap,' he said. 'I wasn't to act as guide until after we were across.' He jabbed one of his long-nailed fingers at the water. 'A lot of your people are down there now, but so too is the rest of my pay. I had neither chance nor reason to betray anyone, priest, and I resent the accusation.'

'He's useful to have around,' Ratimir quipped. 'He can smell the undead before any of us can see them.'

Mahyar ignored the Reclaimed solider and turned towards Soraya. 'Do you speak in the cryptborn's favour?'

Soraya glanced from Zorgrath to Ratimir. 'I speak in no one's favour. The decision is yours to make.' She nodded towards Gaje-vic. 'Only make it quickly before I freeze.'

The priest debated for a moment, then hung his head in defeat. 'What does it matter? Live or die, our quest has failed. What does it matter if one of you is a traitor? Jahangir was the chosen one and without him, our quest is lost.'

As Soraya came forwards to warm the chill of the sea from her body, she found that the wizard's fire did nothing to drive away the chill left by Mahyar's words.

Venteslav clung to the marshmare's mane, his fingers so knotted in the wiry hairs that they stung from lack of circulation. Across the animal's neck he saw that the Azyrite soldier Omid kept a similarly desperate hold. Both men knew the panicked beast was their only hope of survival. By some freak of chance or divine miracle, the marshmare had broken free of its harness and survived its fall from the bridge. An even greater fortune placed it near enough to the soldiers that they were able to catch hold of it as it swam past them.

'The nighthaunts'll be after us next!' Omid cried. He nodded his head to indicate the spectres flitting about the collapsed bridge. When one of them spotted a swimming survivor, it shrieked and dived down on them like some kind of phantasmal vulture. Omid's expression was incredulous when he saw the wolfbloom in Venteslav's hand. 'You think that weed's going to keep them away?' he scoffed.

Venteslav glared back at the Azyrite. The last thing he needed now was some sneering lecture about idle superstitions. He couldn't say how effective the wolfbloom had been at protecting him while fighting on the bridge, but he did know when he hit the water it was his sword rather than the herb that had been knocked from his fingers.

'I think a warrior uses whatever weapon he has in hand,' Venteslav said. He brought the sharp barbs of the wolfbloom slapping against the marshmare's flank. The horse whinnied in pain and plunged ahead in brute panic. He felt sickened by the savage necessity, but if the horse didn't reach shore they were all going to die.

Omid clung tight as the animal swam through the waves. Venteslav didn't need to warn him that if he slipped off there'd be no going back. He could hear the soldier praying, a discordant sound against the wails of the nighthaunts and the shrieks of their victims.

The horse's strength began to wane. Venteslav raked the wolfbloom across its hide again and provoked another surge of motion. How long would the animal respond? How many times could it summon some unguessed stamina to keep moving? How long before it no longer cared if it was hurt and simply gave up? How long before all of them were sucked down into the Drowned City?

Each time he brought the wolfbloom into play, Venteslav felt like a cur. The necessity of cruelty didn't weigh any less heavily on his mind. If he were a wiser man, perhaps he'd know another way. Sigmar! How he wished there was another way.

A shudder coursed through the marshmare. When Venteslav slapped it with the wolfbloom, it didn't make a sound and its lunge forwards wasn't half so far as those that had come before. He knew the poor brute was at the end of its strength. Any moment and it would surrender to the destruction he'd forced it to defy for so long.

'The shore!' Omid cried out. 'We're going to make it!'

Venteslav could see the rubble-strewn beach ahead of them. It was a forlorn and desolate sight as it distinguished itself from the fog, but right now it looked as comforting as his own hearth back in Eastdale.

'Come along, old nag,' Venteslav coaxed the marshmare. 'We're nearly there.' He felt the animal shudder again. Its head sagged under the sluggish waves. He struck it one more time with the wolfbloom, stabbing the barbs deeper than ever before. The marshmare rallied, throwing back its head and snorting in weary protest. It lunged forwards again. This time there was a different kind of shudder that passed through its body. The horse's hooves were touching the bottom now. It was near enough to walk onto the beach.

Omid dropped away the moment his own feet touched the bottom. He shouted for joy as he slogged through the surf. 'By Sigmar, we made it!'

Venteslav curbed the soldier's glee. 'Keep quiet! We don't know what might be listening!' The warning didn't need to be repeated. Omid fell silent and slackened his pace. His eyes roved across every dark patch of rubble, studying them for the merest hint of threat.

Venteslav kept hold of the marshmare even after he found solid footing. He knew if he left the animal it would drown itself even with the beach in sight. It had expended itself past its limit. Only the command of a will outside itself could keep it going. So he walked beside it, cursing and cajoling each step, drawing from the horse that extra effort it didn't know it still had.

Omid was perched on one of the stones that lay strewn about the beach when Venteslav finally led the marshmare up from the water. The soldier had removed his empty scabbard from his belt and was holding it like a club. His tunic was sodden through, clinging to his body like wet parchment. Like Venteslav, he'd divested himself of his armour while clinging to the horse.

'You Reclaimed will waste yourselves on these superstitions,' Omid said. He waved the scabbard at the staggering horse. 'You should have left it. It's just going to die anyway.'

Venteslav stroked the abused brute and glowered at Omid. 'In Eastdale we aren't so churlish as to abandon a benefactor.'

'In Westreach we recognise what's practical and what isn't,' Omid said. He pointed at the wolfbloom in Venteslav's hand. 'That was our benefactor. You kept the beast going when it would have given up.'

Venteslav looked at the herb, its stalks coated in blood from the marshmare. He turned and threw the wolfbloom into the sea, shamed by the very sight of it. 'Sigmar provides,' he said, though the old maxim felt hollow. He started to lead the animal away from the surf, but the horse only took a few steps before it grunted and collapsed. Venteslav had to dart aside to keep from being crushed under its bulk.

'Leave it,' Omid called out when Venteslav moved back to the fallen animal. He flinched when Venteslav glared at him. 'We've got bigger problems. There's a light farther down the beach.'

'What kind of light?' Venteslav asked. 'Does it look like jack-o-wisps?' He trembled as another possibility occurred to him and he remembered the glowing figure standing in the sunken steeple. 'Does it look like *her*?'

Omid shook his head. 'If it's spectral then it isn't like anything I've seen with the Tombwatch.' He hopped down from his perch on the rocks. 'It could mean there're other survivors.'

Venteslav looked down at the marshmare lying in the sand, then back up at Omid. 'Show me,' he told the soldier. He followed him a few yards down the shoreline, far enough that a little flicker of yellow light was visible through the fog. 'You're right. It doesn't look like a spectral manifestation.'

'Whoever they are, we could use their fire,' Omid said.

'Worried they aren't our people?' Venteslav wondered.

Omid nodded and tightened his grip on the scabbard. 'If they're bandits or grots, we'd stand a better chance together than we would alone.'

Venteslav gave a regretful look back at the marshmare. The tide was washing over its flanks but the animal didn't stir. Alive or dead, he realised there was nothing more he could do for it, but leaving the horse behind stung his conscience.

'Let's get moving,' Venteslav said. There was no use lingering and with each passing moment he felt the cold seeping deeper into his flesh. 'Let's find this light. Even if we discover a whole gor warherd, at least we'll warm ourselves by their fire.'

When awareness returned to Kvetka it did so slowly. She observed her surroundings before understanding what she was seeing and hearing. Voices and figures wavered between the familiar and the strange. The effort to seize upon some shred of recognition only made the memories dance off into the confused haze.

Strangely the voice that stirred her from her malaise wasn't one she cared to hear. '…live when others have died. It means Sigmar has some purpose for us.' The words were spoken by Mahyar. She turned her head slowly and looked over at him. He didn't have his warhammer and armour, but there was no mistaking his harsh features and brawny frame. He had that intense, almost fanatical quality in his eyes that always entered them when he was extolling the God-King's might.

'You expect us to keep going?' The incredulous question was uttered by a small, wiry man, a soldier of Eastdale by his look. Kvetka thought she might have seen him before, but couldn't put a name to the face.

'What else do we do? Sit here and wait for the nighthaunts to find us?' The speaker was another soldier, though her dark skin showed she was of Westreach rather than Eastdale.

Another dusky Azyrite responded to her. 'We were all of us lucky to escape the catastrophe,' he said. He gestured with an empty scabbard at a man who was sitting in the sand, a little pillar of fire flowing upwards from his cupped hand. 'If not for the wizard's light, we might all be wandering around by ourselves. Easy prey for... whatever is out there.'

Kvetka focused her attention on the man the soldier called 'wizard'. It took her several heartbeats to realise he was Gajevic. The conjuror smiled at her and quickly lowered his eyes.

'I was worried you wouldn't awaken,' Gajevic said. 'You've been asleep a long time.'

Others were continuing to talk nearby, but their conversation became an indistinct buzz in Kvetka's ears. She held her attention on Gajevic. 'The bridge fell,' she said, trembling as she recalled her plunge into the Sea of Tears. She stared intently at the wizard. 'You saved me.'

Gajevic didn't meet her gaze. He shook his head. 'Mahyar brought you to shore,' he stated. Embarrassment coloured his face. The loss of concentration caused the arcane fire to flicker and die. At once its warmth was banished and the chill breeze wafting over the Drowned City reasserted itself.

Discussion died with the light. Everyone turned towards Gajevic. A moustached captain, a man of Eastdale, demanded an explanation from the wizard. 'Why did you extinguish the light? There may be other survivors out there!'

Gajevic fumbled for an answer. Kvetka knew only too well how awkward he could be when verbally challenged, so she intervened.

'Magic isn't an easy force to command,' she told the captain. 'It takes a toll on those who conjure it.'

Mahyar nodded. Though he looked reluctant to do so, he conceded the point to Kvetka. 'Gajevic has been maintaining that fire for hours now. It was only a matter of time before he had to let the magic fade.'

Kvetka glanced back at Gajevic, shock in her eyes. She knew little of arcane matters, but she knew enough to recognise the impressiveness of his feat. Magic was fickle and any measure of permanence demanded some sort of object to retain the enchantment. Holding a spell like that fire for as long as he had was something she'd have been certain was beyond Gajevic's abilities.

'I wouldn't hold out hope of anyone else joining us,' the Azyrite with the empty scabbard advised. 'Anybody else would've been in the water at least as long as we were, Venteslav. Probably longer.'

'*Captain* Venteslav,' Venteslav snapped. 'You'd do well to remember that, Omid.'

'It doesn't change the facts,' the other Azyrite soldier said. She gave a regretful nod to the rolling waves. 'Each of us barely survived the Sea of Tears. If anyone else was out there, then they can't or won't come to us.'

'Soraya neglects to mention something else,' Omid added. 'The light that can draw survivors to us can attract other things as well. Things we don't want to meet.' He pointed at Kvetka. 'The warmth of the fire revived her. That was what we were waiting for.' He looked around at the others. 'Well, wasn't it?'

A moment of silence passed among the bedraggled group. Soraya sat down on a weathered stone and shook her head. 'I'm not afraid to say it,' she finally spoke up. 'We were waiting for Jahangir. Even now each of us clings to the hope that he'll return.'

'They told us he was the chosen one,' the ferret-faced Reclaimed soldier grumbled.

'None of that, Ratimir,' Venteslav told the man. 'Soraya's right. All of us were inspired by the divinations. We believed Jahangir was fated to break the curse that menaces our towns.' He waved his arms in a helpless gesture. 'Now, that hope is gone.'

Mahyar gave each of them a withering look. 'While there is faith, there is hope. Sigmar will not abandon those who keep faith with him.'

'You'd have us try to do something a small army wasn't able to do,' Omid said. 'That isn't faith. That's madness.'

'Jahangir was the chosen one,' Ratimir repeated. 'If he failed what's the use of us trying?'

'No defeat is so complete as when a man tells himself he is defeated,' Kvetka said, quoting an old Belvegrodian proverb. She held Ratimir's gaze. 'Jahangir was shown to us in the gravesands, but perhaps we didn't understand his role. Perhaps he was marked to only lead us so far.' She turned and stared at Mahyar. 'Perhaps it was fated that others would finish the quest.'

'The God-King delivered us from destruction. He did so for a reason.' Mahyar made the sign of the Hammer as he spoke.

'It's pointless to go on,' Omid declared. 'The only sensible thing is to find a way back to the Twinned Towns.'

Venteslav sighed and ran his fingers through his moustache. 'We left our people cheering us, filled with hope such as they've never known. If we go back, all we can bring them is grief and despair.'

He stamped his foot against the sand. 'I'd rather fight the wraiths again than bring that sort of misery back with me.'

'They'll find out soon enough, if they don't know already,' Ratimir said. 'The garrison on the wall must have heard the fighting and it won't take long to discover part of the bridge is gone.'

'We'd be throwing away our lives,' Omid said. 'For nothing.'

Kvetka lurched to her feet. She swayed uncertainly, but Gajevic caught her and helped support her as she walked towards Omid. 'Not for nothing,' she said. She cast her gaze across the others. 'Lady Olynder tried to destroy the expedition. If we go on, then it is she, not we, who has failed.'

'But what can we do?' Omid demanded. 'Less than a dozen of us. No weapons. No armour. No supplies. We're going to attack the crypt-fortress by ourselves?'

'No, but we can try to find the Veiled Oracle,' Kvetka said. 'Lady Olynder attacked before even that part of the quest could succeed. Perhaps there was a reason. And if we speak with the Veiled Oracle, we might learn that reason.' She gave Omid a challenging look. 'Maybe we'll find out how we can still succeed in our quest.'

The smile Mahyar gave Kvetka was the warmest regard he'd ever shown her. The warrior priest clapped his hands. 'Well spoken. We can still act. We can still strive to accomplish the duty Sigmar has entrusted to us.' He turned to Venteslav. 'In the absence of Jahangir, you are in command. The decision is yours to make.'

Venteslav slowly nodded. 'If we can find the Veiled Oracle we may at least have some answers to bring back to our people.' He turned and stared towards Kvetka. It took her a moment to understand he was looking at someone behind her. Someone she hadn't noticed before.

The cryptborn, Zorgrath, rose from where he'd been sitting. 'The agreement was that I'd lead you to the Veiled Oracle,' he said. 'Just as long as I'm still getting paid.'

'If you can lead us to the Veiled Oracle, the Belvegrod light-house will reward you,' Kvetka assured Zorgrath.

'It will be a hard journey,' Zorgrath reminded them. 'The Barrow-bogs are unforgiving.'

'Which is why we can't even think about this,' Omid said. 'Not without weapons and food.'

Kvetka frowned at the soldier's complaint, for it was a just one. Without weapons and food, they'd have no chance in the Barrowbogs.

'I know where you can find all the supplies you need.' Zorgrath bared his sharp teeth in a predatory grin. 'What you have to ask yourselves is how bad you want them... and how brave you really are.'

CHAPTER SIX

Soraya kept close to Zorgrath as he loped through the scrubland. She didn't trust the cryptborn. In her estimation he was scarcely human. More undead than mortal. Whatever utility he might have, it was dangerous to forget that he wasn't like them. His brain was filled with strange and ghoulish thoughts, his spirit moved by inhuman impulses.

Trusting Zorgrath wasn't Soraya's choice... or her decision. Venteslav was in command. Orders were orders, whether they came from Azyrite or Reclaimed. She'd warned Omid as much when he suggested defying Venteslav. He was captain, and it was their duty to do as they were told. To do less was to violate the oaths they'd sworn when joining the Tombwatch, oaths made upon their honour and which invoked the name of Sigmar. Soraya, for one, would never countenance betraying such a vow.

The scrubland was a cheerless region. The soil was a kind of dun-coloured dirt that liked to form brittle clumps. These would pile up into big clusters to form fragile hills that crumbled into heaps of dust when any weight was put on them. The only solid ground, Soraya soon learned, was where the scrub grew. These were thin, skeletal bushes that seldom climbed more than three feet out of the soil. Their stalks were black as pitch and riddled with purple spines. They liked to prick anything that came close to them, and did so with such tenacious frequency that Soraya was convinced the plants could move when they weren't being watched. She was scratched up and down her body at this point and had left more than a little of her blood to nourish the thirsty vegetation.

She glanced back over the grim terrain. The other survivors were just visible, slowly trudging through the black thorn-bushes. Soraya could see they weren't having any easier a time of it than she was.

'Damn this land,' she swore.

'The only way through,' Zorgrath commented, turning his head as Soraya snapped the branch of a bush that had taken a particularly greedy dig at her skin. 'Their roots are the only thing that binds the ground together.'

Soraya tossed the severed length of branch away and rubbed at her bleeding leg. 'I'd like to burn every one of these vampire-vines.'

The cryptborn grinned at her with his sharp smile. 'Then you'd lose the roots and the whole place would be nothing but dust. Even if we still had our barrel, it wouldn't help us swim through dust.'

Soraya scowled and snapped another spiny branch. 'There has to be a better way to get where we're going,' she grumbled. It was a complaint she'd raised several times since they'd left the beach and started off into the scrubland.

'There are,' Zorgrath said, 'but if we used any of them... well, we might meet up with something we don't want to meet. This way there's a chance, at least a little one, that we won't have to fight.' He stepped down, hard, on a patch of ground where a very small shrub was growing. The clumps, bound only by the fragile young roots, broke apart and the plant fell over as the earth below it became nothing but dust.

'You'd need a dozen of me to match what Thugrah weighs,' Zorgrath explained. 'He won't come out this way. You can depend on that.'

'Why would he make his home in such a place?' Soraya asked.

'For something like him, there's good enough hunting in the Barrowbogs and the Dreadwood,' Zorgrath said. He waved one of his long-nailed fingers. 'He doesn't much care for his own kind, so he built his lodge in a place where he knew others like him couldn't follow. Only a few paths solid enough to support that kind of weight.'

'An ogor,' Soraya muttered, an edge of fear in her voice. Were they really desperate enough to risk fighting an ogor without weapons? Maybe Venteslav thought Gajevic's spells or Mahyar's prayers might make the difference, but she always thought relying on magic was a particularly risky thing to do. Then again, Zorgrath had met with the creature before and walked away. 'Perhaps he will help us.'

Zorgrath killed that expression of hope just as he had when Venteslav suggested it. 'We aren't strong enough to treat with Thugrah. A big merchant caravan with dozens of armed warriors, *that* he'll play nice with. Trade meat for spices or metal or whatever else strikes his fancy. But a ragged bunch like us? No, we're not enough of a threat to parley with him. The only chance you might get to say anything is while he's deciding what pot to cook you in.'

The gruesome image had Soraya's hand whipping down to her waist. Her fingers reached for a sword that wasn't there. That sensation sent a shiver through her. It wasn't fear of the ogor, but of not having a chance to fight back.

'How much farther do we have to go? What landmarks should

we be looking for?' Soraya asked, trying to fix on more immediate problems.

'No use looking,' Zorgrath replied. He wrinkled his nose. 'The hills change too much too often. When we get close enough, I'll smell Thugrah's lodge.' His eyes glittered and a string of spittle dribbled from the corner of his mouth. 'I'll find the lodge. Don't worry about that. I might even be able to pick out his scent, tell if he's there. If we're lucky, he might be out hunting.'

'What if we're not lucky?' Soraya wanted to know.

Zorgrath wiped his mouth with the back of his hand. His eyes lost their glitter. 'Pray we're lucky,' he advised. 'If your Sigmar listens to you at all, pray we're lucky.'

What Zorgrath had described as a mere hunting lodge proved to be as big as Eastdale's town hall. Venteslav's first view of it as he crossed the scrubland was simply a crude jumble of logs and hides lashed together with ropes and chains. It was only as the group of survivors got closer that the true enormity of the structure impressed itself on him. He began to question the plan he'd adopted. The idea of stealing food and weapons from a creature that had to build on such a scale had lost its lustre.

'Can you tell if Thugrah is in there?' Venteslav questioned Zorgrath.

The cryptborn shook his head. 'The smell of ogor... and other things is too strong. Thugrah's been here a long time, so long the very dirt carries the tang of his stink. Then there's all the residue from his hunts.' Zorgrath bared his sharp teeth. 'Whether making trophies or dinner, he's not tidy in his work.'

Venteslav turned to Soraya. She'd kept beside Zorgrath during their slow creep through the scrubland. Before he made any decision, he wanted to know her opinion. 'Do you think the ogor's home?'

'I didn't see anything,' Soraya reported. She waved her thumb at Zorgrath. 'Neither of us could hear anything. I've never heard of an ogor keeping quiet.'

Kvetka ventured to add a reason why that might be so. 'If an ogor has a reason to be quiet, I don't think anybody would be around to talk about it later.' She turned to Venteslav. 'It would be a grave error to indulge the mistaken idea that ogors are stupid. They might be slower to make up their minds than humans, but that doesn't mean they're dumb brutes.'

'Thugrah is sly as a swamp-wolf,' Zorgrath agreed. 'You don't bring down the kind of game he does without being crafty.' He nodded at the lodge. 'If he discovered we were out here, he might be lying low and waiting for us to walk into a trap.'

Venteslav pulled at his moustache while he weighed their options. Going back would effectively put an end to the idea of seeking out the Veiled Oracle. He'd never get this ragtag group back together. He wasn't fond of the notion that a creature bigger than half a dozen men might be lying in wait for them, but they needed weapons if they were going to go any farther. Zorgrath had promised that everything they needed was in the hunting lodge.

'Do you think that's likely?' Venteslav pressed Zorgrath. 'You've met this Thugrah before. If he was aware of us, what would he do?'

Zorgrath scratched the back of his neck with one of his claw-like nails. 'If Thugrah got a good look at us, the way we are, he'd snatch up a club and just mash the lot of us. We're hardly any sort of threat to him… not that he knows anyway,' Zorgrath added with a glance at Gajevic. 'He is only careful when he's dealing with prey he respects. I don't think he'd feel we were worth any special attention.'

'The arrogance of power,' Kvetka said. 'Yes, that would be a failing you could expect from an ogor, even a cunning one.'

Arrogance of power. Venteslav took a more studied view of the lodge with the scholar's words in mind. The skulls of mournfangs and stonehorns were lashed to the tops of the supporting posts. The claws and fangs of other large beasts dangled from long strings that hung off the lodge's walls, rattling in the breeze. The scaly hides of huge reptiles were pinned between the logs, splayed out so there was no mistaking the enormity of the creatures when they had still been alive. Yes, everything about the place bespoke the braggart mindset of the one who built it.

'Spread out,' Venteslav told the others. 'Keep your eyes and ears open. Watch for any sign of life.' Though he was satisfied that Thugrah wasn't lurking inside to attack them, he wasn't ready to throw caution to the wind. He drew Gajevic and Kvetka aside when they would have circled around the lodge with the others. 'Not you,' he told them. 'I want you here with me. It could be I'm wrong and the master of this place *is* at home. If that happens, we're going to have to move fast. Whichever way things turn.'

Minutes stretched away into a lifetime while Venteslav watched the lodge and waited. At first he could hear the others as they crawled through the scrub. When they got close enough to reach the firmer ground on which the lodge had been built, those faint indicators of their progress died away. Sometimes Venteslav would catch a fleeting glimpse of Mahyar or Omid as they moved towards the lodge, but the rest had circled around the structure. The only thing that told him they hadn't been discovered was the absence of terrified screams and ogor roars.

'I'd almost welcome fighting the ogor at this point,' Venteslav whispered as the tension grew more intense than he could tolerate.

Kvetka turned her head and gave him a sharp look. 'Don't wish for ill. You never know which gods might be listening.' She touched her thumb to an iron coin sewn into the sleeve of her robe – an old Reclaimed custom to fend off bad luck.

Venteslav followed her gesture, squeezing a button on his own tunic. 'It isn't impiety, it's uncertainty. Either the ogor's waiting for us, or he isn't. Whichever it is, I want to know. Good or bad. Success or death. A warrior can accept either outcome if he knows which it is he's waiting for.'

'There's something either very profound or very foolish,' Gajevic started to say. The wizard frowned and stared at the ground. 'I mean to say, that sort of acceptance. That willingness to deal with things as they come and adjust accordingly.'

'What would you do?' Venteslav asked. To him, there were only two ways of doing things. Deal with them as they were, or run away.

'I'd try to make the uncertain certain,' Gajevic said. He glanced over at Kvetka. 'I mean, at its most basic level all magic amounts to an effort to make the uncertain conform to a desired outcome.' He looked back to Venteslav. 'Of course, it doesn't always work that way. Magic, by its very nature, is unpredictable. But an experienced wizard knows tricks to shape arcane energies to best suit the desired purpose.'

'And if that purpose was to keep everyone from being eaten by an ogor?' Venteslav pointed at the lodge. 'Do you think your skill would be equal to such an effort?'

Gajevic lowered his head again. 'I don't know. All I can do is try. While I'm trying, at least some of you would have a chance to get away.'

The confession was blunt in its honesty. Venteslav appreciated that, even as he was troubled by the implications. Kvetka was visibly disturbed as well, though she refrained from pressing Gajevic further.

Venteslav was still brooding on the dependability of magic when Zorgrath came creeping back through the scrub. The cryptborn's face was split in a leering smile. 'Thugrah isn't home,' he whispered. 'Fortune favours us. We can slip inside and get what we need.'

'What about traps?' Venteslav asked. 'However arrogant the ogor might be, I can't believe he would leave his home unprotected.'

'I found a few,' Zorgrath admitted. 'So did Ratimir. Between us, they've been disabled. Thugrah was worried about other ogors, not humans, so his traps weren't hard to find.' A worried look pulled at the guide's face. 'Unless, of course, there are others we didn't find.'

Venteslav considered that last point carefully. He looked at Kvetka and Gajevic. 'We've no choice. We need supplies. Every-one just be careful and keep your eyes open.'

'That,' Kvetka assured him, 'won't be a problem.'

In the dark of night, when the moon was low, the priests of Westreach would haul up the great chain to which the town's dead were bound. They would anoint the decaying corpses with holy water and invoke prayers of purity and protection. Then the dead, in all their mouldering horror, would be lowered back into the bay to sleep once more in the black depths. The stench of all those bodies was a pungent horror in Mahyar's memory, his initiation from the cloistered life of a novitiate into the more hazardous duties of a warrior priest. That necrotic reek was the foulest thing to ever assault his nose. At least until he entered the ogor's hunting lodge.

The slippery Reclaimed soldier Ratimir was the first to draw back the heavy flap of uncured hide that served as the lodge's door. His careful inspection had revealed no traps fastened to it. After the deadfalls and spring-launched spears hidden around the structure, Mahyar wasn't sure if he should feel relieved or not. Did Ratimir's inability to find any surprises mean the ogor had lim-ited them to outside or did it indicate that he'd been more careful about concealing the ones inside?

Any idea of relief was forgotten when Mahyar followed Ratimir through the door. The foul reek was horrible, but not half as hor-rible as the scene that provoked it.

'Sigmar's mercy,' Mahyar whispered before pressing his hand against his mouth and nose.

The interior of the lodge was a charnel house. Flesh and offal were strewn about the entry, a vast section of the hut at least fifty feet across and twenty feet high. Support posts propped up the overarching ceiling of skins and hides, and from these a tangle of hooks and ropes hung. Most of these had some sort of carcass fastened to them. Some had been crudely processed, with their skins and pelts removed. Others had been stripped of flesh and bone until all that remained was a shapeless mass of decay. Unwanted scraps were strewn all about the floor in a carpet of dried gore and pulpy slime. Flies and beetles attended the rotting filth while beady-eyed lizards darted about the mess to snap at the insects.

'Look,' Ratimir hissed, his voice muffled by his hand covering his face. The soldier's finger trembled as he indicated a particular carcass. Mahyar saw at once why it warranted special attention. What was dangling from the hook looked like it had once been human.

'The cryptborn warned us this hunter is a man-eater,' Mahyar reminded Ratimir. He glanced around at their ghastly surroundings. 'Let's pray we find weapons before this monster comes back.'

Ratimir nodded. He drew a coin from his money belt, spat on it and then placed it back. Mahyar rolled his eyes at the display of superstition. Considering their surroundings, however, he decided to let the matter rest. Ratimir crept forwards and paused before a flap of hide stretched between two massive leg bones. From their size, Mahyar was certain whatever they had belonged to was something he never wanted to meet. It was unsettling enough to think the ogor had met the beast and vanquished it.

'It's all right,' Ratimir said after he examined the doorway. He pushed aside the flap and moved into the next room.

Mahyar was right behind the soldier. The farther room was equally massive and only slightly less disordered. There were a number of skinning racks along one side. Some were empty, others had animal carcasses chained to them awaiting the attention of the skinning knife. A little beyond the racks were stands for curing hides – the skins pinned to them slowly having the moisture drawn out by smoke rising from a brazier. The priest was comforted to see only the hides of animals, but when he turned to dart a look at the other side of the room, his attitude changed. A great wooden table stretched along that side of the room and on it were a series of butcher's blocks of varying sizes and shapes. Strewn about the blocks were various cuts of meat and gory ropes of entrails. Mahyar spotted something that might be a hand, then saw what was certainly a human head. The battered face stared back at him with its dead eyes and a mouth twisted into a final scream.

'Sigmar's wrath take this foul beast,' Mahyar growled.

Ratimir circled around and pointed to a series of shelves stuffed with a bewildering array of jars, bottles and pots. 'I hate to look at those,' he confessed.

'Preserves,' Mahyar said. 'They can't all be from humans. This ogor has traded with caravans and it would be a desperate merchant who'd feed his men long pig.' He moved towards a heap of bones piled in one corner of the room. It took only a glance to realise they were from both animals and more manlike creatures. The ogor apparently made no distinction. 'We'll have to check everything carefully just the same,' he warned.

'Should I get the others?' Ratimir asked.

'The ogor isn't around,' Mahyar said. 'Every moment we waste now only increases the chance of him coming back. Go tell Venteslav. Everybody gets in, grabs what we need and gets out again.'

The soldier nodded and dashed off on his errand. Mahyar was alone now in the lodge. He looked over the grotesque surroundings and noticed what appeared to be two more doorways. He walked to the table and pulled down a massive axe-like sword. For the ogor, no doubt, it was just a knife to trim cuts of meat, but Mahyar needed both arms to carry it. Still, the cumbersome blade was at least some kind of weapon. When Sigmar answered a prayer, it was blasphemy to look askance at his beneficence.

The nearer of the two doorways was covered by the pelt of a rock-bear. Mahyar had to shoulder his weapon when he ripped the hanging aside. A heavy, bestial stink smashed into his senses. The room beyond was dominated by a huge fur-strewn pallet, a bed for something that must stand three times as big as a man. He saw marks that indicated some sort of animal shared these quarters. Dried branches created a crude lair from which cracked and splintered bones protruded. Mahyar thought whatever the ogor was keeping as a pet must be both large and powerful from the way the bones were damaged.

The priest left the ogor's bedroom and walked towards the other doorway. Curtained off by a strip of shaggy hide he couldn't identify, it was just past the pile of bones he'd noted before. As he moved past the bones, he felt something slide around his foot. Before he could react he was sent crashing to the floor, a loop of rope tightening around his ankle.

The jumble of bones crashed down, bouncing in every direction across the floor. Leaping out of the pile came three short green-skinned creatures, with long sharp noses and wide fang-filled mouths. Each had a wicked-looking knife in its hands as it scrambled towards Mahyar. When he tried to pull himself up to face his attackers, a fourth creature jerked on the cord around his foot and sent him sprawling again. The greenskins laughed, their voices both hoarse and shrill, and dived upon the priest. Knives raked against his skin, drawing blood from his arms as he tried to fend off his foes.

'Grots!' Venteslav's voice cried out from the entrance to the abattoir. The fiendish laughter stopped when the greenskins swung around to see who was shouting.

Mahyar used the distraction to smash his fist into the face of a grot. The sharp nose crumpled under the impact and spattered the area in green blood. The creature dropped its knife and fell back, howling as it pressed its hands to its injury. 'Over here!' Mahyar called to his rescuers.

Venteslav and the others were quick to rush in. The grots, bold when facing a lone victim, were less eager to face such odds. The ambusher still in the bone pile threw aside the end of the cord and tried to bury itself deeper in the heap. The one with the broken nose scurried away, rushing around the room in screaming terror. The ones that still had knives made another try for Mahyar, thinking perhaps to use him as a hostage.

The priest kicked out as they came close. One grot slashed his calf with its blade, but in return it was knocked back with a broken knee. Seeing the fate of its confederate, the other knife-carrying grot turned and ran for the hide wall.

'Don't let it get away!' Zorgrath shouted. The cryptborn was hurtling across the room to get the grot before it could cut a hole in the wall. It was a race he would have lost had Soraya not seized one of the scattered bones and flung it at the creature. The missile struck the grot's head and sent it staggering. Before it could recover, Zorgrath had wrestled it to the ground and was crushing its throat in his powerful hands.

Mahyar dragged out the grot hiding in the bone pile. Any inclination towards mercy ended when the creature spun around and tried to bite him. He settled its antics by wrapping the same cord it had used to trip him with around its throat.

The wounded grots were finished by Omid and Ratimir, neither creature able to present much resistance to human soldiers.

Kvetka and Gajevic hurried over to Mahyar and tried to tend his wounds. He shook them off. He was more angry than hurt, and his anger was fixed in one direction. 'You might have warned us Thugrah had these creeps slinking around!' he snarled at Zorgrath.

Zorgrath licked green blood from his fingers and shrugged. 'He doesn't always have grots around and I don't think I've ever smelled the same one twice when caravans come here. I think Thugrah eats them once in a while and makes do without until more show up.'

'Omid, stand guard at this door,' Venteslav ordered. 'The rest of you, check around and make sure there aren't more. We can't risk any of them escaping and telling the ogor we're here.'

'There aren't any more,' Kvetka told the captain while she was binding a strip of cloth around Mahyar's slashed leg. 'The grots wouldn't have attacked unless they could bring their full numbers to bear. They're sly opportunists and will always do everything to ensure they can win before deciding to act.'

Mahyar was annoyed by Kvetka's surety. 'I don't think they attacked for any reason other than keeping me away from whatever's in that room.' He nodded towards the door he'd been going to before the grots ambushed him.

Ratimir dashed forwards and threw back the hanging. He whistled and shook his head. 'Mahyar's right,' he stated. 'They wanted to keep him from finding all this.'

Ratimir stepped back from the doorway. Beyond him was a room crowded with furs and hides, horns and tusks. Anything valuable that could be harvested after a hunt appeared to be piled inside. Mahyar wasn't an expert in the ways of commerce, but he judged there was a small fortune in the ogor's storeroom. If it could be hauled back to the Twinned Towns, each of them would be rich. He could see that thought was running through the minds of several of the survivors.

'In our circumstances, none of this is any use to us.' Mahyar stepped into the storeroom and started looking around. He soon found what he was seeking, an old sword leaning against the wall. He picked it up so the others could see. 'What we need are weapons, and if the ogor took any from his victims, they'll be in here.'

Zorgrath nodded his head. 'Forget the trade goods and the food. Even the furs. Find weapons. That's what we'll need when Thugrah catches up with us.'

Omid glowered at the cryptborn. 'Catches up with us?' the soldier snarled.

'The ogor's a hunter,' Venteslav stated. 'If he can follow a beast's trail, he can surely follow ours.'

Mahyar shook his head at the simple logic of it – so simple that none of them had considered it before. 'You planned it this way from the start,' he said.

Kvetka gave him a puzzled look, then turned to Venteslav. 'What did you plan?'

'Everyone go in there and find weapons,' Venteslav said. 'Armour if there is any. Anything you can find that can help us in a fight.'

'You expect the ogor to come back,' Soraya said.

Mahyar answered for Venteslav. 'The ogor will come back, and when he does we'll be waiting for him.'

'Waiting for him?' Gajevic gasped. 'Why would we do that?'

'Because whatever we do, Thugrah will know we've been here and will set out after us,' Venteslav explained. He nodded to Zorgrath. 'When this plan was suggested to me, I knew this would have to be part of it. We can't leave the ogor alive to come hunting us later.'

Mahyar picked up a battered helm from where it lay among the furs. 'If we try to run and the ogor finds us, we'll be fighting on his terms and on ground of his choosing. If we stay here, we can give ourselves every advantage Sigmar provides us.

'One way or another, it'll come to a fight,' Mahyar warned the others. 'Let's have that fight here where we're ready for it and the ogor isn't.'

'It's coming,' Zorgrath hissed as he darted back inside the lodge.

The cryptborn's warning had everyone rushing to their places. Kvetka had resented the tireless drilling Venteslav had demanded of them over the last two days, but now, when the crisis was upon them, she appreciated the practice. Before she was even fully aware of what she was doing, she was behind the big butcher's table and had her hands wrapped around the necks of two glass bottles.

Kvetka glanced down at the bottles and felt a moment of hesitation. She'd prepared these concoctions herself, drawing them off from the crude alcohol and vinegar the ogor used to cure hides and preserve meats. She knew the effect she wanted to create with them and had explained her intent to Venteslav so that she would have an active role in the fight rather than simply hiding in the storeroom. She'd convinced the captain her idea had merit, though Mahyar doubted her ability and Gajevic fretted over the risk she was taking.

Two bottles. One for the ogor and one for his pet. From the way the bones had been gnawed and the tufts of fur caught in the animal's bedding, Kvetka thought it was a sabretusk. It wasn't a particularly pleasant thought. A sabretusk was as big as a bear but with the lithe agility of a panther. Its claws could rip open an ox with a single swipe and its fangs really were as long and lethal as swords. The beast would be a formidable foe in its own right even without its hulking master.

Kvetka glanced around the room once more. The soldiers were in their places and ready, each outfitted with whatever they could salvage from the storeroom. Mahyar was off to her right, by the racks of preserves, a gruesome orruk choppa clenched in his hands. Gajevic was back in the ogor's lair, held in reserve until the moment Venteslav called out to him.

Tension-filled silence dominated the lodge. Kvetka thought she could hear the sweat dripping off her brow while she waited, her every sense keyed to the first sign that the ogor was near. The smell inside was worse than ever, aggravated by Zorgrath when he smashed a pot of pickled meat.

'It'll hide any hint of our scent,' Zorgrath explained as he crept around the table to join the scholar. 'Thugrah will think one of the grots broke something. That should make him angry.'

'Aren't things bad enough without making an ogor angry?' Kvetka asked.

'If he's angry, Thugrah won't be careful,' Zorgrath explained. 'He'll barge in here looking for a grot to punish, not enemies waiting to ambush him.'

The cryptborn motioned Kvetka to be quiet. She strained her ears and thought she heard distant footsteps. In a matter of heartbeats, she knew it wasn't imagination. They were footsteps, and as they came nearer she could tell they were heavy and ponderous. The body that produced such footfalls had to be incredibly massive. She glanced back down at the bottles and thought what feeble weapons they were.

The sound of the advancing footsteps grew louder. Now Kvetka could feel a slight tremor in the ground. She held her breath as a deep grunt rose from outside the hide walls of the lodge. Then she felt a change in the atmosphere, an air of impending menace that sent icy shivers through her heart. It was, she imagined, the primal terror felt by the lowest of creatures when it senses a predator approaching.

The ponderous footsteps were in the abattoir now. The inarticulate grunts dropped into a rude and bestial string of words, a harsh tongue that Kvetka didn't know. She figured it was Thugrah calling out to the grots.

In the next moment, the ogor threw aside the curtain and stomped into the room. Kvetka's eyes went wide with awed horror. Thugrah was fifteen feet tall and eight feet broad at the shoulders. His skin had a pale, pebbly look to it, with deep scars evident everywhere. His face was heavy, with a square jaw and a low brow, the features hinting at a dull and simple character. The eyes, however, told a different story, for they were as sharp as a swamp-wolf's and as cruel as a grave-viper.

The ogor wore a mismatch of hides and furs strapped about his massive frame. On his back was the split ribcage of some huge animal, the bones spread out so that they resembled wings. From each rib, a leathery trophy hung. Kvetka could see the dried head of an orruk and the horned scalp of a bestigor dangling by cords of gut and sinew. There were also human skulls and the gold-toothed jawbone of a duardin. Thugrah, it seemed, put the most value in trophies that could appreciate the terror of their final moments when the ogor slaughtered them.

Slinking along beside Thugrah was a monstrous cat. Kvetka had overestimated its size, but only slightly. Its long legs rippled with muscle as it moved. Its blunt, wide head sported eyes that were almost amber in colour and its mouth jutted forwards to support the curved fangs that rose from its lower jaw. Black slashes and spots patterned the sabretusk's dark brown pelt, but the tuft at the end of its long tail was bright white – something to distract prey in that final instant before the cat pounced.

'Attack!' Venteslav shouted the moment the ogor and his pet were inside. The plan demanded swift action, to strike before Thugrah had the opportunity to know what was happening.

Venteslav and the soldiers charged the hunter, slashing and chopping at him with spears and swords. Soraya gashed Thugrah's side and Venteslav landed a cut to the back of his hand. Omid pierced the ogor's leg with a spear, but a sweep of his fist snapped the shaft like a twig and sent the soldier stumbling back. Thugrah bellowed his rage and grabbed the enormous club hanging off his belt. With the weapon in his hands, he glowered at the humans.

Closer to Kvetka, Mahyar rushed out and charged the sabretusk. Even with its sense of smell confused by the stench in the room, the cat's reflexes were too swift for the warrior priest. The animal sprang away from his attack. It spun around in mid-air, and as it did so it swatted him with one of its paws. The claws ground against the armoured breastplate Mahyar had scavenged, scratching the metal but incapable of reaching the man within. The power of the strike threw the priest back and knocked him sprawling. Kvetka gasped when she saw him slam down near some of the sharpened bones they'd planted in the floor.

Mahyar avoided the stakes. The same couldn't be said for the sabretusk. Its spring launched it halfway across the room, its paws impaling themselves on the bones as it landed. The cat yowled in pain, its own weight driving the spikes deep. It leapt again, blood gushing from two of its feet. This time its jump carried it to the top of the table.

'Now!' Zorgrath shouted.

Kvetka didn't need the cryptborn to urge her into action. She cracked the neck of one bottle against the edge of the table and splashed its contents full into the eyes of the sabretusk. Only after the deed was done did she appreciate just how close to the deadly animal she was. She could see the bits of meat caught between its teeth. She could hear the sizzle as the caustic mixture burned the cat's face.

Zorgrath grabbed Kvetka and pulled her down a second before the sabretusk struck at her with its paw. Blood from its injured foot spattered her as she hit the ground. The cat jumped down after her, but the agony of its burning face made it forget its wrath. Instead of pressing its attack, it dragged its head against the ground, trying to wipe off the searing mixture in the dirt.

With a feral snarl Zorgrath jumped onto the sabretusk's back. He had two of the grot knives in his hands and set to work, plunging them deep into the animal's sides. Kvetka watched the savage exhibition as the cryptborn plied the blades, twisting them in the wounds before withdrawing them and stabbing again. The cat roared in pain and struggled to free itself of its tormentor. It rolled onto its back, seeking to crush Zorgrath beneath its weight.

Kvetka brought out the dagger she'd been armed with and leapt upon the struggling beast. In contrast to its otherwise dark pelt, the animal's belly was a snowy white. She turned it crimson. A kind of ferocious panic seized her and she plunged the knife over and over into the brute's chest. Only when Mahyar's hand closed on her shoulder did she relent.

'Enough,' Mahyar told her. He nodded at the dead sabretusk while Zorgrath squirmed out from under it. 'We still have the ogor to deal with.'

'I...' Kvetka choked on her words. She couldn't explain to herself how someone so educated and knowledgeable could descend to this kind of primitive savagery. Instead she turned and grabbed the second bottle – the one she'd prepared to deal with the ogor rather than his pet.

Venteslav and the other soldiers were only just able to keep the ogor at bay. By spreading out and attacking him from every side they managed to prevent Thugrah from focusing on any one of them. The thick boots the hunter wore were too tough for the bone spikes to penetrate and they were crushed to splinters whenever he brought his immense weight down on them. The spiked club, six feet long and as thick around as a wagon tine, was a continuous menace to the warriors. Thugrah would swing it in a wide arc, whipping it around with an ease that belied its destructive mass. Even a glancing blow from that weapon would be enough to cripple a human.

'Gajevic!' Venteslav shouted as Thugrah pressed the captain back towards the skinning racks. The thin wizard emerged from the inner room and faced the ogor. He raised his hands, and from his lips eldritch words escaped into the air. The tips of his fingers took on a frosty glow and from each of them a long shard of ice formed. A final incantation and the shards broke away from his fingers and flew at Thugrah.

The spell looked impressive to Kvetka and went beyond anything she had thought Gajevic capable of. Yet when the icy shards flew at Thugrah, instead of skewering the ogor they exploded into a cloud of frost. Kvetka saw a crude wooden fetish hanging off the hunter's belt flash with light for an instant. Then the monster turned towards Gajevic.

'He has a protective talisman!' the wizard cried out.

Thugrah snorted in contempt. 'Magic-man's bones break soon,' the ogor mocked. He started towards Gajevic, pulverising the spikes in his path.

'Stop him!' Venteslav ordered. The soldiers redoubled their efforts, forcing Thugrah to pause to fend off their attacks. Kvetka could see it was a losing prospect. The ogor was going to get through.

'Leave him alone!' she shouted as she charged at Thugrah. She broke the neck off the bottle before splashing its contents into her enemy's face as she had with the sabretusk. This time, however, the effect was less immediate. An oily sheen dripped down the ogor's face and made him wipe at his eyes. He forgot about Gajevic and turned towards her instead.

'Woman, I let you watch when I grind your legs into meal,' Thugrah snapped.

'*You* won't watch anything,' Kvetka retorted as she backed away. 'Not ever again.'

Distracted by his anger, Thugrah didn't notice Venteslav and

Gajevic charging at him from the side. Neither man carried a sword; instead they each held a clay pot. They flung the contents at the ogor, spattering him with glowing embers.

The mixture of grease, resin and oil that Kvetka had prepared took light instantly. Thugrah's face ignited, his features wrapped in flame. He beat at the fire with his hands, but after wiping his eyes they too were covered in the incendiary concoction and were likewise engulfed. The ogor shrieked as his own efforts spread the fire to other parts of his body.

'Finish him off!' Venteslav ordered as he ducked back to recover his sword. Soraya and the other soldiers rushed in, using spears to thrust at the burning ogor. Blind and tormented, Thugrah was unable to fend off their attacks. Mahyar charged in and shattered the hunter's knee with the orruk choppa.

Thugrah crumpled to the floor. A second swing of the choppa bit halfway through the ogor's thick neck. Dark blood sprayed from the wound. For just a second, the hunter struggled to rise, then his huge body crashed to the floor, the only sign of motion the flames dancing about his burning head.

Kvetka looked down at the huge corpse, amazed that they'd been able to fell this mighty creature. She looked over at her companions and saw the deep respect in their eyes.

'Sigmar provides,' Mahyar told her. 'This time what he provided was you. We won only because you knew what to do to beat this monster.'

Zorgrath limped forwards from behind the table, his body covered in the sabretusk's blood. He gazed down at Thugrah and spat into the hunter's burning face. He gave the others a sombre look. 'I know it was my idea, but let's never do that again.'

CHAPTER SEVEN

'I can't eat this.' Soraya covered her mouth with one hand and tossed the blob of meat back into the cauldron.

Venteslav sympathised. The stringy bit of grey flesh impaled at the end of his knife was far from appealing. However, any soldier knew that it was nutrition, not taste, that was important. He took a big bite, smacking his lips loudly in a show of enjoyment. 'I can assure you that you've had worse if you've been with the Tombwatch any length of time.'

Zorgrath rummaged about in the bag hanging off his belt. 'I found some good spices in the larder...'

Omid glared at the cryptborn. 'It isn't the taste, and you know it!' He stood up and threw his knife into the campfire. His face had a greenish tinge to it.

'Kvetka has examined it carefully,' Gajevic tried to assure Omid and Soraya. 'She'd know if it was human.'

At the moment, the scholar looked anything but certain about her conclusion. She was taking only the slightest, daintiest bites of the meat on her knife. Venteslav thought that any moment she might cast up what little she'd managed to gag down.

'If you don't want any, you can give me yours,' Zorgrath suggested. Venteslav glared at the scout. Every time he opened his mouth he reminded the others of his ghoulish palate and that they might be sharing his diet.

'There's nothing wrong with the food,' Venteslav declared. He stabbed his knife into the pot and withdrew another glob of meat. He made a great show of taking a big bite. 'Tastes like pork,' he said.

'I think you mean chicken,' Mahyar advised him, a warning look in his eyes.

Venteslav nodded to the priest. 'Whatever the meat tastes like, if we're going to press on, we'll have to eat it.' He looked across at the others. 'Stop thinking about it. Think instead about the Twinned Towns and your loved ones. About the people we're trying to save.'

Soraya reluctantly retrieved a new piece of meat from the cauldron. Omid used his sword to fish his discarded knife out of the fire. Kvetka forced herself to take a bigger bite of her food. They ate in silence, resigned to the demands of necessity, all of them trying to blot out the thought of just what it was they'd taken from the ogor's larder.

The ogor's lodge was a day's march behind them now. The scrubland had given way to a ragged forest of thin trees with scrawny branches. Here the ground was firmer and Venteslav breathed a bit easier knowing a misstep wouldn't have him starting a landslide. His relief was tempered a good deal by Zorgrath's warning that this was the Dreadwood, a corridor used by the huge beasts Thugrah hunted when travelling between the lowlands and the high plateau. They would need to keep alert lest they provoke an attack from a wandering cliff-bear or a prowling manticore.

At least now their little band was equipped to meet a fight. The ogor's storeroom had contained enough weapons and armour to outfit the group, even if some of it was of poor quality. Venteslav had found a serviceable longsword and a shirt of mail that was mostly intact. The others had availed themselves of such gear as they needed.

Zorgrath ranged ahead of the group as they marched through the Dreadwood. The rest kept a rough diamond formation as they moved, with Soraya at the fore, Omid and Ratimir on the flanks, and Mahyar bringing up the rear. Venteslav stayed in the middle of the diamond with Kvetka and Gajevic, the better to react to any crisis no matter which direction it came from.

'Are we certain Zorgrath knows where he's leading us?' Kvetka asked Venteslav as they marched. It was a question he'd had put to him many times by different people when they felt the crypt-born was out of earshot.

Venteslav provided the same answer for Kvetka that he'd given the others. 'He found the hunting lodge right enough. I think he knows what he's about. Besides, if he had any trickery in mind, he would hardly have shown us how to get weapons.'

'Why can't he simply draw out a map?' Kvetka grumbled. She waved at the emaciated trees all around them. 'It would help to have some idea of how far we need to go. How long we must spend in the Dreadwood.'

'I don't think he navigates the way you or I would. That's why he doesn't seem to be much interested in maps.' Venteslav caught sight of a black-brushed night fox watching them from the edge of a bush. 'That creature finds its way easy enough without a map,' he pointed out to the scholar. 'The fox sniffs the air and the smell tells it where it is and where it's going. The cryptborn are a bit like that. Their noses are as keen as a jackal's and that's how they find their way in the wilds. Zorgrath can't tell us how near we are to the Veiled Oracle because until he catches the right scent, he doesn't have any reference to judge by.'

Kvetka shook her head. 'I'm anxious to be out of these lands.'

Gajevic gave her a worried look. 'Is it because of the beasts Zorgrath warned us of? My magic will protect you from them. They won't be carrying talismans like the ogor was.'

Kvetka gave the wizard a weary smile. 'No, it isn't the beasts.' She turned her eyes back to Venteslav. 'Do you know much about the Dreadwood?'

'I know our ancestors used to hunt here after they fled Belvegrod,' Venteslav replied. 'The old stories say only a desperate man would hunt game under its boughs. Finally, the entire forest was burned down, ignited by the magic of the tribal warlocks.' He pointed at the trees around them. 'All of this is new, grown since it all burned. The only time any of our people journey here now is to observe Middelfeast and hunt an animal to offer in sacrifice to Sigmar.'

'Dreadwood is older than the exile of our ancestors,' Kvetka stated. 'It was once known as Shiverbloom and was written of extensively in the old texts. It was avoided then, regarded with fear by even the most learned in the city. They spoke of strange forces and sinister powers, energies that were hostile to intruders. Those who trespassed within the borders of the forest sometimes brought back wonderful things. More often they didn't come back at all.'

'Whatever force once governed here, it's gone now,' Venteslav said. 'Cleansed by the purging flames.' He gave an uncertain glance to the trees around them, wondering if after all there might not be some malevolent power waiting to strike at them. He wished Kvetka hadn't mentioned the old stories. His fingers closed around an iron coin, rubbing it to fend off ill fortune. 'We'll be through the Dreadwood soon enough,' he told Kvetka. 'The Veiled Oracle's citadel lies beyond the Barrowbogs.'

Kvetka shook her head. 'That is why I wish Zorgrath had drawn a map – anything with some sort of scale. I've seen the old maps in the books and Shiverbloom was a great forest, bigger than what we've seen here.'

'Meaning?' Venteslav asked.

'Meaning that even when we're out of the Dreadwood, we might not be out of what was once Shiverbloom,' the scholar said.

Venteslav could hear the anxiety in Kvetka's tone. He didn't know much about these old accounts she'd read, but if she felt there was something to be afraid of, that was enough to make him worry. The Barrowbogs were intimidating enough without adding ancient hostile forces into the mix. He could almost wish for another ogor. At least Thugrah had been a foe of flesh and blood who could be battled with cold steel and a strong heart. Unseen curses were a far different menace.

'We have to press on,' Venteslav stated. 'Whatever the danger, we have to at least speak with the Veiled Oracle. If we can't achieve that much of our quest, what hope can we bring back to our people?'

To that question, even the learned Kvetka offered no answer.

Kvetka wished the old texts had been more explicit in their accounts of Shiverbloom. It had been named, so it was said, after the wondrous flowers that had been taken from its hidden glades: living jewels that shone with all the brilliance of the stars and which were coveted as nothing else by Belvegrod's wealthy. Eager for riches themselves, many had penetrated the forest in that first year to bring back flowers for the tables of nobles and the corsages of ladies. Then, after a season, no more flowers came out of the forest. Nor did any of the men who went seeking them. A terrible force had been awakened and it would no longer suffer these intrusions into its domain.

The thin-boled trees with their withered branches were but a shadow of the lush forest Kvetka had read about. No, not a shadow. A ghost. A remnant that refused to surrender the land. The ancestors of the Reclaimed had burned the old forest and turned it into Dreadwood, but had they completely eradicated the power they so feared?

'You're imagining things,' Kvetka told herself the first time she caught a blur of motion from the corner of her eye. She turned her head and saw a great black oak with massive branches coated in dusky leaves. Its trunk was thick and scarred by age, red-leaved creepers winding around it as they leached its sap. The scholar rubbed her eyes, but the oak was gone, replaced by nothing more than another of the thin Dreadwood pines.

The illusion came again; this time it was a tall silver ash that appeared at the edge of her vision. When she tried to look directly at it, the tree was gone, but she was almost certain it had been there. Kvetka stopped in her tracks. Either some magic was affecting her, or she was losing her reason.

'What's wrong?' Gajevic asked, noting her troubled look.

'The trees…' Kvetka stopped herself. How could she explain it? How could she make Gajevic understand something she didn't understand herself? 'It… Nothing, just a moment of weariness.'

Gajevic's eyes had an intense quality to them as he stepped closer. 'You've seen them too,' he whispered. 'Trees that aren't there. Other things that shouldn't be there. Watching us. Hating us.'

Kvetka shuddered. She knew all practitioners of magic developed a kind of enhanced vision. Witch-sight was the name many used for it. They could see things nobody else could see, wisps of sorcery left behind by some powerful spell or the boundaries of a magical ward. Gajevic might very well have seen more than she had.

'Hating us,' Kvetka muttered. She was certain now that she'd seen a towering elm this time. It had lingered a bit longer than the others had, allowing her to be sure its appearance was no trick of her eyes. It had been there, just for an instant. A flicker of time.

Ratimir suddenly cried out. He fled from his post on the right flank and ran into the centre of the formation. He had his sword in his hand and was gesturing wildly with it towards the trees. 'It was there!' he shouted. 'It was there and then it wasn't!'

'Stay where you are,' Venteslav ordered the others. He seized Ratimir and shook him. 'What are you babbling about, man?'

Kvetka could see the raw terror in Ratimir's eyes as he struggled to answer. 'It... it was like a tree. But it wasn't a tree! There for just a moment! I saw it watching me, watching me with all the hate in the world in its eyes!'

'Where is it, this thing you saw?' Venteslav demanded, scouring the forest with his gaze. 'Where did it go?'

'It didn't go anywhere,' Ratimir said. 'It just vanished! One moment I could see it, and the next it was gone!'

'Superstitious nonsense,' Omid sneered as he listened to Ratimir's cries. 'He's given himself the frights with all the garbage he believes.'

Kvetka rounded on the Azyrite soldier. 'I've seen something too.' She pointed to Gajevic. 'We both have.'

Venteslav relaxed his hold on Ratimir and walked towards Soraya. 'You've been in the lead. Have you seen anything,' he hesitated over his choice of word, 'strange?'

'Only the trees,' Soraya reported. 'None of them have vanished, if that's what you want to know.'

'I've seen nothing because there's nothing going on,' Omid said. He made no effort to disguise his contempt when he looked at Kvetka. 'The Eastdalers are jumping at shadows.'

'Enough of that,' Venteslav warned. 'We're all in this together. Together is the only way we'll accomplish anything.' He turned to Kvetka. 'I thought it was my eyes playing tricks, but I've had fleeting glimpses of things that were there one moment and gone the next. What do you think it means?'

Kvetka was quiet for a moment, then posed a question to Mahyar. 'Have you noticed anything unusual?'

The warrior priest shook his head. 'Nothing like what you think you've seen,' was his gruff reply.

'Then whatever's happening, it isn't affecting the Azyrites,' Kvetka said. 'Only the Reclaimed.' Omid grunted his amusement at the statement, but the scholar ignored his derision. 'Venteslav, it was our ancestors who burned Shiverbloom. If there was some remnant of the power that once held sway, what would be more natural than for it to hate us?'

'You mean… gheists?' Ratimir trembled as he forced the word out.

'Not gheists as we think of them, but a kind of lingering energy,' Kvetka explained. 'Something old and hateful towards us.'

'Would it be strong enough to act?' Venteslav inquired. 'Or is the worst of its tricks to make us see phantoms?'

'I don't know,' Kvetka admitted. 'In the old books there was sometimes mention of the green-folk who lived within Shiverbloom. Humans seldom saw them, but they were said to be fey and magical beings. What we've experienced could be some lingering spell they evoked before the conflagration.'

'If it is a spell,' Gajevic offered, 'then it must be a powerful one to linger so long. The hunters of Middelfeast would spend only a few hours in the Dreadwood. We've been here for over a day. It could be the spell draws energy into itself. Our intrusion activated it, but our continued presence feeds it. The longer we remain, the stronger it might grow.' The wizard tapped his chin and supplied another possibility. 'It could also be that the spell isn't simply reactive. That there's some manner of intelligence guiding it. Maybe not a living mind but an arcane semblance of one, an ancient spirit of malevolence. Now that it has been aroused it may be debating what it's going to do.'

'Either way,' Kvetka said, 'our course is clear. We have to get out of the Dreadwood as quickly as we can. If what we've seen are only illusions, then the Azyrites can steer us true since this force is only interested in the Reclaimed.'

Venteslav nodded. 'Agreed,' he said. 'We'll bring in the pickets. If anybody spots something, ask an Azyrite if it's really there.'

'Let's hope Zorgrath hurries back and tells us he's found the end of the forest.' Kvetka waved her hand at the surrounding trees. 'Because if Gajevic's right, then the longer we're here the more danger we're in.'

They set up camp only when it became too dark to march. For her own part, Soraya would almost have preferred to keep going. While it was true that she'd seen nothing, it was clear something was upsetting the Reclaimed. If it had just been Ratimir or Gajevic, she might have been able to chalk it up to nerves or imagination, but not all four of them and certainly not a capable captain like Venteslav. There was something more going on than mere superstition, as Omid claimed.

Certainly the continued absence of Zorgrath was more than imagination. The guide had last put in an appearance around midday. After that, there hadn't been a trace of him. Soraya didn't care for the cryptborn any more than the first time she'd laid eyes on him in Eastdale, but she had developed a grudging respect for his abilities as a scout. While it was possible he'd got lost, she considered it unlikely. That meant something else had happened – perhaps an encounter with one of the wild beasts that ranged through the Dreadwood. Or maybe a less nebulous manifestation of whatever was bedevilling the Reclaimed.

'Look at those Eastdalers,' Omid said to Soraya when he joined her at the edge of the camp. 'If they huddled any closer to that fire they'd set their hair alight. Wouldn't that be a laugh to watch that pompous Venteslav trying to douse his moustache?'

Soraya gave Omid a stern look. 'Captain Venteslav is in command,' she reminded him.

'An Eastdaler,' Omid scoffed. 'Head full of bugaboos. You see how careful he was about how the stones for the fire were positioned? Probably some superstition about that, too. These Reclaimed have a moronic custom for everything.'

'Their ancestors survived the horrors of Shyish by themselves for a long time,' Soraya said. 'So maybe some of their customs aren't as stupid as you think.'

'There's only two things to put your faith in,' Omid disagreed. 'Sigmar and cold steel. Leave the old wives' tale to old wives.' His gaze shifted back to Venteslav. 'This whole affair is foolish. Jahangir had a small army. The smart thing is to go back.'

A thin smile took shape on Soraya's face. 'You sound more afraid than the Reclaimed.'

'At least I have good reason to be afraid,' Omid said. 'I'm not jumping at shadows like they are.' He laughed when he noticed Ratimir turn pale and cover his eyes. 'I wonder what shadow's making him jump right now.'

A moment later it was Omid who was jumping. From the darkened forest near them they heard the sound of wood cracking. The Azyrite soldier sprang back several feet, his sword half drawn. Soraya chuckled at his distress.

'Some animal prowling past the camp,' she chided him. At the same time, she made certain her own weapon was at the ready, a metal bludgeon the ogor had used to tenderise meat. Omid could do with being humbled, but Soraya decided she wasn't going to entirely discount the threat that might be out there in the dark.

The sounds of brush being disturbed persisted. Whatever was out there was coming closer. 'Omid, go warn the others,' Soraya told her companion in a low voice. He didn't argue, but jogged over to alert the Reclaimed.

The sounds slowed, assuming a furtive quality. Whatever was making them was clearly coming straight towards Soraya. She firmed her grip on the bludgeon. She'd make certain that anything trying to attack the camp would regret running into her first.

'Keep calm,' a familiar voice hissed from the night. 'It's me, Zorgrath.'

Soraya took a step back. She could hear some of her companions moving up to support her. The voice was Zorgrath's, but with the weirdness the Reclaimed attributed to the Dreadwood, she didn't want to take chances. 'Come into the light where I can see you,' she ordered. 'And be slow when you do it.'

Obediently, a figure advanced out of the blackness. It took Soraya a moment to recognise the figure as Zorgrath. The guide was bloodied, his clothing torn. His chest bore several deep scratches and there was an ugly bite on his shoulder.

'What happened to you?' Soraya asked.

'Pack of swamp-wolves,' Zorgrath replied with a twisted smile. 'They were downwind. I didn't smell them before they smelled me. Had to kill the pack leader before they'd leave me alone.'

The others gathered around Zorgrath. Kvetka inspected the cryptborn's wounds while Mahyar produced a small bottle of ale he'd liberated from the ogor's larder. Zorgrath took a long pull from the bottle, his sharp teeth scratching its neck. The priest waved aside his efforts to return the remainder to him.

'The wolves are why you've been gone so long?' Venteslav wanted to know.

Zorgrath took another pull from the bottle and shook his head. 'No. It was something different that did that.' He gave the captain a steady look. 'By Nagash's Crown, I swear to you I've never lost a track or trail the way I did today.' He gestured with his hands. 'It seemed like the ground changed as soon as it was out of sight. The way back was just as unfamiliar as the way ahead. It even smelled different,' he added, tapping his nose. 'It was all changed, like something was trying to get me lost.'

Kvetka paused in wrapping a bandage around the cryptborn's shoulder. 'With Zorgrath lost, we'd all be lost,' she said with a glance at Venteslav.

'How did you find your way back?' Soraya asked.

'The fire,' Zorgrath said, pointing at the flames. 'I could see the light. That's how I know... how I know the trees have been moving. The only constant was your light. Without that I'd never have made it back.'

'The forest doesn't want to let us go.' Kvetka shuddered. She turned to Venteslav. 'That's why we've only seen glimpses and images. Its true power has been worked to keep Zorgrath from guiding us out.'

'Twaddle,' Omid growled. 'The cryptborn got himself lost, that's all...' His words trailed away and he pointed towards the trees. Out in the darkness, dozens of glowing eyes had appeared. They had a lustreless green colour to them, like old jade buried in the ground.

'What are they?' Soraya asked.

'The sins of the past,' Kvetka answered. 'Now that Zorgrath is with us, the spirits of Shiverbloom can focus their full attention here.'

Mahyar strode towards the glowing eyes, the orruk choppa clenched in his hands. 'Now that they've shown themselves to all of us, they shall regret doing so. By Sigmar, no spectre of the night is going to keep us from our task.'

Soraya caught Mahyar's arm before he could walk into the

darkness and confront whatever was out there. 'It could be a trick,' she cautioned him. 'They mean to draw you out, keep you from protecting the rest of us.'

'We stay together,' Venteslav declared. 'Whether we make our stand here or go out to fight, we do it as one.'

'There's another way,' Gajevic said. His visage was grave. 'It will be dangerous and I'll need all of you to guard me while I perform the ritual I have in mind.'

'What are you going to do?' Kvetka asked.

Gajevic pointed to the eyes watching them. 'Perhaps you have forgotten, but the green-folk were said to have such eyes. They were also said to have powerful magic. Maybe some of them survived the conflagration. If so, it might be possible to communicate with them.'

Soraya stared in disbelief at the wizard. 'There's nothing alive out there.'

'Then I will seek to appease their spirits.' Gajevic smiled.

'That would be flirting with necromancy,' Mahyar warned, menace in his voice.

Kvetka laid her hand on Gajevic's shoulder. 'There must be another way.'

'Can we think of one before this power becomes strong enough to act against us?' Gajevic retorted. He looked to Venteslav. 'Please, captain, let me try before it's too late.'

'Sigmar have mercy on us all,' Venteslav said as he nodded his head.

While the wizard began his preparations, Soraya watched the trees. There were more sets of eyes now. Many more. Dozens had become hundreds. She even thought she saw shadowy bodies attached to the eyes, gnarled and twisted shapes that were anything but human.

Whatever spell Gajevic was going to try, Soraya hoped it was a quick one. Because it looked like the spirits of the forest were becoming impatient.

Mahyar observed from a distance as Gajevic prepared his ritual. If they had been back in the Twinned Towns, he wouldn't have hesitated to arrest the wizard for even suggesting such magic. Aside from the foul devices of Chaos itself, necromancy was the most profane brand of enchantment. In the realm of Azyr, the dark art was actively suppressed. Here in Shyish it had proven much more difficult to restrain. The energies that fuelled necromancy were everywhere in this realm, waiting to be harnessed. Innocent children unaware of their affinity for the arcane would accidentally tap into that fell power. A dead pet would rise as a decayed zombie or a lost parent's gheist might be conjured up from the underworlds. The perils of necromancy were many, its practitioners often deluded that they could control the power and harness it towards good rather than the evil that was innate within it.

Gajevic was trying to do good. Mahyar didn't even question that his motivations were pure. What he questioned was the magic itself. Could anything good be drawn from evil? That was a lesson even the God-King had been forced to ask himself when he invited the Great Necromancer into his pantheon, only to be betrayed by Nagash. Evil will always revert to its true nature.

'Sigmar forgive us,' Mahyar prayed. He kept his eyes on the ritual. It was left to Zorgrath and the soldiers to guard against the spirits in the woods. His place was here, guarding against a different kind of danger.

'Place the candles there,' Gajevic directed Kvetka. There was no timidity in his voice now, only a grim resignation. Perhaps Mahyar had been unjust in his opinion. It was possible the wizard was fully aware how dangerous this ritual was.

Kvetka put the black candles down as Gajevic reached into his bag and drew out a lump of salt. Mahyar felt the hairs at the back of his neck prickle at the sight. He'd seen the wizard walk out of the Sea of Tears, but to know his spell had gone so far as to keep even a lump of salt from dissolving struck him as in some way beyond the pale. He watched as Gajevic crushed the salt between his hands and quickly poured a line between the two candles before crouching down in front of the display.

'Kvetka, I will need your dagger,' Gajevic said. The scholar started to hand the blade to him, but then hesitated. 'Don't be alarmed. The ritual needs only a little blood.'

Of course it does, Mahyar thought to himself. All black magic required the essence of life. The difference between a blood offering and a full sacrifice was only a matter of degrees. The taint was the same. The corruption was the same. He took a step towards Gajevic, ready to end this before it could start. Then he thought of Westreach and all the people waiting, depending on them. If there was any chance to accomplish what Jahangir had set out to do, they had to take it. He thought again of Sigmar and Nagash. For a time, at least, good had come from the Lord of Undeath.

'No,' Kvetka cried out. Gajevic had stabbed the point of her dagger into his palm. She moved to grab the blade away from him, but Mahyar drew her back.

'Let him try to work his magic,' Mahyar told her. The words were uncomfortable on his tongue. Almost blasphemous considering what Gajevic was trying to do.

Gajevic twisted the dagger in his wound until he drew a sufficient quantity of blood. Then he slapped his hand into the very middle of the line of salt. Red mixed with white when he withdrew and leaned back. Strange words, low and sinister, rose from his throat. Mahyar saw the wizard's eyes roll over so that only the whites were visible.

'Something's happening!' Venteslav shouted. 'The… shapes… are coming closer now!'

Blood! It was the blood calling to them! There was no savour the undead craved, be they spectral or physical, so much as the blood of mortals. Mahyar started forwards, again intent on stopping the ritual. Some inner voice held him back. A compulsion he couldn't explain.

'It's gone wrong,' Kvetka said. 'We have to stop him.'

'Not yet,' Mahyar said, unsure why he said it.

Before them, Gajevic had thrown his head back. Strange wisps of light swirled around him, weaving about in ever-tightening circles. The wizard began to speak. 'The green-folk are gone. Burned away in the fires of fear and ignorance. Their ashes have been scattered to the winds. But their spirit remains, the great spirit which was within them all. It lingers still, a howling whisper that cries out. Cries out in mourning and in wrath.' A ragged scream of pain was ripped from his mouth and blood dripped down his chin.

'Stop it! We have to stop it!' Kvetka struggled in Mahyar's restraining grip.

'Not yet,' the priest repeated. 'Gajevic,' he called to the wizard. 'You sought to appease the spirits. Can you speak to them? Can you gain us passage through the forest?'

From the soldiers watching the trees more shouts of alarm rang out. The forest-shapes were drawing closer, the hate in their jade eyes shining bright in the darkness.

'There is a harmony,' Gajevic muttered. 'Faint. So very faint. It drifts away when I try to catch it. I'm not meant to catch it. It is not meant for humans to know.'

'Try,' Mahyar told Gajevic. 'Try to get hold of it.' He was stunned by his own words, provoking the wizard to delve still deeper into this profane magic. It was testament to his commitment to their quest that he'd embrace even such sorcery if it meant ending the curse.

Another scream rang out. Now the wisps of light were flying so close to Gajevic that they were singeing his clothes. His eyes changed colour, fading into the same dull jade as those of the spirits in the forest. 'I hear!' Gajevic screamed. 'I hear the great Spirit Song! I hear its glory! Its magnificence! Its horror!' His flesh took on an eerie colour, a pallid and sickly green. Beads of blood dripped from his fingers like crimson sweat.

'Stop him!' Kvetka yelled. 'It's too much! It's killing him!'

Mahyar kept his grip on the scholar and shouted to Gajevic. 'You can hear them. Now make them hear you!'

For the third time, a wail of unspeakable suffering was ripped from Gajevic. The jade light vanished from his eyes and the wisps dancing about his body winked out. Even the candles were extinguished, as though an unseen hand had snuffed them out.

'They're gone!' Ratimir shouted. Mahyar turned his head and looked towards the soldiers. It was true. There was no trace of the jade eyes now. No suggestion of strange figures assembling in the shadows.

While he was distracted by the changing situation, Kvetka broke away and ran over to Gajevic. She dropped down beside the wizard and lifted his head off the ground. She darted a venomous look at Mahyar. 'He's still alive, no thanks to you.'

Mahyar walked over to them. 'He knew the risks he was taking.' He gestured to the now empty forest around them. 'Whatever was out there, it's gone now.'

'But will it stay gone?' Venteslav asked as he came running up. The others had been left to watch in case the menace returned.

'They're gone,' Gajevic said, his voice a weak whisper. 'I spoke with them. With their remnant. What was left behind by our fires.' He opened his eyes, drawing a gasp from Kvetka. Mahyar observed the transformation in grim silence. The wizard's pupils had changed to a light green colour.

'Will they be back?' Venteslav asked again.

Gajevic smiled at him. It was a terrible smile. The grin of an idiot. 'The seeds are sown here no more,' he said, ending his speech with a crazed titter.

'Mad,' Venteslav gasped and backed away.

Kvetka glared at Mahyar. 'You did this to him.'

Mahyar had time for neither Kvetka's accusations nor Venteslav's fright. 'Gajevic, try to think. What did you say to them? What did you tell them to make them leave?'

'Everything,' the wizard answered. 'I was a part of the song. Everything I know, everything I am, was part of the song. I heard them and they heard me.'

'Leave him alone,' Kvetka snapped. She recovered her dagger from where Gajevic had dropped it.

'Not until we know,' Mahyar said. 'Otherwise all of this, everything he's gone through will be for nothing.' He leaned closer to Gajevic. 'Will they let us leave the forest? Can we leave?'

The wizard didn't look at him, but Mahyar noted there seemed to be conscious effort on his part when he framed an answer. Some part of Gajevic knew how important it was to speak.

'They will let us leave now,' the wizard said. 'Now that they know our quest, they will let us leave.'

CHAPTER EIGHT

After Gajevic's ritual, Zorgrath was easily able to lead the group out from the Dreadwood. There'd be no reason to spend another night under its haunted boughs. That is, Kvetka thought, if the whole of Shiverbloom had been contained within the withered forest.

Now their path took them into a dank, marshy terrain. They moved through water that rose up above their knees. The few trees that grew in the stagnant water were older and thicker than those of the Dreadwood, but even sicklier in their appearance. Their trunks had a scaly texture that suggested serpents rather than vegetation. Hairy moss hung in matted clumps from their branches, the largest of them evoking images of severed heads dangling by their hair.

'Scalp-wort, they call it,' Zorgrath informed the scholar when he saw her studying the moss. 'Makes a good ointment for keeping leeches away.' The scout gave her a ghoulish grin. 'Of course, you'd be best not to use it since it also attracts blood-bats. Best to let the leeches take a little than have the bats take it all.' He snickered at his morbid jest and continued back down the line of march to report to Venteslav.

'We'll yet rue trusting that jackal,' Mahyar commented. The warrior priest was just ahead of Kvetka. Strapped across his shoulders were ropes attached to the litter they'd fashioned for Gajevic. The wizard was in no condition to walk on his own. Of them all, Mahyar was the one who had the strength and stamina to drag the litter behind him. It was a task he seemed to take on with a sense of duty. After forcing Gajevic to continue the dangerous spell, Kvetka supposed that it was only right Mahyar should be the one to tend the wizard. It did make her feelings towards him more than a bit confused – antipathy alternating with gratitude.

'He knows the Barrowbogs,' Kvetka said, but decided that was perhaps a bit too generous. 'At least he's been here before. That is more than any of us can say. The old texts don't mention them at all.'

Mahyar stopped suddenly. It took him a moment to pull his leg out from the mud. He shifted over to his right and wagged his finger in warning towards the left. 'Stay clear of that,' he advised. 'Felt like a toothless mouth sucking on my foot. Sigmar's grace it wasn't stronger.'

Kvetka looked along the dank creek they were following. It was one of many that snaked their way between weed-covered patches of firmer ground. 'We should be up there,' she said. 'No leeches and no sinkholes.' She gave another uncertain look at the stagnant water. 'No wondering what's slithering around under the surface.'

'Zorgrath's worried about our scent,' Soraya reminded her, coming up from behind the scholar. 'The cryptborn might have the right of it, too. In the water we don't leave a trail behind us. Up there we would. He's worried about swamp-wolves and jabberslythes.'

'At least we should fight them on solid earth,' Mahyar stated. 'Zorgrath said all you need to do to rout wolves is kill the leader.'

'What about a jabberslythe?' Kvetka asked. 'Those are monstrosities spawned by Chaos. They care only about destruction and death. Such an abomination wouldn't run simply because you struck it with a sword.'

Mahyar shook his head. 'Sigmar provides. If you put your faith in the God-King, there will always be a way to prevail. It is simply that we often lack the wisdom and humility to submit to his will.'

Kvetka bristled at the pious talk. 'Was it Sigmar's will that Gajevic be driven half-mad?' she demanded.

'Perhaps that was a mercy,' Mahyar said. 'The wizard invoked magic he himself knew to be profane. It may have been merciful that he communed with the forest-spirit's remnant rather than drawing the attention of even darker forces.'

'I don't accept that,' Kvetka told him.

'That is your choice,' Mahyar said. He turned and looked at her over his shoulder. 'You think you know much, but all you know has come from books. You haven't gone out and experienced things for yourself. You haven't seen with your own eyes the reality you've read about.'

'And you have?' Kvetka asked.

'In some things,' Mahyar said. 'Some matters I think I could tell you more of than your books. I can tell you of the power of Sigmar and the strength of faith because I have seen it. I've also seen the evil certain magic can bring. There's a catechism that says magic is a malicious servant and a fearful master. Even the most innocuous wizardry must be conducted with caution, and there are some invocations that can be justified by only the most extreme need. The danger is that great.'

'What manner of danger?' Soraya interjected.

'I've seen what happens when witches try to bring messages

from the dead to the living,' Mahyar stated, his voice grim. 'They might succeed in their foul art nine times out of ten, but it is their failure that undoes any good they might have wrought – spectres drawn from their tombs to haunt the living, the undead called up from their graves. Do not ever forget that necromancy is the magic of Nagash and that all which is accomplished through it is done only because it suits his malefic purposes.' He clenched his fists and shook his head. 'I should never have permitted such a foul ritual. I too bear the fault.'

'Gajevic is no disciple of Nagash,' Kvetka snapped.

Mahyar looked down at the wizard lashed to the litter. Even in sleep, there was an expression of suffering on his face. 'That is the most insidious thing of all. One doesn't have to follow Nagash to do his bidding.'

'Your people came from Azyr,' Kvetka said. 'Ours are of Shyish. There's no hiding from the Great Necromancer's power here. To survive, Nagash's dominion must be acknowledged. There is a saying that the Lord of Undeath should be invited to every feast, but every feast should have a long table.'

'Nagash's dominion is the dead, not the living,' Mahyar declared. 'Sigmar is our protector. However long your table, if you seek to propitiate Nagash you flirt with blasphemy and embrace delusion. He cares for the living only so much as they further the reign of the dead.' He gave Kvetka a challenging look. 'Do you think any prayer or offering rendered to Nagash would move him to protect our people from the Lady of Sorrows? She is one of his Mortarchs. Her curse could be lifted by the merest gesture from Nagash. But this will not happen. No matter how you beg and grovel.'

'Our people survived many generations before the Stormcasts came and the Twinned Towns were founded,' Kvetka countered.

'You scratched a living from the shadows and existed in constant fear of the walking dead,' Mahyar stated. 'It was the strength of Sigmar that allowed you to live with dignity again. To know once more the joy of hearth and home.'

Kvetka was about to offer a rejoinder to the priest, determined to defend the customs and traditions that had kept her ancestors alive since the destruction of Belvegrod. Before she could, she felt her foot step down into a mucky hole. At once she stumbled forwards and her other foot encountered nothing but mud. She tried to pull herself up, but the mire was too strong. Instead of freeing herself, she felt herself dragged farther down. The image Mahyar had painted of a toothless mouth was horrifyingly appropriate to the sensation that now held her.

Soraya rushed to catch Kvetka. She gripped the scholar under her shoulders and tried to pull her up. Instead, Kvetka was only sucked deeper. Her waist was already beneath the surface.

'Omid! Ratimir!' Mahyar shouted. He started to turn, to move to help, but the wizard's litter made him aware he would be risking two lives if he did. 'Soraya, hold on to her! Omid, get these straps off me and take care of Gajevic!'

Kvetka's fingers clutched desperately at Soraya. Vainly she tried to pull herself up from the sucking mire. The soldier staggered and would have pitched forwards had Ratimir not seized her arm and dragged her back. The detached, rational part of her mind told Kvetka she needed to calm down, that her panic was imperilling the very people trying to save her, but the downward pull of the mud spoke far louder. She couldn't shake the terror of being sucked beneath the surface and drowning in the muck.

'Get a rope around her!' Venteslav ordered. He threw a long length of cord to Ratimir.

Soraya shifted her grip while Ratimir looped the rope around Kvetka's body. The merciless pull of the mud had drawn her down to her belly now. 'Don't leave me! Don't leave me!' Kvetka shouted when both Ratimir and Venteslav turned away. They were hurrying to one of the trees with the other end of the rope. Again, she knew they weren't abandoning her, that they were going to use the tree to act as leverage. But panic made no allowances for reason.

'Help Venteslav,' Mahyar told Soraya. The warrior priest took over from the soldier, slipping his arms underneath Kvetka's and holding her fast. For just an instant, as the two Azyrites traded places, Kvetka felt the suction increase. She screamed as the stagnant surface of the water rose to just below her neck.

'Don't let me drown,' she pleaded with Mahyar.

'Keep your eyes on me.' The warrior priest grunted with the strain of holding onto her. 'If the bog takes you, it takes me too,' he said. 'But by Sigmar, that won't happen!' He was bent nearly double to keep his grip and each moment saw him lean forwards a little more as the pull of the mud dragged Kvetka down.

Kvetka tried to control her panic, to not make Mahyar's task worse by her struggles. With more resolve than she knew she possessed, she focused on the priest's eyes: the one constant in a world that was gradually sinking away beneath her.

'Sigmar lend me strength,' Mahyar prayed. As he said the words, it seemed to Kvetka that his hold on her tightened. She actually felt herself inching upwards, being drawn out of the hungry muck.

'We're ready!' Soraya shouted. The rope around Kvetka's body tightened. The breath was forced out of her as the cord snapped taut. Now she was rising swiftly, being pulled up and out from the hole. Mahyar lurched sideways, adjusting his position so that he wouldn't stagger into the mire. Never did he loosen his grip and never did his steadfast, determined gaze leave Kvetka's eyes.

The water was down around Kvetka's waist again. She felt herself being pulled up and back by the rope. She managed to draw short, sharp breaths into her lungs, sneaking them past the squeezing pressure of the rope. Her panic lessened, the stolid presence of

Mahyar tempering the fear that raced through her mind. She was able to think again, able to recognise when it was solid ground rather than sucking mud under her feet.

For a moment, Kvetka continued to stare into Mahyar's eyes. Then, almost simultaneously, each broke the contact and looked away.

'I'm out,' Kvetka gasped as she stood away from the sinkhole. The words came in little more than a croak and were followed by rapid, panting breaths. The soldiers by the tree stopped pulling on the rope. Mahyar quickly untied the cords wrapped around her and his fingers pressed against her ribs. She winced at the contact, her skin bruised and tender from the bite of the rope.

'Nothing feels broken,' Mahyar said. He gave Kvetka an uneasy look. 'Are you able to walk?'

'I'll try,' Kvetka said. Gingerly she took a step to her right, her eyes darting from where she was going to the sinkhole that had almost sucked her under. 'Yes, I think I can walk.'

'We'll need to be more careful,' Zorgrath told them. The guide left Gajevic with Omid and moved towards one of the trees. He started chopping away at a branch with one of his knives. In a short amount of time he had a long stick which he thrust into the water around him. 'We use these to test the ground before we walk,' he said, looking towards Venteslav.

'You might have suggested that before,' the captain snapped. 'We nearly lost Kvetka. Might have lost others trying to get her out.'

Zorgrath shrugged. 'The other times I've gone through the Barrowbogs, the caravans had skiffs to cross the channels,' he explained. 'If you would rather find the Veiled Oracle's citadel by yourself, that is your choice.'

Kvetka turned towards Venteslav. 'We know the danger now,' she said, repressing a shudder. 'I don't think any of us will make the same mistake again.'

'My worry is that there may be other dangers in these swamps,' Venteslav replied. He cast another doubtful look at Zorgrath. 'Other things that our guide "didn't know about".'

'There may be any manner of unexpected things ahead,' Zorgrath countered. 'I've seen the citadel you're looking for, but only from a distance. I can't say what hazards there might be nearer to it. None of the caravans wanted to get any closer to the Veiled Oracle than they had to.'

'Why would that be?' Kvetka asked. 'Do they fear the oracle's powers that much?'

Zorgrath walked towards her and handed her the stick he'd cut. 'There are many strange stories about the Veiled Oracle.' His voice dropped to a grim whisper. 'Some of them hold that it is an aelven mystic. Others say that what dwells within the citadel is a vampire.'

The Eastdalers reached for the charms they carried. Mahyar made the sign of the Hammer and invoked the name of Sigmar. He turned to Kvetka. 'Certainly if the oracle were a vampire the gravesands would have revealed that. Certainly it would have been spoken of before.'

A knot grew at the back of Kvetka's throat. She didn't like the answers she had for Mahyar's statements. 'The gravesands reveal only what is immediate to the moment of tomorrow they contain. As for the Veiled Oracle, there is disagreement in the texts. All that is certain is that she is old. Either the role is passed from one seeress to another, or else... she isn't entirely mortal.'

The Barrowbogs somehow managed to become less pleasant and more intimidating the deeper into them the small group marched. Slogging through the stagnant water, prodding every foot to be certain the next step wasn't going to be another sinkhole, they made slow progress. Venteslav only had to mention the prospect of spending the night in the swamps to keep his people moving.

Nobody wanted to be in this forsaken landscape when it grew dark, not if there was even the merest chance of winning through before sunset.

Venteslav kept a careful watch on Zorgrath. The cryptborn should have spoken about using skiffs on his earlier visits to the Barrowbogs. It bothered him not only because of the accident that nearly killed Kvetka, but because now there was a nagging doubt in his mind. If their guide had kept that detail back, then what other things wasn't he telling them? Maybe he knew more about the citadel and the Veiled Oracle than he was admitting. Maybe everything to this point had been to get them here for some unsavoury purpose. The cryptborn, after all, were a degenerate breed. The taint of the ghoul was in their blood and in their brains.

Or it needn't be so nefarious. Zorgrath might simply have taken a pragmatic outlook. The disaster on the bridge certainly made the prospect of success dubious, to say the least. Venteslav considered that the scout might be thinking his chances of getting paid were too slight to bother with. Zorgrath might be thinking that getting free of the Shadoom was about the only good that would come to him from this venture. If such were the case, he would be looking for a chance to slip away. Maybe only the fear of pursuit had kept him around this long. Maybe he was just waiting for lands safe enough to venture in alone before abandoning them?

The mind of a cryptborn, after all, didn't work like that of someone truly human.

Soraya was marching close to Venteslav and noticed the subject that kept drawing his gaze. 'You believe he's leading us into a trap after all?' she whispered.

Fully aware of how sharp Zorgrath's hearing was, Venteslav only gave the briefest nod. He allowed the severity of his expression to convey his true feelings when he answered with words much milder than he might otherwise have used. 'The incident has shaken my confidence in his abilities. We've depended on him so much that it upsets the faith I've put into him that such an accident could beset us.' His eyes were hard as he looked forward to where the guide ranged ahead of the column, poking the slime of the channel's bottom with his stick. 'It would almost be more comfortable to think it was deliberate.'

'The argument still stands that he did lead us to weapons and food,' Soraya objected.

'If I wanted to do something, I'd do it when and where the odds against me weren't seven to one,' Venteslav said. 'I'd need to give enough genuine help to keep us going to where things might be very different.'

'The swamps,' Soraya muttered, a tinge of dread in her voice.

'He could slip away and leave us,' elaborated Venteslav. 'With Gajevic in such condition we wouldn't be able to call on magic to see us through.'

'That's why you told Zorgrath to stay close,' Soraya said. 'Not so we could help if he stumbled into a sinkhole, but so we could keep an eye on him.'

Venteslav tugged at his long moustache. 'If we're vigilant we might avoid more accidents.' His expression became even more severe. 'I think he might have made a mistake when he mentioned vampires to Kvetka. Perhaps he was trying to be clever, to tell me what was in his mind so that I'd be less likely to suspect him.' He stopped and gripped Soraya's arm. 'Your people aren't of Shyish. Your ancestors never had to hide in the dirt when the flesh-eaters came! Great packs of ghouls led by the most debased and monstrous vampires, all of them hungry for human prey!'

As he spoke, Venteslav saw alarm rise in Soraya's eyes. She tried to draw back from him. She was speaking words to him, but they were just so much noise.

'Have you gone mad?' Soraya gasped. 'How can you think such things?'

'That is what I'd expect someone colluding with the cryptborn to say,' Venteslav countered with a snarl. 'Try to make me doubt what I see with my own eyes. Make me think I am the one who's mad.' A bitter laugh rose from his throat. 'You're mad if you think you can save your life by helping Zorgrath. Once you're no longer useful, he'll kill you and eat you, just as he will the rest of us.'

'It isn't true,' Soraya insisted. There was fear now in her eyes. For just a moment, Venteslav wondered if he was wrong. If he was hurling baseless and vile accusations against a loyal soldier.

Venteslav's mind raced with new suspicions, but as his fears became ever wilder and more fantastical, he felt a tremendous sense of futility. They were all traitors. Not just Zorgrath and Soraya, but all of them. He was the only loyal one who'd survived the battle of the bridge. The only one left to complete a quest he couldn't accomplish alone. He would have been better off if he'd died with Jahangir.

Venteslav let go of Soraya and staggered back, his mind reeling with the enormity of his failure. Had he thought he could somehow achieve even a part of what the chosen one was incapable of doing? Had he been presumptuous enough to think he could defy the might of Lady Olynder? He was a disgrace, a mockery. The magnitude of his failure would be borne back to Eastdale to become the shame of his family for generations to come.

'Something's wrong with the captain,' Soraya called out. Venteslav could only vaguely make sense of her words. He was dimly aware of others hurrying over to him. Kvetka was the first to reach him. Behind her he could see Mahyar lumbering fowards, dragging Gajevic behind him.

Sight of Gajevic was like an inundation of icy water. Venteslav felt a sharp shock race through him when he looked into the wizard's vacant, crazed visage. The suspicion and despair that wracked his brain didn't vanish, but their grip on him lessened. He could recognise them now as an influence acting upon him from somewhere outside himself.

'Stay back,' Venteslav warned, holding up his hands. 'Soraya's right. Something's wrong. Something working against my mind.' He found he was now at the centre of a ring of worried faces. He motioned to Ratimir and Omid. 'Rush in together and get hold of my arms. Soraya, when they have me take my sword away.' He ground his teeth against the surge of raw terror that pounded through him as the paranoid visions screamed at him, trying to convince him that he was exposing himself to enemies.

'What's happening?' Kvetka demanded.

Venteslav didn't try to frame even the semblance of an answer until the soldiers grabbed his arms and Soraya took the sword from his belt. He struggled to free himself. Only when he knew his efforts were useless did his mind calm enough for him to speak. 'Thoughts that aren't mine,' he growled. 'Terrible things that can't be real.' He fixed his gaze on Kvetka. 'I think you were right. It was more than just the Dreadwood which was once Shiverbloom. I think the hate of the green-folk must be here too. Their old magic is trying to destroy me from within.'

'What can we do?' Ratimir gasped. 'Gajevic can't cast a spell and make them go away again!'

Kvetka made a close study of Venteslav, leaning close to peer into his eyes. 'These alien thoughts, they tell you that everything is hopeless, that no one can be trusted?' She stepped back, her face going pale. She must have found her answer just by looking at him. 'I have felt the same disturbing influence working against my mind.'

'It is the green-folk,' Omid snarled. 'Striking out again at the Reclaimed.'

Soraya doused her fellow Azyrite's statement. 'I've felt it too,' she said. 'Even before Venteslav started to express suspicions of treachery, I felt the same ideas tugging at me. Trying to poison me against the rest of you. Trying to tell me it was all hopeless. Making me think the best thing to do would be to fall upon my own sword...'

Omid's hold on Venteslav tightened. His eyes had a fearful cast to them. 'No, it is the Reclaimed they want,' he insisted. 'If we give the spirits the Reclaimed, they'll leave the rest of us alone.'

Venteslav tried to pull away when he saw Omid reaching for his knife. Shocked by the sudden escalation, Ratimir didn't react at all, but simply retained the hold he already had. It was from a different quarter that help came. Before Omid could draw his blade, he was struck from behind by Zorgrath. The cryptborn drove his shoulder into the frantic soldier and sent him sprawling. He splashed headfirst into the water and quickly rolled onto his back. The knife was in his hand and murder was in his eyes when he glared up at Zorgrath.

'You'll pay for that, ghoul,' Omid swore. Before he could make a lunge for Zorgrath, Soraya's boot cracked against his wrist and sent the knife skipping away into the swamp. He turned his fury on the other Azyrite. 'Traitor,' he hissed. He sprang from the water and had his hands locked about her throat before Soraya could react.

'Stop it!' Venteslav ordered. Even as he did, there was a part of his mind that exulted in the scene. Two traitors destroying one another. Whichever died, he'd have one less enemy. Better still, both might die. He looked over at Ratimir. 'Stop them,' he said. The tone of command in his voice penetrated the shock. Ratimir released Venteslav and started towards the other soldiers.

A golden light shone out, burning through a thick grey mist that surrounded them all. Venteslav was more alarmed by that mist than the supernatural glow. He knew the moist fog was uncanny, though he couldn't say how. Neither could he say with even the vaguest accuracy when the mist had appeared. Had it only recently come upon them or had it been there since before Kvetka stepped into the sinkhole?

'All of you will stop!' Mahyar's stern voice boomed like the crack of thunder across the swamp. There was a force of authority and conviction in his words that had woven within it more than the merely mortal. Forcibly it was impressed on Venteslav that a true priest of sincere faith was a living conduit between the mundane and the divine.

The golden light shone brighter even as it diminished in size. From a shapeless glow it condensed into the form of a small hammer. Venteslav's eyes widened with amazement when he saw that the hammer was nothing less than the holy icon Mahyar wore. The sacred light blazed from that simple metal pendant, burning with a purity that thrust itself into his mind. He felt it washing across the destructive impulses that strove to control him, forcing them back and back again, compelling them to recede into the last corners of his awareness. He knew they were extinguished, but he didn't feel them leave. They simply dissolved into nothingness, diminished until there was too little to sense when the last threads of despair were finally eradicated. Venteslav was even more convinced now that these thoughts hadn't been his own, for there was no sense of pain as they were burned from his mind. Instead, there was a feeling almost of euphoria, a sense of cleansing that left him refreshed.

Mahyar pulled Soraya and Omid apart. 'Sigmar commands you to relent,' the priest told them. Venteslav watched as the same process that had freed him worked upon them. He saw the change in their faces. Ferocious one moment, they shifted into melancholy and then to a blissful calm. It was that calm which still ruled their countenances when Mahyar turned from them. He moved towards Ratimir and repeated the same words to him.

Venteslav curled the small fingers of his hands together and bowed his head – a customary gesture for the Reclaimed when acknowledging the presence of Sigmar. Surely it was the power of the God-King that enabled Mahyar to banish the baneful influence that had afflicted them.

The grey mist, only moments before so dominant, now began to dwindle. Venteslav watched as it was reduced from a mighty wall to only a few tattered strands. These slithered away deeper into the Barrowbogs, sliding across the water like giant snakes. He whispered an old charm against witchcraft as they vanished into the distance.

'The green-folk,' Venteslav said. 'Their spirits must have been regathering their strength to strike at us after Gajevic's ritual.'

'If the Barrowbogs were once part of Shiverbloom, their power would reach here as easily as the Dreadwood,' Kvetka said. The others were ready to agree with the idea, but Mahyar presented a dissenting voice.

'It is not the spirits of the green-folk with which we contend,' Mahyar stated. 'This was a manifestation of a far more evil power.' He pointed to Venteslav. 'Think a moment upon the instruments with which your willpower was subverted. Treachery and despair. These are the tools of an enemy we know only too well. The Mortarch of Grief. The Lady of Sorrows.'

'You are saying then that this attack was directed against us by Lady Olynder?' Venteslav felt his heart go cold.

'Perhaps not directed,' Mahyar said. 'It could be some ancient malice left to haunt these swamps. But I feel certain it originated from her. How long ago would be a question only a wizard might answer.' He looked over his shoulder at Gajevic's litter.

'Praise Sigmar you were able to drive off the power, whatever it was,' Soraya said. 'Without your intervention…'

Mahyar nodded. 'That is another reason I am convinced the

attack was necromantic in nature. Where your minds were dominated by this force, I felt only its most tenuous touch. My faith repelled it. The light of my devotion to Sigmar left it no foothold to gain with me.'

'We'll need your protection if such an attack happens again,' Venteslav said. For just an instant he saw uneasiness in Mahyar's face.

'In Shyish there are things that may obstruct the primacy of Sigmar.' Each word came reluctantly to the priest's lips. He pointed his hand up at the sky. 'We were fortunate that this attack happened by day. At night the fell powers of necromancy are ascendant and the light of Azyr shines with difficulty.' His eyes were hard when he looked at Venteslav. 'We need to leave these swamps before nightfall. I'm certain the force that attacked us will strike again once the sun has set.'

Mahyar's warning was still howling through Venteslav's mind hours later. The whole group had been moving with a desperate haste, striving to outpace the dying day. They slogged through the channels with recklessness now, barely bothering to check the ground before hurrying across it. Being sucked down by the mud seemed a happy death beside the soul-rending insanity brought on by the spectral mists.

Zorgrath ranged farther and farther ahead of them, often vanishing from sight entirely. Venteslav found himself unwilling to call him back, worried that such notions might not be his own but rather some tiny bit of Lady Olynder's magic that hadn't completely left his mind. He felt almost an obligation to trust his companions now, if only to prove the maddening mists wrong.

'We're losing the race,' Kvetka groaned. She was walking beside Venteslav, but her face was turned skywards.

'Even the most devout of Mahyar's prayers won't turn back the sun,' Venteslav said. 'We should hope instead that Zorgrath will find the edge of the swamp soon.'

'The mists!' Omid shouted. He'd been posted at the back of their formation, but now he came hurrying forwards, sloshing past Mahyar and Gajevic to reach the captain. He waved his hand frantically at the darkening swamp behind them. 'I saw the mists again. They're coming back, glowing like jack-o-wisps!'

For just a moment Venteslav stopped. Everyone else did too, turning around so they might see for themselves.

The truth came in slender ribbons of vapour slithering across the water. They were still a dull grey in colour, but now there was a ghostly flicker within them that made them shine in the dark. Before, the miasma had set upon them without warning. Now it seemed as if it took sadistic pleasure in announcing itself. Venteslav was certain it was not imagination when the mists stayed still, freezing in place above the sluggish water like a dragon evaluating its prey, bold in the belief that it could not be opposed.

'Run,' Venteslav hissed. He fell back to help Mahyar with Gajevic. Kvetka hurried along to lend her support. Together they lifted the litter completely out of the water and with Mahyar leading the way they were able to make good progress, though still not enough to keep pace with the others.

In the distance Venteslav could hear the howls of swamp-wolves as they welcomed the dying of the sun. The sky above wasn't entirely dark, the last of the day struggling against the grip of night. A struggle that was decided with agonising slowness, almost as though Shyish itself were toying with them and prolonging their torment.

'The miasma's moving again!' Kvetka yelled.

Venteslav risked one look back as they all tried to run faster. What he saw chilled him to the bone. The mists weren't simply moving, they were expanding! The slender ribbons were billowing outwards, roiling and undulating into a great cloud of fog that appeared to swallow everything behind them. It felt like trying to outrun the end of the world as the mists roared after them. Already he could feel the despairing thoughts trying to claw their way back into his mind. Subtlety had won them entry before, but now that he was aware of it, the influence was seeking to tear its way inside with phantom talons. How long he could resist, he didn't know.

'Keep going!' Mahyar bellowed. 'Fight it! Fight it!'

Until the priest cried out, Venteslav hadn't realised his pace had slackened. So had Kvetka's. So too had Omid's. Venteslav looked again, surprised that the soldier had fallen back to help them. Then he saw Soraya and Ratimir as well. They hadn't fallen back and Mahyar's words hadn't been just for him and Kvetka. Everyone was slowing; and it wasn't merely fatigue that drained their energy.

'It's the miasma!' Venteslav shouted. 'It's making us slow!' He was stunned by the vile craftiness of the necromantic force. The violent efforts to force itself into their minds had let it slip in more subtle compulsions. Like mental spiderwebs, the malignant power had ensnared them.

As before, simply being aware of what was happening wasn't enough to break free. Indeed, Venteslav thought it made the influence harder to resist. What had Mahyar said? That the power of Lady Olynder was that of despair? So it was that the very hopelessness he felt was only strengthening the hold upon him.

Darkness was truly settling upon the swamps. The moonlight shone fitfully through the trees, illuminating just enough to reveal the uselessness of trying to resist. Venteslav had to force every ounce of willpower to keep hold of the litter. If not for Mahyar's lead, he didn't know if he'd have been able to move his own legs.

'Fight it!' Venteslav shouted, trying to force Mahyar's words into his mind, trying to compel himself to believe them. The others took up the cry. Even Gajevic mouthed the words, though only a garbled sound escaped his mouth.

Up ahead, a gangrel shape loped into view. At first glance, Venteslav thought it must be a swamp-wolf scouting for its pack. Then a thrill crackled through his blood. It was a scout, but a scout of a very different sort. 'Zorgrath!' he cried. 'It's Zorgrath!'

Never would he have believed that sight of the cryptborn could instil such excitement. Such... yes, Venteslav had to use the word, hope. And as that sense of hope rushed through him, he felt energy pour back into his legs and the clawing influence recede from the walls of his mind.

'This way,' Zorgrath called, waving his arms. 'The citadel's this way.'

The citadel? The home of the Veiled Oracle! The site they'd come so far to find. Venteslav's heart pounded in his chest. He could almost hear the snarl of frustration as the destructive influence slipped away entirely. He could hear the relief of the others and knew that they too were inspired by a new hope.

Then Venteslav looked back. The miasma was hurtling towards them with redoubled intensity, speeding across the water like a gargantuan serpent. 'Hurry! It's after us!' Far from being won, it now seemed that their desperate race was doomed to tragedy.

Zorgrath waved his arms, shouting encouragement to the others. Though Venteslav expected the miasma to engulf them at any moment, he wouldn't relent. He would keep going. The malevolence wouldn't take him without a fight. He could see from the intensity of Kvetka's face that the scholar felt the same. They would not submit.

The soldiers were ahead again now. Zorgrath motioned them off to the right and up a slimy embankment. Soraya and Omid made the climb, but Ratimir slammed down into the water. His face was a mask of terror when he picked himself up and glanced back towards Venteslav and his companions. Frantically, Ratimir turned and leapt up the embankment. Venteslav didn't dare turn his head to look at what was behind them.

'Drop the litter and save yourselves,' Mahyar told them. 'I'll carry the wizard.'

'No,' Kvetka snapped. 'We all make it or none of us will.'

Venteslav felt it would be the latter. He prepared to order everyone to leave Gajevic, despising the necessity of such a choice. They were all obliged to the wizard for getting them out of the Dreadwood, but as things looked now the very lives he'd saved would be lost because of him.

Before he could speak, something bright and shining went flying over his head, sailing back into the miasma. Venteslav felt rather than heard the wail of agony that shuddered through the swamp.

'That was my pendant,' Mahyar declared. 'Perhaps it will hold the force back for a little while.'

None of them wanted to test how long that might be. Venteslav strained as much as any of them as they hurried to the embankment. Zorgrath helped them cut the straps and lift Gajevic's litter to the soldiers above. Then the rest of them made their own desperate ascent.

The mist had drawn back because of Mahyar's holy icon, but now it came swirling onwards with a vengeance. Venteslav pictured Ratimir's fall back into the water. If any of them lost their grip now, it would be something far more perilous that closed around them.

By the grace of Sigmar and their own frantic efforts, all of them reached solid ground. Venteslav gave a worried look back to the channel, but the mist appeared to be restricted to the water. It roiled below like an angry beast cheated of its prey.

'It doesn't look like it can chase us,' Venteslav said. Neither did it appear that the influence was able to project itself up to where they stood, unless it was again trying to be subtle.

Venteslav turned to speak with Zorgrath. 'We'll have to find another way back...' The rest of his instructions to the guide faltered on his tongue. The others had already forgotten the miasma. They were looking at the hill which loomed above them and at the structure that rose up from its summit.

'The citadel of the Veiled Oracle,' Venteslav muttered.

CHAPTER NINE

The hill atop which the citadel stood was only an extended finger of a much larger range that rolled off into the distance. The hills were all characterised by their sharp, craggy contours and rocky surface. Unlike the Barrowbogs or even the Dreadwood, nothing alive scratched out a presence as far as Soraya could see. They were desolate and barren.

'What do we do? Climb the cliffs?' Ratimir wondered as he stared up at the hill. It was an uninviting prospect. The jagged rocks had split at such severe angles as to leave each with a knife-like edge.

Soraya craned her neck and tried to study the citadel. From this vantage it was just an indistinct structure rising above the peak. 'There has to be another way,' she said. 'I don't think the builders of this place expected visitors to make such an ascent.'

'If the builders expected anyone to come here at all,' Kvetka said. 'Perhaps no one was meant to visit this place. Not an outpost but a prison.'

Venteslav pulled at his moustache for a moment before shaking his head. 'We've come too far to turn back now. We're here, and we're going to see the Veiled Oracle.'

'There may be a less demanding approach,' Zorgrath offered. The cryptborn indicated the broad expanse of the hill itself. 'We should spread out and see. There might be a path that isn't immediately obvious.'

'That notion sounds reasonable,' Soraya agreed. She turned to Venteslav to see if he thought so as well.

'It would be better to find out now than discover an easier path when we're halfway up the hillside,' Venteslav decided. 'Everyone keep within eyesight of one another while you're looking.' He darted a worried glance back at the Barrowbogs where the glowing miasma could still be seen. 'There may be other dangers lurking about.'

Soraya headed off to take position on the extreme left flank. The rest of the survivors spread out, with Zorgrath at the other extreme. Mahyar with Gajevic stayed at the spot where they'd climbed up from the swamp, acting as both anchor and reference point for the searchers. Despite their ordeal with the mists and their harrowing efforts to elude them, none of the survivors thought of rest. Not with their objective so near.

It was after a few hours of poking at the rocks with her stick, inspecting every shadow for anything untoward, that Soraya made her discovery. So cunningly placed within the angles of two tall boulders that she didn't see it until she was right on top of it, there was a narrow path. She could see it arcing away from the base of the hill, winding off around its side in a gradual ascent banded on either side by the jagged rocks. It looked artificial, a deliberate construction. She confirmed this when she inspected the tall boulders and found that they were fragments of a still bigger stone that had been hewn in twain by some incredible process which looked to have both split it and pushed it apart. Soraya wasn't sure what could have that sort of power. She wasn't so sure she wanted to know.

Soraya took her stick and wedged it between the rocks beside the path to mark her discovery. Then she worked her way back around the base of the hill, alerting each person she passed of what she'd found. They followed her back to where Mahyar was waiting. After collecting the searchers on the right side of the hill, Venteslav reached a quick decision.

'The path Soraya's found is what we've been looking for,' he said. 'That some effort was made to conceal it from a distance only convinces me that it must communicate with the summit. We'll see if we can't reach the citadel.' Venteslav frowned at the sharp rocks that jutted out from the sides of the hill. 'At all lengths, however far it goes, it'll save us at least a little climbing.'

The small band followed Soraya back to the path she'd marked. Zorgrath took the lead, inspecting the ground between the tall boulders. After a close scrutiny of the path, he turned and shook his head.

'No scent, no tracks,' Zorgrath told Venteslav. 'I can't say if this trail leads anywhere, but I can tell that nothing's been using it for a long time.'

'Let me go first,' Soraya suggested. She pointed at Zorgrath. 'My eyesight is better than his. If there's something wrong, I'd be able to see it before he could.'

Venteslav nodded slowly. 'Be careful and try not to disturb the ground too much. Zorgrath will follow behind you. He might not be able to see as far as you, but he can recognise a track better than any of us.' He glanced again at the hillside. 'It could be someone was here but they didn't find this path until they'd climbed the rocks for a while.'

'I'll be careful,' Soraya affirmed. She started up, passing between the two boulders. This close to them she was again impressed by the curious way in which the rock had been split. Zorgrath let her get a dozen yards ahead of him before striking out. The cryptborn would pause at intervals and study the ground for any tracks that weren't the soldier's. A good dozen yards behind Zorgrath, the rest of the group made their ascent.

The going was easy at first, but soon Soraya found that the path angled at a steep slope. Even the excitement of finally reaching the citadel wasn't enough to bolster her against the laborious hike. The muscles in her legs protested against the effort. They felt as though they were burning under her skin, trying to sear their way out of her body. The pain mounted, wracking her senses and making her head reel. She started to swoon, and for a terrifying moment she lurched out over the rocks that lined the path.

Fear flushed all dizziness from her. She was staring down at the slope of the hill. A hundred feet of sharp rocks awaited her if she lost her balance, and then a plunge into the dank murk of the swamp. She doubted if the rocks would leave anything for the Barrowbogs to claim. From this vantage they looked like crooked teeth waiting to gnash and tear at her.

'Sigmar grant me strength,' Soraya prayed. Carefully she turned so that instead of pitching over the side, her reeling body flopped against the path. She heard Zorgrath cry out and start rushing up towards her. A new fear raced through her mind. In his haste the cryptborn might lose his balance and fall victim to the danger that had almost claimed her.

'It's all right,' Soraya called out, waving Zorgrath back. 'Just a moment of dizziness. I'll be all right in a moment.' She was relieved to see the guide stop his hurried ascent. Zorgrath turned and passed her reassurance along to the rest of the group.

Soraya rose from the ground and looked out over the hillside. By her estimate she was halfway to the summit now. A little farther and they would be where they needed to be. They would be standing at the citadel of the Veiled Oracle.

Still as weary as she'd been before her swoon, Soraya resumed her climb. The slope was so steep now that she used her hands as well as her feet to navigate the path. Her promise to be careful and to leave the path undisturbed for Zorgrath to inspect was impossible to keep. She felt like a lizard climbing a wall, creeping along on her belly in little spurts of frantic activity, then stopping to rest before the next frenzy of motion.

Now, to the fiery pain of her legs was added the agony of her arms. Soraya felt as though hot needles had been stabbed into them and every effort to move only magnified the pain. She desperately wanted to stop, to rest. Yet each time she wanted to surrender to her fatigue she'd glance down. She'd see how small the swamp was and how high up the hill she was. If she tried to rest on the steep trail, how far would she slide back down? How much of her progress would she lose only to repeat the ordeal all over again? The summit couldn't be much farther now. The summit, where the ground would have to be level to support the citadel. A place where she could finally rest in safety.

Dawn's first glow was an ugly bruise behind the range of hills. Night withdrew with sullen resentment, clinging to every shadow as though to retain some presence through the coming day. Soraya turned her head and looked towards the Barrowbogs. She could just make out the glowing miasma as it dispersed, slinking back to whatever holes it hid in when it wasn't abroad seeking victims.

Soraya turned her gaze upwards and blinked her eyes. She was almost unable to believe what she was seeing. A moment before it had seemed the climb ahead was every bit as immense as that which was behind her. Yet now she saw that it wasn't so. The path stretched only a few dozen yards farther and then... then there was the peak! She cried out in triumph. 'Thank you, Great Sigmar, for sustaining me in this ordeal.'

Her prayer of thanks faltered when she glanced back down. Not at the swamp, but at the hill itself. Soraya had been climbing all night, as had all of them. She'd seen for herself that they must have followed the path for thousands of feet, not simply around the hill but up it as well. The very steepness of the trail bespoke how high they had to have ascended. Yet when she gazed down, she could see the base of the hill was only a few hundred feet below!

Vertigo hit her and she swayed once again. She was utterly disoriented, not by the height, but by the lack of height. It was impossible! Utterly impossible! Soraya groaned, then pitched over. She saw the sharp rocks grinning at her as she hurtled towards them.

Then all was blackness.

Mahyar watched over Soraya and Gajevic while the rest of the group slept. The climb up the hillside had exhausted everyone, but fortunately only Soraya had slipped into the rocks. The fall was less than a dozen feet, but the sharp edges had cut her badly. Zorgrath and Ratimir were the ones who'd gone down and carried her up. The perverse thing about the accident was that she was only a few yards from the summit when she fell.

Kvetka had staved off fatigue long enough to help Mahyar tend the soldier's wounds. Indeed, she'd only taken a few steps after winding the last bandage around Soraya's leg before she'd collapsed. Mahyar carried her a few feet away where she'd have room to stretch out.

'Sigmar watch over you,' Mahyar prayed as he looked down on his charges. He supposed it was only natural that he'd be tasked with looking after Soraya after he became custodian of Gajevic. One was wounded in body, the other in mind. Kvetka was reasonably sure Soraya would recover. The wizard's affliction, however, was anyone's guess. All the knowledge from Kvetka's books couldn't give an answer. Even she had agreed that prayer was the only thing they could do for him now.

Mahyar turned and looked across the summit. It was two hundred yards across, in his estimation, but unlike the jagged slopes the ground here was dirt rather than rock and flattened into a kind of plateau. Nothing grew here and there was no sign of life, not even birds. The only thing of import was what they'd come so far to find. The citadel.

It rose from almost the centre of the plateau, a grey tower fifty feet wide and twice again as tall. From below it had seemed constructed, perhaps not the work of humans, but certainly built by someone. This close, Mahyar was no longer sure. The stone – if stone it was – which constituted the walls of the citadel had a strange, grainy look to it. Though as grey and lifeless as granite, it suggested to him the pattern of tree bark. That impression only increased when he looked at the peak of the tower and the ragged, irregular striations there. They were unlike any crenellations he'd ever heard of, wildly varying in size and width and with apparently random gaps between them. He thought of what Kvetka had said about Shiverbloom and the green-folk and the strange magics associated with them.

The great door at the base of the citadel was clearly built rather than grown. Mahyar couldn't decide if it was as old as the tree-like stone around it, but the door had been there a long time. It was shaped from a great block of marble flecked with veins of gold, the archway around it edged in polished obsidian. The capstone was a carving and even from a distance there was no mistaking the god represented by that crowned skull. Unconsciously, Mahyar reached to his neck for the holy symbol he wore. It took a moment for him to remember that he'd thrown it away.

The priest frowned and turned his back to the tower. 'I abandoned a symbol, not my faith,' he said. 'I had to save these people and lacked the wisdom to see another way.' Though he no longer looked at it, he imagined the skeletal carving of Nagash was laughing at him. The thought only further darkened his mood. How he wished, even for only a moment, to walk in the lands of Azyr where it was the God-King who ruled and not the Great Necromancer.

Mahyar's thoughts were grim as he looked over the land. He thought he could dimly make out the edge of the Dreadwood, but of the Sea of Tears and the Twinned Towns there was not so much as a hint. It was a sombre thought to consider how far they'd travelled. It was a long way to go only to fail. It wasn't a lack of faith that made him consider the likeliness of that end. He had long ago resigned himself to the understanding that Sigmar's power worked to a plan far greater than the needs of the individual, even the needs of an entire community. The God-King was striving to restore civilisation and order to all the Mortal Realms, to drive back the foulness of Chaos. To that noble purpose, sacrifices had to be made. What presumption to assume that the Twinned Towns were of such importance that Sigmar would marshal all his powers to preserve it, forsaking who knew how many others in the process?

No, Mahyar told himself, when the God-King's might was absent it was because that strength was needed elsewhere. Somewhere where it would serve an even greater good.

The warrior priest ruminated long upon this theological subject. So intent was he upon the matter that sleep stole on him unawares.

It was late in the afternoon when Mahyar was awakened by Venteslav. 'You should have woken someone else to take over your watch if you felt tired,' he reprimanded the priest. 'Anything could have happened while we slept.'

'I tried to stay awake, but I was unequal to the effort,' he said, contrition in his voice.

'We saw no tracks coming up here,' Zorgrath said, interceding on Mahyar's behalf.

'Not everything would leave tracks,' Venteslav countered. 'The things which serve Lady Olynder are spectral. They could set upon us and leave no mark on the ground.'

Kvetka had been studying the citadel, but when she heard him speak she turned and walked over. 'Nighthaunts are named such for they shun the light of day,' she said. 'Oh, to be certain, a powerful necromancer or undead lord might be able to force them to stir in the sunlight, but it could be done only with the greatest magic.'

'Need I remind you that our enemy is the Mortarch of Grief herself?' Venteslav asked.

'All apologies, captain,' Kvetka said, 'but if the Lady of Sorrows was aware of us and wanted to destroy us, she'd already have done so. We've far less protection than the column did when we were caught on the bridge.'

'Unless she has other reasons for staying her hand,' Mahyar mused. The thought was stirred by his ruminations of the night before on the workings of the divine. If the holy could work to greater designs, why not the unholy as well? 'Venteslav is right, I put us all at risk.'

Venteslav was pensive for a moment, pulling at the end of his moustache. 'Worms in a casket,' he cursed. 'We were all done in after the race through the swamp and the climb. Anyone you woke up would've been just as tired.' He clapped Mahyar on the shoulder. 'What's done is done. Forget about it. As we say in Eastdale, "Sufficient for today the evil thereof." Come along, we might need your help if Ratimir can't figure out this door.'

Venteslav led Mahyar over to the citadel where Ratimir and the other soldiers were gathered. Soraya looked stiff when she moved, but at least she *was* moving, so perhaps her injuries were more superficial than they'd seemed.

'Any luck?' Venteslav asked when they got closer to the door.

Ratimir frowned and shook his head. 'It is the damnedest thing I've seen. There's no sign of lock or hinge, but from the way the inside of the arch is scratched, I'm convinced it must move. The trick is figuring out how.'

'You're supposed to be an expert scrounger,' Omid chided Ratimir. 'Surely you can figure out a door easier than you can figure out how to steal wine for a whole company.'

'Soraya,' Ratimir said, 'your cur is barking at me again.'

Venteslav stepped between Omid and Ratimir. 'The next one of you who snaps at the other one is going to regret it. We might not be much of an expedition, but I will have discipline.' The two soldiers glared at each other but were wise enough not to say anything further.

Mahyar found his gaze drawn to the sculpted skull. The impression of mockery from the night before returned. The Lord of Undeath was amused by the struggles of the living and that disdain was evoked in the obsidian statue.

'There appears to be writing here,' Kvetka said when she joined them. She reached out and indicated a string of carved symbols on the edge of the door, almost imperceptible.

'I thought they were just scratches.' Ratimir shrugged. 'Certainly no letters that I've ever seen.'

'Next you'll be telling us you can read,' Omid muttered under his breath.

'Yes, I am certain this is writing.' Kvetka leaned closer, her eyes roving across the line of symbols. Her face turned pale and she glanced back at Mahyar. 'This is Mordant,' she stated, fear in her voice.

'The forbidden script of Nagash's priests,' Mahyar informed the others. His gaze was hard as he looked at Kvetka. 'It is an act of heresy to study that writing for any but the death-priests. How is it that you recognise it?'

Kvetka lowered her head. 'The lighthouse,' she confessed. 'There are books there, books from old Belvegrod, that were written in Mordant. It was necessary to learn the language to translate them.'

'I will have words with Ivor when we return,' Mahyar swore. 'For a wise man, he should know how reckless it is to do such things.'

'It doesn't matter,' Venteslav declared. 'Maybe in the Twinned Towns, but not here.' He turned to Kvetka. 'You recognise the script – can you read the words? Does it tell of how to get inside?'

'Yes,' Kvetka answered. 'But the meaning is itself a riddle. It says that those who would enter the tower must hand their faith to their god.'

The explanation brought a buzz of discussion from all the survivors. Only Mahyar was silent. His eyes returned to the grinning skull. Its jaws were parted. Not wide, but there was a space between the teeth. Now he thought he understood the riddle, but the answer was far from comforting.

'I think all of us have faith in Sigmar after escaping the Sea of Tears,' Venteslav stated when the others had all said their piece. 'No, it can't be faith alone. There must be some mechanism or trigger.'

'You invoke the wrong god,' Mahyar stated. 'When this door was built and that inscription carved, think about who they were. "Their" doesn't mean our god Sigmar, but the god of the builders.' He pointed at the crowned skull. 'Black Nagash, that's the god they mean. The god to whom faith must be handed.' He swallowed and took a deep breath. He held out his left hand and walked towards the obsidian skull.

Kvetka moved to stop him. 'Don't do this,' she pleaded. She glanced over at the skull and the gleaming black teeth. 'Volcanic glass,' she said. 'Able to cut through flesh like butter. Think about what kind of people would invoke Nagash in such a way. How depraved they would be.'

'I only know that my faith is being questioned,' Mahyar said as he gently pushed her aside. 'Those who built this door think to mock me. Well, I will show their perfidious spirits that I'm not afraid. That my faith in Sigmar is greater than their evil.'

Mahyar didn't hesitate, but pushed his hand into the partly opened mouth. He stared into the empty sockets of the obsidian skull and braced himself to feel its sharp teeth chomp down. When the archway shuddered he expected the mechanism he'd set in motion to cleave his hand from his wrist. Instead there was only the mocking aspect of Nagash, amused by his relief – as though sneering at something that wasn't faith so much as it was resignation.

'It's opening!' Ratimir cried as Mahyar staggered away from the skull. The marble door withdrew into the citadel, drawn back by some force none of them could see. In a matter of moments, the entrance was clear. The gloom of the tower beckoned to them.

'Make torches,' Venteslav ordered. 'Be quick about it. We don't know for how long the door will stay open.'

'Now that we know its secret, we could just open it again,' Ratimir pointed out.

'Elder Mahyar's faith was enough to open it,' Soraya said. 'That doesn't mean any of us could do it.'

'It is foolishness to test faith frivolously,' Mahyar said, working the fingers of his left hand, still surprised it was attached. 'Perhaps if I had to repeat the ordeal, I would be found wanting.' He tried to keep any hint of doubt from his voice, but the look Kvetka gave him said that at least as far as she was concerned, he'd failed.

'My eyes see better in the dark,' Zorgrath said. He didn't wait for the torches, only a nod from Venteslav, and then he was scrambling through the doorway. A moment later his voice called back from the interior. 'It's empty. Just a stairway leading up to a door.'

'Another door,' Mahyar mused. He balled his left hand into a fist to keep it from shaking. His eyes were drawn back to the crowned skull.

More than ever before, it seemed like Nagash was mocking him.

The interior of the citadel was even more uncanny than the outside. It was the hollowed-out trunk of a colossal tree, one that had been petrified long ago, perhaps even before Belvegrod was drowned by the Lady of Sorrows. Only the doorway and the stairs appeared to be artificial, the latter a great spiral of carved stones that rose to another portal of gold-veined marble. Except for the steps, the chamber was empty. The ceiling twenty feet above their heads looked to be more petrified wood, a layer of the ancient tree that hadn't been stripped away.

'It's clear the Veiled Oracle isn't down here,' Venteslav said. He swung his torch around and waved it at the stairs. 'It looks like our only choice is to ascend.'

The group started towards the stairs, Mahyar in the lead with Zorgrath trailing at the rear. Soraya and Omid had remained outside with Gajevic. Kvetka shook her head as she thought of the wizard lying there, a deranged husk of himself. If things went badly here, Soraya and Omid wouldn't be able to take him with them. It would be hard enough getting back to the Twinned Towns on their own. At least she could console herself that they'd make sure he didn't suffer when the end came.

'More carvings,' Mahyar called to Kvetka. She pushed past Venteslav and Ratimir to inspect the door. Once again, the forbidden script of Mordant was before her eyes.

'It is a kind of poem,' she told the others. 'It reads, "I am the one who shunned all belief and who cursed all reverence, I am the one who shook my fist at the heavens and who spat upon the holy. Who am I?"'

Kvetka jumped back, for as she completed her translation, the image of a hand appeared in the marble door, aglow with a spectral light. Her flesh crawled as the manifestation drained the warmth from the air around it.

'Another riddle,' Venteslav said. He pointed to the image of the hand. 'It expects one of us to place a hand against the door.'

'But which of us?' Kvetka asked. When she did, she thought she saw a troubled look on Mahyar's face. She gave him a curious stare. 'You?' she whispered. The priest shook his head, but she could see there was sweat on his brow.

'What would happen if the wrong person touched the door?' Zorgrath wondered.

'I'd imagine it would be best not to find out,' Kvetka said, her eyes still on Mahyar. Something wasn't right. The priest looked more anxious now than she'd ever seen him.

'No need to worry,' Ratimir proclaimed. He strode past Mahyar and gently urged Kvetka to step away from the door. 'The riddle is clearly asking for me. I've been a scoundrel since I was old enough to chew my own food. I've stolen from temples and pickpocketed priests. If there's a transgression that can't be laid at my door, then I certainly don't know about it.' He chuckled in amusement. 'Probably the only moment in my life when any of that stands me in good stead!'

'Are you sure?' Kvetka asked.

Ratimir smiled at her. 'No, but I'll try anyway. Can't have the Azyrite there opening all the doors.'

Kvetka saw Mahyar flinch. Then her attention was focused on the Reclaimed soldier. He spat twice in his hand, trying to call all the luck he could muster. Then he clapped his palm against the door. The ghostly outline shifted to encompass only Ratimir's hand.

For an instant, there was nothing. Then a deafening howl ripped through the citadel. Ratimir screamed; Kvetka could see his head thrown back in agony, but the sound was devoured by the monstrous wailing. The spectral light expanded, swirling around the soldier's body. Faster and faster it spun, and with each spin a layer of Ratimir's body was peeled away. Thin slivers of cloth and skin, then bloody shreds of flesh and muscle. Mahyar lunged forward to try to free him, but as soon as he touched the whirling ectoplasm he was hurled back, swatted aside by the spectral force.

When it was finished, the flayed corpse of Ratimir toppled off the stairs to crash against the floor below, exploding into fragments of bloody bone. The walls and floor around the doorway were plastered with gore. Kvetka could feel bits of the dead soldier dripping down her clothes. Mahyar was coated in the man's blood.

'Black horrors of Nagash spare us!' Zorgrath whined. The cryptborn crouched against the stairs, gnashing his teeth in terror.

'You were wrong!' Venteslav shouted at Kvetka. 'You must have mistaken its meaning! There's no way past that!'

Kvetka was sickened at the accusation. Had it been her doing? Had she caused Ratimir's ghastly death?

'She isn't wrong,' Mahyar's firm voice declared. His face was a mask of guilt when he looked at Kvetka. 'She isn't mistaken. She read the riddle right. Ratimir was wrong to try. He was uncertain. The man who answers the riddle has no doubts. He knows who it means.'

'You?' Kvetka repeated in a stunned whisper.

Mahyar nodded. 'It is my deepest shame. I was but an initiate in the Temple of Sigmar. My parents, people who had done everything for me, whose love knew no limit... they were afflicted by an undead spirit, a fiend that set upon them in the night and drained off their vitality. Not enough to kill them outright. No, instead they slowly withered, dying bit by bit each night. How I prayed for their deliverance! How I begged and pleaded with Sigmar to save them! But try as they might, the Tombwatch couldn't find the gheist preying on them. They couldn't stop it. All the prayers couldn't stop it.' He marched to the door and held out his hand. 'When they died, I cursed Sigmar for not saving them. There was no blasphemy that did not fall from my tongue. I cursed the God-King – in my pain I spat upon everything I held holy.'

The warrior priest set his hand against the door. Everyone held their breath as the glow surrounded his hand. This time, however, it remained only there. It didn't reach out to engulf Mahyar, but only flickered around his fingers. Then the light was gone and the door slowly slid aside.

Mahyar looked back at them. Kvetka could see the shame and regret in his eyes. 'After my parents died, the Tombwatch were able to track the thing that killed them back to its lair. They found not just it but a dozen more of its kind that had been feeding on the people of Westreach. They destroyed all of them. The deaths of my parents saved hundreds of others. I repent my lack of faith in Sigmar every time I pray. I doubted his wisdom, and there is no greater shame a priest can carry within himself.'

Venteslav's expression was grave as he walked past Mahyar. He gave the priest a withering look. 'Your reticence cost a man his life,' he said as he pushed ahead through the open doorway. 'Add that to your shame.'

CHAPTER TEN

Mahyar followed Venteslav into the room beyond the door. It was a chamber exactly like the one below, with identical dimensions and a stairway that curled its way upwards. At the top of the steps was another marble door.

'Think for a moment,' Mahyar told the captain. 'All of this reeks of blackest sorcery. First there was that impossible climb round the hill, the summit only coming within reach when the sun rose. Now we have these riddles, tricks to be solved only by whomever they were meant for.'

'I don't pretend to understand,' Venteslav said. 'I only know that if you'd acted, Ratimir wouldn't have had to die.' He scowled at the priest. 'Your guilt killed him as surely as the spell did. I had faith in you. I thought that of all these people you were the one who I could trust.'

Kvetka and Zorgrath entered the chamber. The guide prowled about the periphery and inspected the floor and walls. 'The dust is thick here. No one has been here for many years. I can't catch the scent of so much as a mouse.'

'Be careful,' Mahyar warned Kvetka as she started up the steps. He hurried over to take the lead. Too late to save Ratimir, he might be able to keep the others from harm.

'Unless you can read Mordant, I have to go first,' Kvetka stated. She thrust her finger at the door and indicated the writing carved into it. 'Worry about your own affairs and leave me to my work.'

'There's something wrong about this,' Mahyar said. 'These inscriptions, they couldn't have been put here by chance.'

He could see from Kvetka's expression that she wasn't ready to accept the idea. She began to translate the inscription. Her voice rose as she projected the words to the room below. 'Another poem. "From the vault I come, to the vault I go. Breast that I suckled and bones that I gnawed. Who am I?"'

A cry of horror rang out. Zorgrath darted towards the room's exit, his retreat prevented only when Venteslav tackled him to the floor. Mahyar hurried below to help as the cryptborn struggled to squirm free. The priest banged Zorgrath's head against the petrified floor, stunning him. As his body grew limp, Mahyar helped Venteslav pick him up and carry him to the stairs.

'No mystery who this riddle means,' Venteslav said, disgust in his voice. 'Walks and talks like a man, but the appetite of a ghoul.'

'What that poem suggests would sicken anything even partly human,' Mahyar replied. His eyes swept across the interior of the citadel. 'Whatever magic was set to protect this place knows our darkest secrets. It guards by making intruders cower from the truth they carry inside themselves.'

Kvetka stepped aside as they brought Zorgrath to the door. Again, the glowing outline of a hand appeared. Venteslav started to push the cryptborn's hand towards the door, but Mahyar held him back.

'I think it will only work if he chooses to do it,' the priest warned.

Venteslav nodded and glared at Zorgrath. 'Open it,' he ordered. 'Put your hand there and open it.'

Zorgrath was still partly stunned and blood trickled from a gash in his scalp, but his eyes were bright with horror. 'No! I wasn't so hungry that I'd do that! It was the others. The others did it. They broke into the vault. It was they who ate her corpse. They who waited for the meat to ripen.'

'Who? Who did they wait for?' Kvetka asked, her voice trembling.

One word, uttered in a ghastly whisper. One word that in the circumstances was more monstrous than the Dark Gods themselves.

'Mother.'

Venteslav let go of Zorgrath and backed away, sickened to his core by the cryptborn. 'His own mother,' he gagged. A few shaky steps brought him to the support of the wall. His eyes were filled with loathing, unable to leave the guide.

Mahyar kept his grip on Zorgrath's arm. 'What is past cannot be changed,' he told him. 'To deny what we've done is only to pile shame atop shame.' He glanced back at Venteslav. 'All that is left to us is to seek to atone for what we've done, to redeem the wickedness of the days behind us.' He coaxed Zorgrath to stare at the door and the spectral imprint of a hand. 'Facing what you've done is the beginning of redemption.'

Zorgrath managed a brief nod. He lurched forwards and pressed his hand to the door. Just as the previous riddle had been Mahyar's to solve, here it was Zorgrath who opened the way. The cryptborn slumped against the steps, his head curled down against his chest and a sound somewhere between the sob of a man and the whine of a jackal shuddering from his throat.

'Leave him,' Mahyar told Venteslav when the captain started up the stairs.

'He's a monster,' Venteslav growled, his hand tightening about the grip of his sword.

Mahyar looked into the room ahead of them, then turned back to Venteslav. 'We may find we're all monsters before we reach the Veiled Oracle,' he said. 'I can see another stairway in there, with a marble door at its top.' He shifted his gaze to Kvetka. 'Unless I'm mistaken, there will be another inscription. Another riddle challenging one of us to confess a secret shame.'

Kvetka and Venteslav joined Mahyar as he entered the room, while the desolate Zorgrath remained crouched on the stairs behind them. The scholar started up towards the closed door with the priest following close behind her. Venteslav hung back, his eyes roving about the room, trying to spot anything out of the ordinary.

'There is writing,' Kvetka said when she reached the door. 'Just like the others.'

'Another riddle hidden in a poem,' Mahyar suggested. Kvetka nodded slowly. He could see her studying the inscription with more intensity than she'd done before. He noted the shudder that passed through her. She reached towards the door. Mahyar grabbed her shoulder and pulled her back.

'It means me,' Kvetka said. 'I'm the one it wants.' She tried to pull free, but Mahyar held her fast.

'You aren't thinking clearly,' he admonished her. 'Look again.' Mahyar nodded at the door. 'The glow, the outline of the hand isn't there. This citadel, it is governed by strange magics. Magics that only respond when the formula that controls them is complete.' He gave her a sympathetic look, knowing only too well the weight of shame and the pain of humiliation. 'You must recite the poem. I think it serves as some sort of incantation. Only then does the spectral hand appear.'

Kvetka shook in horror. 'I can't,' she hissed. 'Please don't ask me.'

'It isn't me who tells you to do this, it is the sadists who placed these barriers.' Mahyar frowned and waved his hand to the doorway below. 'If you can't, then the quest ends here. We won't be able to go further. We won't see the Veiled Oracle.'

'All we've endured will mean nothing,' Venteslav said as he mounted the steps. 'We'll return to our people – if we're lucky – with nothing but woe and despair. No hope, only the promise that the Lady of Sorrows will come again and set her hordes against the Twinned Towns.'

'I can't,' Kvetka protested again. She closed her fingers around an iron button pinned to her cloak, clenching it tight.

'I order you to,' Venteslav snapped. 'You cannot fail now.'

Mahyar didn't like the captain's haughty tone and the arrogance of his words. 'If it was your shame that would unlock the door, could you easily confess it for all to hear?' He looked aside at Kvetka. 'We'll withdraw to the room below.'

The offer moved Kvetka. 'No,' she said, laying her hand on Mahyar's. 'That might be part of the ritual. That others should hear.' She turned and looked at the door. 'Just as there are ranks within the priesthood or army, so there are ranks among the learned who study in the Belvegrod lighthouse.' Her voice cracked with emotion, but she forced herself to continue. 'There are examinations to determine who is wise enough to rise in rank. Those who advance are allowed to consult books forbidden to the lower grades of scholar. They're permitted to study subjects that reach to the very fabric of the realms.' She pressed her hand to her chest. 'I was ambitious. I wanted to learn these things, but I was too impatient to wait until I was truly ready. I contrived to cheat in the examinations.'

Kvetka's finger trembled as she pointed to the Mordant inscription. 'The poem evokes what I've done. "Silvered word and dishonest heart to secure the way. Broken heart and spattered blood will pay the price. Who am I?" The answer is me.' There were tears in the scholar's eyes when she looked back at her companions. 'I loved another scholar, a brilliant man who had surpassed me in his studies. Perhaps we might have started a family but for the relentless thirst for knowledge that burned inside me. I did love him, but I loved the thrill of discovery more. When the examination was made, I copied his work. The deceit was discovered, but he took the blame and claimed *he* had copied from *me*. He was expulsed from the lighthouse, taking on himself the disgrace that should have been mine. That night he took a dagger and plunged it into his own heart.' She looked from Mahyar to Venteslav. 'You see, his disgrace was such that there could be no further association between us.'

Behind Kvetka, the outline of the glowing hand had appeared. She was oblivious to its presence, continuing to explain herself to her companions. 'I've tried to excel, to truly excel, ever since. Not for my own sake, but to make up for what I've done. To accomplish something, some good that will benefit civilisation. Something that will pay a debt that can never be paid.'

Mahyar gestured at the wall behind her. 'Perhaps now you have your chance to repay that debt.'

'We must be at the top of the citadel,' Venteslav said. 'The Veiled Oracle's chambers must be above.'

Kvetka nodded. She set her hand within the spectral outline. 'Right now I shouldn't care if I ended up like Ratimir,' she said.

No arcane curse reached out for her. Mahyar moved forwards as the marble portal slid aside. 'It takes courage to confess our crimes,' he told Kvetka. 'Only by recognising what we've done can we try to be better.' She showed a brief smile as he walked through into the next room.

The chamber was exactly like those below, an empty room with a winding stair that ended at a marble door. Mahyar felt a clammy sensation crawl across his skin. He began to suspect a magic more pervasive than just the doors and their riddles.

Venteslav entered and confirmed his worst suspicions. 'It isn't possible,' he gasped. He waved his torch at the floor and indicated marks in the dust. 'Those are the same marks in the room below!'

'I suspect you'd find them in the room below that as well,' Mahyar said, his tone grim. 'Footprints left by Zorgrath when he was checking for any sign of inhabitants.'

'That isn't possible,' Venteslav repeated.

'Yet that's what's happened,' Mahyar stated. He glanced about the chamber. 'The ceilings are twenty feet high, the floors between are five feet thick. This is the fourth level. The only thing above us should be the roof.' He pointed at the marble door. 'Yet I suspect when we open that, we'll find something much different.'

Kvetka stepped into the chamber, her sleeves damp where she'd used them to dry her tears. 'You think the citadel is somehow *growing*?'

Mahyar nodded. 'The same way the hill itself did until the dawn broke its spell. I don't pretend to understand how such a thing can be. Perhaps Gajevic could explain it. I only know that I'm convinced these chambers are manifestations of some dark and powerful sorcery.' He pointed again at the door. 'A riddle for each of us. Unless I'm mistaken, this one will reveal something about you, Captain Venteslav.'

Venteslav stiffened his back and glared defiantly at the door. 'Whatever it demands of me, I will meet its challenge.'

'We'll see,' Mahyar said. He started up the steps and motioned the others to follow. 'Kvetka, translate the poem and we'll see what kind of monster Venteslav is.'

Venteslav watched Kvetka as the scholar inspected the carving on the door. He already knew what great shame he'd have to confess to. He supposed he had to be honest enough to admit it wasn't any better than what the others had done. Even if he set aside the instinctive revulsion of necrophagia, was Zorgrath's graveyard cannibalism any less shameful than his own sin? At least his crime had been against the dead. Venteslav's had been against the living.

'"Eager to action, quick to strife. The lost command with a lost commander. Who am I?"' After Kvetka read the poem, she turned and stared at Venteslav. Mahyar did the same.

'I'd just been appointed captain,' Venteslav said. The only thing he could think of to salvage even a measure of respect was to confess his misdeed without hesitation. 'I was, as you say, eager to prove myself. I led a patrol of the Tombwatch and we pushed deep into the ruins seeking the hiding place of some nighthaunts that had been stalking Eastdale. I knew I was leading them too far from the settlement, but I was so certain, so confident that I took them in anyway. We found the lair, catacombs under a manor. On my command, we tried to cleanse the crypts. The undead were too powerful for us. My soldiers were killed, one after another. I hid inside a casket to save myself. I stayed there, listening to my men dying all around me. I was the only one who survived. When I returned, I was feted for my bravery.' He strode over to the door where the spectral glow now emanated. 'Until now, I never told anyone what really happened.'

Venteslav closed his eyes. For a moment he was back in those catacombs, his ears ringing with the screams of his soldiers. If he'd been worthy of his command, he would never have brought them there. If he'd been any kind of hero, he would have died with them.

Venteslav clapped his hand against the glowing light. He felt the chill of the grave rush across his fingers. Then the door was sliding open. He opened his eyes. At once he saw that the room beyond was different. There was light inside – pallid and wan, but light just the same.

'Something's here,' he told Kvetka and Mahyar. Venteslav didn't wait for a response but went ahead. After his confession, he felt he had to prove he was more courageous than he'd been in the past. That he was no longer the kind of leader who'd abandon his followers.

The room beyond the door was similar to the others only in its dimensions. Tall sconces lined the walls, each topped by a transparent globe within which pale light flickered. To Venteslav it looked like someone had trapped jack-o-wisps inside them.

A rich rug stretched across the floor, its pile deep and lush though its colours were faded. Cloth stretched across the ceiling and streamed down in long folds that billowed out to rings set into the walls. The hangings were thin and gauzy, distorting rather than hiding what lay beyond them. Venteslav squinted as he noted what looked like a dais. He pushed his way through the hangings, feeling them brush across his face as he moved. The sensation reminded him unpleasantly of cobwebs from the catacombs.

'Venteslav, wait,' Mahyar called after him. Venteslav was deaf to the priest's concern. He had to prove his valour and regain their respect. Otherwise how would he be able to command?

At length, Venteslav found his way through the hangings and stood at the foot of the dais. It was fashioned of gleaming obsidian, just like the archway at the citadel's entrance. Thirteen steps rose from the floor to the platform. Here he could see what looked like a basin carved from ivory and a great throne-like chair cut from rose-coloured crystal. Resting on that seat was a figure draped from head to foot in black. A flowing dress edged in curls of lace, its skirts billowing out in layers, swathed the lean body while the head and face were hidden behind a shadowy veil.

Venteslav wasn't certain how long he simply stared at the tableau. Defeat soured his heart. They'd come this far and braved so much only to find it was for nothing. The Veiled Oracle was dead. To all appearances, she might have been dead for hundreds of years, spared the ravages of time by the protection of her citadel.

'Too late,' Venteslav moaned. Then his eyes widened with horror. The shape seated upon the chair stood up. The veiled face stared down at him, and he could feel the eyes behind the shadow studying him.

'You arrive precisely when I expected you,' a voice soft as spring rain assured him. The Veiled Oracle held out one of her gloved hands and motioned to Venteslav. 'Come to me and make your purpose known.' She turned her head as Kvetka and Mahyar emerged from the curtained maze. 'All of you,' she said, extending the invitation. 'It has been a very long time since anyone has come to seek my wisdom.'

Kvetka stepped forwards, suspicion in her eyes. 'You... you are the Veiled Oracle?'

A musical laugh trickled from the black-clad prophetess. 'Was I not who you expected to find?' She laughed again as she looked down on them. 'Perhaps you expected someone grander? An aelven lady arrayed in a gown of silver and diamond? A demigoddess of such divine beauty that she must be hidden away from mortal eyes?' The veiled head shook from side to side. 'Alas, there is only me and I fear I am not who you expected me to be.'

'Are you flesh or spirit?' Venteslav asked, putting into words the fear that he knew all of them shared. Was this a living woman or an undead horror?

Again, the Veiled Oracle laughed. 'Am I alive?' she rephrased. She sat back in the rose-coloured chair and looked around the chamber. 'Yes... I suppose this is a kind of life. Though I often weary of it, I fear what waits me should I abandon it.' Her veiled face once again turned to Venteslav. 'When I am taken into the grave, then will my enemies gain power over me. While I remain in this citadel, I am safe. Tired. Alone. But safe.' She lifted her hand and gestured at the basin atop the dais. 'I have peered into a thousand thousand yesterdays, watched countless lives play to their end. I can watch all the things that for me will never be. But, then, if I could not, none would ever brave the journey here.'

'It's true,' Venteslav said. 'We wouldn't have risked coming here if not for your wisdom. We've come...'

The Veiled Oracle lifted her hand and motioned for him to be silent. 'Your accent proclaims you to be a Belvegrodian,' she said. Then she shook her head. 'No, it has been a long time since the Drowned City was alive. There is a sea now where once people thrived, but in that sea there is an island. A place where the descendants of a vanquished race now build their homes.'

'We are all of us from the Twinned Towns,' Mahyar informed the prophetess. 'By the grace and strength of Sigmar, life is being built upon the ruins.'

'Only once did I ever hear speech such as yours,' the Veiled Oracle said. She waved her hand before her, as though to conjure a distant memory into focus. 'There came an emissary from another realm to the court. His skin wasn't so dusky as yours and his hair was gold like the sun, but he had the same voice. His words were like iron, strong and firm. He came to us from the wondrous city of Azyrheim and told us of the marvels of the God-King's glory.' The wistful tone darkened into sorrow. 'He was too pure for Shyish. The minions of the Dark Gods lurked even among the noble houses. One night they fell upon him as he slept. He was able to slay eight of his assassins, but to survive he needed to prevail against nine.'

The Veiled Oracle stirred from her reverie and again focused upon Venteslav. 'If you are from the Twinned Towns, then I can guess your purpose. You seek a way to protect your people from the Lady of Sorrows.'

To hear her proclaim the objective of their quest so abruptly stunned Venteslav. He stared in bewilderment for a moment before he could offer any kind of answer. 'That is indeed why we've come here,' he stammered. 'We set out with a small army, but the Lady of Sorrows came against us with a host of night-haunts. Only a few of us escaped.'

'Lady Olynder,' the Veiled Oracle hissed. 'We share an enemy, you and I. Her deceit and treachery brought me to this place.'

'The Belvegrod lighthouse has a perspicillum that can watch the gravesands as they fall at the edge of Shyish,' Kvetka said. 'The scholars and wizards have been able to glean glimpses of the future from the patterns of the falling sands. The divinations called on us to seek you out.' Her voice grew solemn as she recounted the rest of what the sands had revealed. 'We were to be led against the Lady of Sorrows by a hero chosen by fate, a champion of both our peoples.'

'Jahangir,' the Veiled Oracle provided the name. 'Do not be so shocked. I see many things here. As I have said, if it were not so, none would seek my wisdom.'

Venteslav climbed the first few steps of the dais. 'Jahangir was our leader, the chosen one. He was the hero who would break the curse of Lady Olynder. Without him, we are lost.'

'Only those who lack hope are lost,' the Veiled Oracle warned. She wagged her finger at Venteslav. 'More than anyone, the ene-mies of Lady Olynder cannot entertain the spirit of despair, for it is the poison that drips from her fingers. Nagash appointed her the Mortarch of Grief, but she exploited the despair of oth-ers long before that. Even when she was alive, she was a creature of treachery and manipulation.'

'But Jahangir was the chosen one,' Kvetka persisted. 'It was he who was foreseen to break the curse. What can we do?'

'Perhaps nothing. Perhaps much,' the Veiled Oracle said. 'You have come to me. That is a feat few have managed in the long time I've been here.' She held out her hand and pointed to the door. 'You have withstood the tests and proven yourselves to possess courage and virtue... yes, for only virtue can recognise and confess the deepest shame. Do not allow humility to blind you to your own value.'

The Veiled Oracle beckoned to them. Venteslav climbed the steps. Behind him he could hear Kvetka and Mahyar following. When they reached the top of the dais, the Veiled Oracle rose up from her chair and led them to the ivory pedestal. He could see the reflective surface of the basin, but what he thought was a pool of liquid was in fact a sheet of glass. The glass had been cracked at some time in the past and a spiderweb of jagged breaks marred its surface.

Venteslav peered intently when he saw images appear in the glass. Each cracked pane acted like a strange window, showing people and places and things that he instinctively knew belonged to regions throughout Shyish.

'Yes,' the Veiled Oracle told him. 'This is how I have grown so wise. My pool shows me whatever I would see within the realm.' One of her gloved fingers tapped against the glass, disrupting a scene of green-armoured warriors stalking through a desiccated forest. In its place there arose a scene of a man and a woman near a misty lake, a knight in golden armour stalking towards them with upraised sword. 'Glass from the lost city of Shadespire,' she said, tapping her finger again to banish the picture and summon another. 'Each fragment reflects a piece of Shyish.' Her voice darkened and her hidden face turned to her visitors. 'One must be careful what is conjured in the glass. There are sights too horrible for most to endure.' She shook her head. 'After enough years, even the unendurable becomes tiresome.'

'Just how long have you been here?' Mahyar said.

'Since before Lady Olynder brought doom upon the empire of Dolorum, this place has been my refuge,' the Veiled Oracle said. 'I was there, when the Mourning Bride was to be married to the son of the high king.' Sorrow trembled in the soft voice as an ancient hurt resurfaced. 'I warned my brother against her. I warned him that she was scheming and ruthless and would balk at nothing to further her ambition. But, like so many others before him, he was charmed by her beauty, enticed by her poise and wit, enraptured by her grace. They were to be wed, and all the empire celebrated the coming union. The banns were read in the great temple of Nagash, the betrothal affirmed before the gods of Dolorum. That very night, both my brother and my father disappeared. In their absence, after the custom of the empire, Lady Olynder became queen.

'Others accepted Lady Olynder's show of grief, but I was not so easily deceived. I knew she had eliminated the prince and the high king, the only ones who stood between her and the throne.' The Veiled Oracle curled her hands into fists. 'Before she could destroy me, I had those priests and warlocks who had not been swayed by her feigned remorse build this citadel. The magic which guards this place was such that even Lady Olynder could not defy it.' She pointed again at the marble door. 'How could she confess the vile shame that saturates her spirit or admit to her many crimes?'

'You have been here all that time?' Venteslav marvelled.

The Veiled Oracle shook her head. 'There is no time within this citadel. Within these walls, hours do not build into days, days do not rise into years. There is only ever this single moment. Never anything more. It is how I have endured for so long and defied the death that would render me into the power of Lady Olynder.'

'Then you are a prisoner?' Kvetka asked.

'By choice as much as by necessity,' the Veiled Oracle said. 'Outside these walls, I would age as all else ages. An hour in the hills draws an hour from my allotted span. But an hour away from this citadel exposes me to the malice of Lady Olynder. She will never forget me. She will always be waiting to wreak her vengeance.'

She nodded and swept her hand across the glass, changing all the scenes shown within the fragments. 'Only something of the gravest moment could bring me to leave my refuge.'

Venteslav stared at the glass. Each fragment showed a different view of the same place. He was gazing upon what seemed at first to be an immense city, but as he concentrated, he saw that the colossal walls surrounded a gigantic funeral complex: streets of crypts and tombs, monoliths and sepulchres, all of them surrounding a towering mausoleum adorned with crystal statues and alabaster columns. One of the statues was a figure he knew only too well, the shrouded shape of the Lady of Sorrows. When he saw it, he knew what the structure was.

'The crypt-court of Lady Olynder,' Venteslav gasped.

The Veiled Oracle nodded. Again, her hand swept across the glass. This time the fragments showed craggy mountains and deep gorges. A narrow trail wound its way through the brutal terrain, ending in the black mouth of a cave. 'It would need an army unseen since the hordes of Chaos ravaged Shyish to storm Lady Olynder's tomb-fortress,' she proclaimed. 'But there is another way. A secret way. A way that a handful of enemies – if they are brave and determined enough – could use to sneak into the Mortarch's innermost sanctum. That is where the curse laid upon the Twinned Towns can be broken.' She tapped her finger against one of the fragments. A stone casket loomed into view, its surface etched with grave-roses but absent of any other inscription.

'But the perspicillum claimed Jahangir was the only one who could break the curse,' Venteslav said.

'The future is always in motion,' the Veiled Oracle replied, 'just like the gravesands at the edge of the realm. What is certain one moment becomes impossible in the next. Jahangir may have already fulfilled his purpose simply by causing you to come here.' She nodded to the basin and the images it revealed. 'I have shown you a way that *you* may seize victory from defeat. This secret is known by only a few. Now the secret is yours. What will you do with it?'

Venteslav turned and looked into the eyes of his companions. 'It is likely madness to try, but if there's even a chance of stopping the Lady of Sorrows and breaking the curse, I feel we have to take it.'

Mahyar nodded solemnly. 'Sigmar favours the bold and the brave. We've been given a chance. Lady Olynder will not expect us to strike at her after destroying the army on the bridge.'

'Then we're all in agreement,' Kvetka said. 'We know the death and suffering the curse has inflicted upon our people. We can't shirk an opportunity to spare them such misery.'

'How do we find the path that leads to the cave?' Venteslav asked, pointing at the images in the glass.

'It would be better if I showed you,' the Veiled Oracle said. Again, her crisp laugh echoed through the room. 'Do not be so surprised. I told you we share an enemy and that only a matter of the gravest import could move me to leave my refuge. I can think of nothing more important than a chance to spoil one of Lady Olynder's oldest vendettas.'

Kvetka and Mahyar smiled, their expressions brightened by the confidence shown in them by the Veiled Oracle. Venteslav's own spirit was darkened by a voice that whispered in his ear. The voice of the prophetess.

You will fulfil the prophecy, the whisper said, *but only if you beware treachery from within.*

CHAPTER ELEVEN

Night stretched across the hills, bearing with it a cold and clammy breeze. Kvetka shivered and drew her cloak close. She looked over her shoulder at the citadel but the thought of taking shelter within its sorcerous walls sent another shiver through her that had nothing to do with the cold.

The scholar turned back to the little camp their band had made atop the plateau. Soraya and Mahyar were tending the fire with wood Omid and Zorgrath had gathered from the edge of the Barrowbogs. The soldier and the guide were lying on the ground a little distance from the flames, trying to sleep where it was neither too hot nor too cold. The frequency with which one or the other would stir and adjust his position bespoke how difficult finding such a spot was.

Venteslav and the Veiled Oracle were farther away from the fire. Both of them sat beside Gajevic's litter. The captain had a pensive, worried look on his face as he watched the mystic minister to the wizard. Kvetka understood how he felt. There was something nebulously obscene in the way the black-gloved fingers stroked Gajevic's face. It was like watching a lean, hungry spider toying with its prey, teasing the last dregs of terror from the victim trapped in its web before pouncing in a final burst of annihilating violence.

Kvetka shook her head and tried to disabuse herself of such morbid imaginings. The Veiled Oracle was trying to help. She was attempting to stir Gajevic's awareness and heal the damage wrought upon his psyche by contacting the spectral vibrations left by the green-folk.

'You should be resting,' Venteslav told Kvetka when he noticed her approaching. 'It will be a long march tomorrow.'

'How can I sleep when he is fighting for his life?' Kvetka said. 'No, more than his life, his very mind.' She stared down at the wizard and for just a moment there was a touch of affection in her eyes. 'I don't think he would have risked himself if I hadn't been there. He lacks a wider range of knowledge and experience, but in matters of the arcane he's well versed. He must have known the danger he was exposing himself to.'

'He did,' the Veiled Oracle said without looking up. 'It was for love's sake that he took the danger on himself. His motives were far less impersonal than your quest or saving your towns. He knew the strange and inhuman ways of the sylvaneth, but he exposed himself to their psychic legacy in the hope he could save someone more dear to him than his own life.'

Kvetka felt a kind of sick guilt. She'd known Gajevic had great regard for her, but never had she imagined his feelings ran to such commitment. The knowledge stung all the deeper because his was a regard she didn't feel in return. That part of her life had been closed long ago. It was a dead part within her that even the wizard's magic couldn't rouse from its grave.

'Will he recover?' Venteslav asked. His expression was cold, his eyes like chips of stone. 'He will slow us if we try to take him farther.'

'You wouldn't abandon him,' Kvetka gasped. 'You couldn't just toss him aside like a worn-out boot.'

Venteslav glowered at her. 'I must do what is necessary,' he said. 'Perhaps Gajevic had no thought of the Twinned Towns and our mission when he exposed his mind to the green-folk, but I cannot afford that luxury. We have a chance to break Lady Olynder's curse. This is an opportunity that may never arise again and can't be jeopardised. Not for him. Not for me. Not for anyone.'

'If we abandon our friends, what are we fighting for?' Kvetka demanded.

'Our people. The thousands of innocents who will never have to fear the spectral hand of Lady Olynder or wonder when the nighthaunts will come to bear their children away to unquiet graves.' Venteslav sighed and turned to stare into the fire. 'We do this for people we'll never see or know – the generations who will live after us, who will live in a better world than the one we've known, who won't have the spectre of the Lady of Sorrows ever hanging over their heads. We do this to free them from the terrors of the dark.'

Kvetka stared down at Gajevic, at the crazed and distant look in his eyes. For her sake, the Veiled Oracle had said. 'It isn't fair,' she whispered.

'The ways of the gods are seldom so,' the Veiled Oracle told her. 'Even the most benign of the gods works to a plan greater than even the wisest mortal can fathom. An evil, a great hurt, is allowed in one place so that in another a noble good can be achieved.' She turned her head towards Kvetka. It seemed to the scholar that there must be a smile on her hidden face when she spoke again. 'Take heart, little one. My magic has found the shadows to which your friend's mind has retreated from the jade light.

I will be able to whip those embers into a mighty flame that will burn the green growth that chokes his spirit.' She waved one of her gloved hands at Gajevic's brow. 'It will take me most of the night. Do as your captain says and get some sleep. In the morning, it may be that I have returned your friend to you.'

Kvetka wanted to reject the Veiled Oracle's suggestion, but she found that an inexorable lethargy had stolen up on her. She knew it was unnatural, some sort of spell conjured by the mystic. At the same time, its hold on her was so firm that she didn't care about its nature. All that mattered was sleep and rest. In the morning, things would be different.

In the morning...

The first light of morning emerged from the cloud-ridden sky. Venteslav could see the leathery shapes of blood-bats speeding away from the dawn to gain their nests deep within the Barrow-bogs. Somewhere a swamp-wolf gave a last desultory cry to the dying night. The chill wind of evening dissipated, leaving the air still and sombre.

The captain had slept little during the night. The burden of command weighed heavily on his mind and made it impossible to quieten his thoughts. Venteslav had been sincere when he told Kvetka he had to look to the larger perspective and focus on their quest rather than sentimentality. That didn't make it any easier for him to reconcile himself to leaving Gajevic behind. Indeed, he didn't think he could just abandon the wizard. A knife between the ribs would be a kindness when compared to forsaking him in this desolation.

Venteslav's decision was all the harder on him because of the warning from the Veiled Oracle. He'd been watching his companions much closer than before, trying to spot the one who'd betray their mission. Gajevic was the only one he knew was above suspicion. No traitor would have done what he'd done. He couldn't accept that such self-sacrifice was possible from a man of feckless loyalty. Gajevic was the only one he could trust… and he was reduced to an insane idiot.

The captain walked away from the fire to where the Veiled Oracle crouched beside Gajevic. The mystic hadn't slept, nor had she left her patient's side all night. He could hear the whispered incantation as her thin fingers pressed against the wizard's skull.

'Save your efforts,' Venteslav told her, his voice gruff. He nodded at the growing dawn. 'We'll have to start soon. You think we can reach this hidden path before nightfall?'

The Veiled Oracle shrugged. 'It is possible if we are not hindered along the way,' she said. 'It would be best to reach the tunnel while it is still daylight. The processions of nighthaunts will be less active and alert when the sun is out. They will be easier to contend with.'

Venteslav stared down at the wizard. 'Then it is time to leave him,' he said. His hand gripped the knife on his belt.

'Leave him?' the Veiled Oracle asked. 'I do not think that will be necessary. I have worked long to mend his mind and he has responded.' She took her hand away and pointed at the wizard. 'This sleep is to speed his healing, but the healing has already begun. He will be able to fend for himself when he wakes.'

'How soon will that be?' Venteslav asked. 'I don't know how long we can tarry.'

'Whenever you like, I can wake him,' the Veiled Oracle said. There was a hint of unease in her voice that Venteslav didn't allow to pass without explanation.

'If something's wrong, I need to know about it,' he told her.

The Veiled Oracle wagged her finger at Gajevic. 'He responded quickly to my magic. More quickly than I expected. It could simply be because he is aetherically attuned. He is, after all, a wizard.' She turned and Venteslav could feel her hidden eyes studying him. 'There's another possibility. Some part of the sylvaneth spirit may have been absorbed into his own and it is that which has caused him to rally so speedily. When I awaken him, he may not be entirely the man you knew before. There might be something else there too.'

'Will he be a danger?' Venteslav wanted to know.

'The sylvaneth, what you call the green-folk, are a strange and fey race,' the mystic replied. 'It is difficult to predict what their intentions are and often dangerous to make assumptions about their purposes. All I can say is that they are hostile to all the kindreds of the undead. So if they have gained some influence over Gajevic, it will not make him any less an enemy to the Lady of Sorrows. But it may make him less of a friend to you.'

Venteslav was quiet for a moment as he ruminated on what the mystic told him. His fingers tapped against the hilt of his knife. If he struck before Gajevic woke then there'd be no question about who he was now or where his motives lay. At the same time, from what the Veiled Oracle said, even if his mind was no longer fully his own, the wizard remained an enemy of Lady Olynder. The only one who could be depended on not to betray the mission.

'Wake him,' Venteslav decided, his hand falling away from the knife on his belt. 'I want to get moving before much of the morning is spent.' He turned from the Veiled Oracle and walked back towards the fire. Omid was still on guard and he employed the Azyrite in helping him to rouse the others. All of them slept but lightly, and they were soon on their feet.

True to her claims, the Veiled Oracle soon had Gajevic standing on his own. The wizard wore a dazed, confused expression, but his recovery brought cheers from the others. After the death of Ratimir, Gajevic's return provided a much-needed boost to their morale. Kvetka took pains to help the wizard and lend him support. Even Omid managed to overcome his prejudice to express a warm sentiment.

Venteslav wanted to share in the general mood, but he had too much to do. He snapped curt orders to the survivors and readied them for their march into the hills beyond the citadel. They'd adopt the same diamond-pattern style of march, this time with him acting as the rearguard. Zorgrath would resume his role as scout and guide, though the cryptborn warned that they were now entering a region unfamiliar to him. Kvetka and Gajevic would remain in the middle, this time with the Veiled Oracle as their travelling companion.

The group descended the hillside, now using the approach that faced away from the Barrowbogs. As they began to climb down, just for an instant Venteslav was afforded an unsettling glimpse of Gajevic before the wizard started down the slope.

Was it a trick of his imagination, or had Venteslav seen a flicker of jade light shining from the wizard's eyes?

When he looked back, Mahyar could barely make out the distant speck that was the Veiled Oracle's citadel. They'd covered a lot of ground since leaving there. He knew his own stamina was up to the gruelling pace Venteslav demanded of them – the Temple of Sigmar had a way of encouraging its warrior priests to continually test their limitations – but he was surprised Kvetka and Gajevic were keeping up. When they'd started out, the scholar had been helping the wizard. Now those roles had been reversed. Perhaps Gajevic was using his magic to bolster his vitality.

If there was some question about magic allowing Gajevic to maintain the pace, Mahyar had no doubts concerning the Veiled Oracle's ability to endure the gruelling march. By her own admission, it had been years since she'd set foot outside her citadel. Draped in black cloth, still mourning her murdered family, hers was hardly an image that could be called hale and hearty. Yet she kept up with them just the same, gliding across the rocky hillsides with such graceful ease that she might have been waltzing in a ballroom. Even Zorgrath had remarked on the eerie sight when he slipped back to advise the others as to what lay ahead of them.

'The witches of the Skullkeeper tribes move like that,' Zorgrath muttered. 'They draw into themselves the malice of their Blood God and then slip away from their huts to slash the throats of anyone they find until the madness leaves them. I have seen it! They move without sound and leave no mark upon the earth.'

'No slave of Khorne would be so restrained as she is,' Mahyar assured the cryptborn. 'She'd have had to draw something's blood by now to avoid the Skull Lord's ire. I've been watching her, and she's not paused to strike down so much as a lizard since we left the citadel.'

Zorgrath nodded, but his beady eyes were dubious. 'I'll leave the question of gods and daemons to the priests then,' he grumbled. 'But a cautious eye might prevent a slit throat just the same.' The guide loped back off into the rocks, following the rough path they'd been on for several hours.

Mahyar gave the cryptborn's advice more thought than he liked to admit. The machinations of the Dark Gods were complex and intricate. Though Nagash had turned against Sigmar and his pantheon, the Great Necromancer remained a dire enemy of Chaos. Forgiveness wasn't a quality Nagash was known to possess and the realm of Shyish still bore the scars from the conquests of the Dark Gods. Their minions yet retained footholds even in this land of the undead: the Skullkeeper tribes, who built ziggurats from the heads of their enemies to prevent the dead from returning; the Order of the Fly, extending the putrescent fecundity of Nurgle in a crusade against the necrotic dissolution of the tomb-lands. Was it possible that the Veiled Oracle was a servant of Chaos, pitting one enemy against another? The idea, as unlikely as it was, couldn't be entirely dismissed.

Quietly, Mahyar prayed to Sigmar for wisdom, for the perception to see past all subterfuge.

Hours fell away, bearing with them the sunlight. Dark clouds boiled up across the horizon, turning the afternoon grey. The hills were a dreary land, a place of rocks and dead weeds, spiders and beetles. Sometimes the vague outline of a foundation gave evidence of past habitation, little more than a discoloured smear painted on the ground. Sometimes there would be furtive noises and shadows darting behind boulders, signs that the land wasn't completely deserted. Mahyar noted that these skulkers never drew too close to their group. They appeared to lose interest once they got a good look at the band. Either the prospect of confronting them was too formidable, or the creeping watchers discovered something to frighten them off.

'Kinfolk of Zorgrath,' Kvetka suggested when she spotted one of the shadowy figures peeking from behind a boulder. 'Unless they can bring numbers to bear, they won't attack until they have the cover of darkness to protect them.'

'They have numbers,' Mahyar said, keeping a close watch on the rocks as he marched. 'I've counted scores of them since we got deep into the hills.'

The Veiled Oracle added her own thoughts on the subject. 'They're afraid to attack,' she stated. 'The ghouls stay up in these hills where there's little to eat because they still fear the remnants of Shiverbloom. The sylvaneth were merciless towards their packs when they tried to pass through the forest to haunt the catacombs of Belvegrod.'

Gajevic responded to the intimation in the mystic's statement. 'You're saying they're keeping away because of me? Because somehow I carry some taint associated with the green-folk?'

'You could answer that better than I could,' the Veiled Oracle told him. 'It needn't be anything overt. Perhaps as inconsequential as a change in your aura or an alteration in your scent.'

'You've seen already how different Zorgrath's senses are from our own,' Kvetka reminded the wizard, 'and he's only half-ghoul.'

Mahyar shook his head. 'Whatever is keeping them back, I don't like it.'

The Veiled Oracle laughed. 'You should not say something so impious, priest. You are devoted to the God-King and bear His light wherever you tread. How often, do you suppose, even a mote of Sigmar's power is seen in these lands? Your mere presence could be the very thing which makes the ghouls cower in the shadows.'

The mystic's humour faded and she continued in a more sober tone. 'Or it could be that they are waiting for something. Something they expect to happen.'

'Like what?' Mahyar wanted to know, his pride stinging from her laughter.

'If I could tell you that,' the Veiled Oracle said, 'I should be much easier in my own mind. There's danger here for us, but a danger we have yet to see.' She raised her head and stared off down the winding path. 'Or perhaps only some of us have yet to see it.'

Her words brought Mahyar's mind back to Zorgrath. The crypt-born claimed these lands were unknown to him. But was that true?

'It'll be best if we keep moving,' Mahyar said, gesturing at the darkened sky. 'Venteslav wants to reach this hidden route into the tomb-fortress before night, if it's possible.' He paused and looked back at the Veiled Oracle. 'Is it possible?'

'All things are possible,' the mystic answered. 'The difference lies in what is likely and what is unlikely.' She nodded her head. 'If nothing causes undue delay, it is likely we reach the tunnel before night overtakes us.'

'Then all the more reason to hurry,' Mahyar declared. 'If there's a chance, then it is a sin to squander it. Sigmar extends no favours to the timid.'

The warrior priest left the other part of the old proverb unsaid, for it continued with a sentiment perhaps even more appropriate to their situation: *Sigmar forsakes the foolish.*

Many a hero, Mahyar reflected, had come to ruin for being unable to tell the difference between courage and folly. He prayed again, this time not for the wisdom to see through deception, but the wisdom to recognise both bravery and foolishness.

Even if they reached the hidden entrance, did they have any real chance of breaking the curse? Could so few challenge the Lady of Sorrows and prevail?

To Mahyar's dismay, there was no answer to his prayer, only the moan of the rising wind as the day continued to die and the funereal breeze returned to wrap them all in its clammy embrace.

Soraya was first to spot Zorgrath when the guide came scrambling back to rejoin them. The cryptborn scurried out from among the boulders with such abruptness that she had her sword raised before she recognised him.

'I almost cut you down,' she snapped at him. 'I thought you were a ghoul.' As soon as she said the words, Soraya frowned, but the half-breed took no notice of her discomfort.

'I went up to speak with one of them,' Zorgrath said. 'There's something ahead of us that puzzled me and only they could give me an answer.' He turned his head and glanced around at the marchers. 'I'll go talk with Venteslav. You should come too in case anyone else thinks I'm a ghoul.'

Soraya followed Zorgrath back to the captain and alerted Mahyar to keep an eye on her side of the path. Venteslav looked curious when he saw the guide approaching him with an escort.

'There's trouble ahead of us,' Zorgrath said. 'I found a valley a mile from here that has hundreds of gallows standing in it.' The cryptborn paused before adding mystery to his macabre report. 'There are bodies hanging from the gallows-trees.'

Soraya felt her skin crawl. They'd seen for themselves that these hills were infested with ghouls. No carrion should have been left alone by the scavengers. As soon as a corpse first started to exude the smell of decay, a hungry ghoul would be on it. Only the most regimented of their packs had the discipline to let their meals rot before indulging in necrophagia.

'Why would the ghouls leave the bodies alone?' Venteslav asked, echoing Soraya's thoughts. He looked at the soldier. 'Bring Omid in from the flank. I have questions I want to put to the Veiled Oracle.'

Soraya did as she was ordered. Omid was hardly cheered by her explanation of why he'd been summoned. They found the others gathered in the middle of the path in a cluster. At a signal from Venteslav, the two Azyrites fanned out and positioned themselves to either side of the group. She noted that they were equally close to both the Veiled Oracle and Zorgrath.

'We are close to the entrance now,' the Veiled Oracle said. 'What your scout has seen is the Hanging Glade. Long ago Lady Olynder massacred a rebellious tribe. Their bodies were left to swing as a warning to others and as a vivid reminder of both her authority and power.'

'Surely they should have rotted into dust by now if they're so old,' Kvetka pointed out.

The Veiled Oracle shook her head. 'The Lady of Sorrows is not content to simply punish her enemies in this life. She must make her wrath felt on the other side of the grave.'

Zorgrath turned to Venteslav. 'I was able to ambush one of the ghouls and get him to speak. He said the corpses are bewitched and none of his kind, no matter how hungry, will dare to touch them.'

'If they're so afraid, then why have the ghouls been following us for so long?' Mahyar asked. 'If there's a taboo on the place, I'd expect them to shun it.'

'There's no danger by day unless the bodies are disturbed,' Zorgrath said. 'It is at night that the danger comes. The spirits of the dead arise to kill anyone they find in the Hanging Glade.' He lowered his eyes, unwilling to look at any of them while he explained the reason the ghouls were lingering in the rocks. 'The ghouls expect the spirits to kill us. Then they'll come down from the rocks when it is safe and collect our corpses.'

Omid took a step towards the cryptborn. 'What's your angle? Lead us in there and then take breakfast with your people?'

Soraya laid her hand on Omid's shoulder and drew him back. 'If Zorgrath had such a plan, he wouldn't come back here to warn us.'

'We could wait for morning before entering the Hanging Glade,' Gajevic suggested. 'Then the danger would have passed.'

'Or it would be worse,' the Veiled Oracle countered. 'If even one of the spirits should roam away from the valley and discover us, it would bear the tidings back to the Lady of Sorrows. Then your chance would be lost. The Mortarch would move her processions against us. She might even remember the secret way into her crypt-fortress and seal it off.' She turned towards Venteslav. 'Your one chance is to get into the hidden tunnel before nightfall.'

Venteslav was silent while he weighed his options. 'Zorgrath, the ghoul claimed that so long as none of the bodies were disturbed the spirits wouldn't rise until nightfall?' His gaze swept across the others. 'Then our chance is this. While we still have the light we hurry through the Hanging Glade. We leave the bodies where they hang and pray to Sigmar that we are fast enough to get through.' He curled two of his fingers together in a gesture the Reclaimed believed could catch good luck.

'If we're going to do it this way, then we'd better do it,' Soraya stated before anyone could discuss the plan. She pointed at the sky. 'Time is the last luxury we can claim right now. We either do this or we don't. Make the choice now.'

'We go,' Venteslav said. 'Keep moving and touch nothing.' He nodded to Zorgrath. 'Lead the way,' he told the guide.

Soraya thought there was a certain reluctance about Zorgrath when he started back down the path, an uneasiness in his eyes that hadn't been there before. Whatever was waiting for them ahead, it was clearly something to disgust even a cryptborn.

They were losing their race against night when they finally reached the Hanging Glade. Soraya glanced over her shoulder at the red smudge on the horizon that marked the slow creep towards sunset. There were times when the sun seemed to struggle against the darkness, fighting to claim a few extra minutes of dominion over the realm. She hoped this was one such time. She felt they'd need every speck of sunlight the day could bestow on them.

The path widened from a miserable goat-track into a narrow valley. The slopes here were strewn with rubble and Soraya could see from their irregular contours that once they'd sported terraced gardens and fields. The floor of the valley was also littered with piles of ancient debris, but far more prominent was the morbid forest that stood before them: hundreds of gallows, built from a crimson wood Soraya had never seen before. While the wood appeared fresh and new, the metal fastenings that held the beams together were so caked in rust that it resembled mould on a slice of spoiled bread.

'Sigmar preserve us,' Soraya prayed as they started into the valley. She saw that the Reclaimed were pressing their fingers to iron, following their superstition about warding off evil spirits. Mahyar made the sign of the Hammer before entering the Hanging Glade and Soraya could not recall ever seeing such an expression of grave intensity on his face before. Even the Veiled Oracle appeared to hesitate before resuming her graceful, gliding gait.

'We're mad to come here,' Omid growled under his breath. 'As mad as those Eastdalers thinking a bit of iron will make the undead ignore them.'

'Venteslav is captain and we follow his orders,' Soraya reminded her fellow soldier. 'Jahangir would expect nothing less from us.'

'Jahangir's dead and we will be too if we go in there,' Omid persisted. The others were ahead of them now. It would be easy to slip back and return along the path.

'We'll be dead if we don't,' Soraya advised Omid. She nodded at the boulder-strewn hillsides behind them. 'The ghouls are still up there and you heard Zorgrath. They didn't attack before because they expected us to die here. What do you think they'll do if they see us back out now?' She gave him a grim smile. 'I'd rather risk myself trying to accomplish something than running straight into a ghoul's belly.'

Omid glared at her. 'Damn you,' he hissed. She could see that he knew she was right. There wasn't any choice except to press on. He took a deep breath, then started after the others.

Soraya brought up the rear. She could see shadowy figures on the path behind them now and feel their hungry eyes watching her. She tried not to think further than that. Whatever happened, all she could do was resist and fight until the last breath fled from her body. After that, what did it really matter if her bones were picked by vultures or gnawed by ghouls?

On either side, the grisly sight of the gallows met her gaze. Soraya was sickened by the merciless cruelty of the massacre. Lady Olynder had decimated the rebellious tribe root and branch. Old and young, none had been spared. More horrible still was the obscene enchantment invested into the massacred populace. Like the crimson wood of the gallows, the corpses looked as fresh as when the rope had first strangled the life from them. Their necks bore the purplish bruises of the noose, their tongues protruding from their mouths, their eyes rolled back so only white remained. They stank of death at the moment of its arrival, foul and obscene.

The line of hanging corpses seemed to stretch on forever. Soraya broke into a run, striving to put the hideous tableau behind her. Simply escaping the scene was more important to her than even the thought of angry spirits eager for the blood of the living. The others likewise increased their speed until all of them were hurrying through the horrible valley.

'There!' the Veiled Oracle proclaimed, and waved a gloved hand at the slope which ran above the Hanging Glade. 'That is where the entrance is!'

Soraya could just make out the suggestion of a trail running along the ridge above. She couldn't be sure, but she thought there was a darker patch in the hillside that might be the opening of a cave. It mattered little to her now. What was vital was that it lay outside the valley and away from the hanging corpses.

The group started up towards the ridge. The sun was quickly fading from the sky and night again was stealing over the land. The horror of the Hanging Glade now assumed a more sinister quality, an air of immediate threat. Soraya could see mist begin to seep up from the earth and gather about the dangling feet. The unholy powers of the valley were rallying to the darkness, gathering their energies. But they'd be too late! Their tiny band would be away before the malevolent spirits could stir!

As she ran, Soraya noticed Zorgrath standing under one of the gallows. There was a strange look on the cryptborn's face as he looked up at the body swinging from the noose. Before she could shout a warning, his hand was reaching out to brush the cold, dead foot.

'Get away from that!' Mahyar shouted. The warrior priest turned around and lunged at Zorgrath. His tackle sent both men tumbling through the dust. Soraya hurried towards them, uncertain if the conflict would escalate.

'Zorgrath!' Soraya shouted as she ran. 'What are you doing?'

'Get him away from there!' Venteslav yelled. The captain gestured with his sword, pointing it at Zorgrath and Mahyar.

Both men rose. Mahyar reached for the orruk choppa lying in the dirt. Zorgrath fumbled for the knives on his belt, an almost piteous look of confusion on his face. Before they came to blows, Soraya's attention was drawn away from them and towards the hanging corpses.

'Look!' she shouted. The glowing mist wasn't simply seeping up from the ground now. It was streaming up, like steam exploding from a volcanic vent. It inundated the bodies, engulfing them completely. The corpses absorbed the vapour. For a moment they twitched and thrashed about at the ends of their nooses. Then a grotesque shudder swept through them.

'Run! Run!' Gajevic roared. The wizard was pushing Kvetka up the slope, away from the Hanging Glade. Instead of following her, he turned back to help those who were left behind.

'Leave them,' Venteslav snarled at the wizard as he and Omid ran for the ridge. While Omid continued upwards, the captain muttered a curse and turned around.

'Something's happening.' Soraya spun Mahyar around and pushed him back towards the ridge. She glared at Zorgrath.

'I... It looked so much like... my mother...' the cryptborn mumbled. Soraya gave him a shove and sent him stumbling towards the slope.

The hanged corpses gave one last shiver. There was no glowing mist about their feet now; it had all been absorbed into their cadaverous flesh. Silence gripped the valley, so complete that Soraya could hear the blood rushing through her veins.

In the blink of an eye, the scene exploded into horror. From each corpse, a black shadow burst forth, rushing out from every pore like smoke rising from a burning log. Behind them they left their rotten bodies swinging at the end of their ropes. The apparitions had no interest in the flesh they'd once inhabited. It was the flesh of the intruders that called to them now!

'They're coming for you!' The shout echoed down from the rise. So lost was Soraya in her fear that she didn't know who spoke. She was only grateful that the sound of a human voice snapped her back to reality and broke the paralysis that held her.

'Run!' Soraya snarled the word at Zorgrath and gave him a shove towards the rise. The cryptborn didn't need further encouragement. He sprang away, a moan of abject terror rattling from his throat. In his rush to escape, he slammed into Mahyar and knocked the priest to the ground.

'Misbegotten cur!' Mahyar spat. He stumbled up onto his feet and started to lurch after the scout, even as one of the wraiths sped towards him. The orruk blade the priest carried chopped down through the apparition, scattering its wispy essence. While he dispatched the first of the undead, another phantom rushed at him from behind. Its spectral talons wrapped themselves about his neck. He screamed, and Soraya could see a hideous pallor stealing across his flesh. The wraith was draining his life force with its grip.

'Leave him alone!' Soraya sprang at the phantom. She stabbed at its head, piercing the mist-like essence. The apparition flickered, its malignance disrupted enough so that Mahyar could break away. Soraya put herself between the wraith and the priest as he staggered up towards the others.

Soraya looked back at the phantom she'd struck. It stood motionless, its ethereal shape gradually sealing the wound she'd dealt. Soraya shuddered and turned to flee, but she knew it was impossible to escape. The nighthaunts were more than a match for mortal flesh and bone. They would fall upon her like a pack of wolves and rend the life force from her beating heart. She would die and her body would be left to the hunger of the waiting ghouls.

One of the phantoms, a ghastly shape that carried in its hands a gleaming axe, flew at Soraya. Its wail of misery rang in her ears as it raised its weapon and brought it swinging down. She expected to feel the annihilating bite of the wraithblade, the chill of an edge forged in the underworlds. Instead there was a searing blast of light. The ghostly headsman shrieked in pain, its shrouded shape wreathed in silvery fire. Soraya blinked in amazement as the flames consumed the creature's essence.

'Hurry!' Gajevic shouted to her. Soraya didn't need further encouragement. She ran towards the wizard as other nighthaunts took up the chase. It seemed to her they'd hung back only to allow the headsman to claim the first kill, for now they came in a seething tide of malice.

Mahyar rushed back and met the first of the wraiths with the orruk choppa. The crude weapon had a golden energy surrounding it now, a manifestation of the priest's faith that allowed it to bite with far greater effect than the rough iron from which it was made. Venteslav plied his own sword against the spectres, but his steel could only drive the things back for the briefest moment. Gajevic cast more spells into the horde, but for every spirit he immolated, half a dozen more came rushing in.

Soraya could see there was no chance of winning the fight. Yet what else could they do? The nighthaunts wouldn't give them the chance to withdraw to the ridge and that was the only way to escape from their valley.

The wave of angry spirits surged towards them, threatening to drown them beneath an inundation of enmity and bloodlust. Soraya drew what she was certain would be her last breath. But before the undead tide could come crashing down, it was hurled back. The phantoms recoiled as though the entire horde had been swatted with the club of a gargant. Soraya blinked in disbelief. The nighthaunts also appeared disoriented, uncertain of what had just happened. They started forwards again, only to be hurled back once more, rebuffed by a tremendous but unseen force.

'Climb to the ridge,' the Veiled Oracle told them as she strode towards the enraged phantoms. She had both hands raised. One was open, the fingers splayed wide apart. The other was clenched into a fist. When the nighthaunts tried to charge once more, the mystic opened the fist and closed the other hand. Again there was that uncanny sight of the entire spectral host being flung back. The Veiled Oracle turned her head and urged the others to make haste. 'I cannot keep them back long.'

'What about you?' Soraya demanded.

'I can defend myself more easily than I can defend you,' the Veiled Oracle replied. 'Now go!'

Mahyar caught hold of Soraya's shoulder and spun her around. Together they ran for the slope. The others were already hurrying up to the ridge. Whether the Veiled Oracle spoke true or not, all knew that to remain in the Hanging Glade was to embrace death.

When Soraya gained the top of the ridge she turned around to see the mystic's fate. All in their little party were caught by the same grim fascination, giving no thought to further retreat.

'She's going to get killed,' Kvetka groaned.

'No,' Venteslav corrected her, pointing his hand at the Veiled Oracle. Slowly she was backtracking towards the ridge. Each time the horde started towards her, she would repeat the gesture with her hands and hurl them back again. It was only when she reached the slope that danger threatened. She had to turn to make her ascent. Unable to face the apparitions and unleash her spell, she could do nothing as they surged towards her once more.

Gajevic stepped forwards. Soraya saw the flash of eerie jade light that crackled through his eyes as he made arcane gestures with his hands. From his fingertips, ribbons of lightning snaked down into the nighthaunts. The vanguard of the horde was wracked by the wizard's magic, incinerated into smoke and shadow.

The destruction bought the Veiled Oracle the time she needed to complete her ascent. Before the rest of the undead could reach her, she was out of the valley and with the others on the ridge.

'They will not follow us,' the Veiled Oracle proclaimed. 'They have expended too much of their energies in rising so swiftly from their gallows. They lack the strength to stray from the valley now.' She nodded to Venteslav. 'Whatever roused them, it has left them too weak to report our presence to Lady Olynder. At least for tonight.'

Soraya glanced over at Zorgrath. The guide was paler than usual, his head hung down in guilt. He cringed among the rocks where he'd fled from the nighthaunts. He refused to meet the glowering gaze Mahyar trained on him.

'It was the cryptborn,' Omid accused. 'I saw him touch one of the bodies. He deliberately walked over to it and touched it.'

Zorgrath shook his head. 'I don't know what came over me,' he moaned. 'It seemed to me… the body was…'

'You thought to let us be murdered by the spirits,' Omid pressed, 'leave us all as carrion for you and your ghoul friends to eat!' The soldier's eyes blazed with hate and his hand clenched tight about the grip of his sword.

'Omid, you don't know what you're saying,' Soraya told him. She stepped between the soldier and the scout to try to defuse the situation.

There was an anguished gasp from behind her. She spun around to see Zorgrath coughing blood. The cryptborn slumped to his knees, more blood gushing from the wound in his chest.

Venteslav pressed his foot against Zorgrath's back and drew his sword free. He wiped the stained blade clean and returned it to his belt. His eyes were cold when he met Soraya's shocked gaze. 'By his own admission, he almost destroyed us all. I couldn't take the chance it was more than an accident.' For just a moment, his gaze lingered on the Veiled Oracle. 'We can't risk having a traitor among us. We've a chance to save our towns. I'll not let anyone or anything threaten that.' Venteslav pointed to the trail above the valley and the cave that yawned at its end.

A stunned silence gripped the band as they started for the cave. The sudden, brutal violence had shocked all of them.

'Wait,' Soraya said. She pointed at Zorgrath's body. 'We can't just leave him like this.'

'What would you have us do?' Omid sneered.

Soraya bristled at his tone. 'Bury him.'

Omid laughed at that. Venteslav gave him a dark look that silenced his mockery. His eyes were sympathetic to Soraya. She thought perhaps there was even a trace of guilt there. 'Your sense of decency does you credit, but there's an old saying in Eastdale. The wolf only pretends to befriend the dog. He betrayed us, would have seen all of us die. Leave him. Forget him.'

Mahyar stepped forwards and laid his hand on Soraya's shoulder. 'Pray that his soul finds peace, but understand there is none for his body. Even if we buried it, his kinfolk would dig him up. There's nothing we could do to prevent that.' He glanced down at the body. 'It would be a gesture only. Something for us, not him.'

The priest's words touched Soraya. She looked across at the others, her gaze flitting from the Veiled Oracle to Kvetka, seeking some understanding from the other women. 'It feels wrong.'

'It is wrong,' Kvetka agreed. 'But sometimes what is wrong is what's necessary. Mahyar's right, the flesh-eaters will only dig him up again.'

The group started into the dark tunnel. Soraya looked back once over her shoulder at Zorgrath's corpse, unable to reconcile herself to the callousness of necessity.

CHAPTER TWELVE

The cave led into a noisome tunnel, dark and dank and reeking of decay. Kvetka couldn't decide if the walls were natural or simply the product of a crude and slovenly excavation. She remembered things she'd read in restricted tomes about the perfidious ratkin and their works. The tunnel might be a product of their construction. She found herself studying the walls for any trace left by pick or claw, any betraying mark left behind by inhuman builders. The skaven were known to be thieves and looters. The crypt-fortress of Lady Olynder would doubtless make a tempting prize for them.

Kvetka tried to concentrate on the walls, but her gaze kept straying back to Venteslav. She was still in shock from the swift judgement the captain had visited on Zorgrath. Was he so certain that the cryptborn had betrayed them? Her thumb pressed against an iron button while she prayed that it was so. She didn't want to believe he would kill if he was unsure.

The scout's death had left all of them in a grim mood. They advanced in single file down the narrow passage, cautious in the gloom. Except for the Veiled Oracle, each of them carried a sputtering torch, but the omnipresent darkness receded only resentfully and never as far as it should. It drew back from the flames and compacted itself into pitch-black depths, pacing like a wild beast just beyond the firelight. Waiting for its chance to come rushing in and smother them all in its cold shadows.

Soraya was in the lead now. The Azyrite soldier picked her way carefully, always probing ahead with her torch before pressing on. After her came Mahyar, the heavy orruk weapon resting on his shoulder, the words of a religious litany whispering from his lips. Venteslav and the Veiled Oracle came next, the captain keeping close to the mystic and frequently tilting his head towards her as though to listen to hushed words. Kvetka was next in the line, but she never was able to catch whatever instructions – if any – the Veiled Oracle was relating to Venteslav.

She glanced back. Behind her, Gajevic picked his way through the blackness. The wizard held his torch out away from him so that it was as far from his body as possible. She thought there was a hint of anxiety in his face whenever he chanced to look towards it. A lingering effect from his contact with the residue of the green-folk, or was it something more?

Last of all came Omid. With Soraya taking the lead, the other soldier had been sent to act as rearguard. It was a post he resented and had tried to refuse. He kept turning about and watching behind them, a ready grip always on his sword. Kvetka had no great liking for the Azyrite. He was an intolerant and pompous man. But in this matter, she could sympathise with him. She had confidence in the Veiled Oracle's assurance that the night-haunts couldn't leave the Hanging Glade. That same limitation wouldn't apply to the ghouls from the hills, however. Now that the flesh-eaters had lost the prospect of letting the spectres kill their prey for them, the threat of them entering the tunnel and hunting the party down was a very real one. It would be Omid's lot to dis-cover the cannibals first if they came charging out of the darkness.

Kvetka drew closer to Venteslav and expressed her concerns. 'The ghouls may follow us into the tunnel. If Zorgrath intended to betray us...'

Venteslav cut her off with a wave of his hand. 'The cryptborn betrayed us when he touched the corpse and awakened the night-haunts. There's an old saying of our people, "By your deeds shall your heart be proven." Zorgrath proved himself a traitor.' He glanced past Kvetka to where Omid walked. 'The flesh-eaters may follow us,' he said, 'but the best way to escape their attention is forwards, not back. The closer we get to the crypt-fortress the less likely those scavengers are to keep to our trail.'

The Veiled Oracle nodded. 'A rude semblance of life lingers in the veins of ghouls. Corrupt, polluted by the black necromancy of Nagash, but life just the same. Antithetical to the malevolent spirits that serve Lady Olynder. Just as the phantoms that lurk in the Hanging Glade would attack the flesh-eaters, so too would the nighthaunts that infest the crypt-fortress.' She waved one of her gloved hands, the motion just visible in the sputtering light. 'Ahead is the best way to avoid their attentions. When you are far enough into the tunnel, they will be scared to follow.'

The question appeared settled as far as Venteslav was concerned. Kvetka was less convinced. She remembered when a ghoul had been captured and brought to the Belvegrod lighthouse. The scholars had examined it closely. Degenerate and vile, the resem-blance between it and the normal human form only increased the horror it provoked. All ripping fangs and tearing claws, with a con-stitution robust enough to defy most poisons, the creature was a ghastly specimen. Most vivid of all in her memory was when the ghoul had escaped its cage and run loose in the lighthouse; how it had moved faster than its human pursuers, outdistancing even the dogs that were set upon it. Now she imagined a whole pack of the monsters hounding them, desperate to catch them before they could reach the region into which the ghouls would not trespass, or at least so the Veiled Oracle declared.

'There may be danger following us,' Kvetka advised Gajevic when she drew back to speak with him. 'I worry that we've got ghouls on our tracks.'

'You agree that Zorgrath betrayed us to the flesh-eaters?' Gajevic asked.

'Whether he did or not, the ghouls expected us to be killed in the Hanging Glade,' Kvetka said. 'Since we escaped, it would be presumptuous to think they'll give up easily.'

'You've discussed this with Venteslav?'

Kvetka nodded. 'He and the Veiled Oracle believe our best chance is to keep going. The nearer we get to Lady Olynder's domain, the less likely they are to pursue.' Her gaze hardened as she looked back down the tunnel. 'Gajevic, I've seen how quick these things are. They can catch us easily if that is their intention.' She pointed at the torch in his hand. 'They wouldn't need light either. They could find us simply by smell.'

Gajevic might have offered words of reassurance, but before he could speak a scream rang out from behind them. The wizard swung around and thrust the blazing torch towards the noise. Eldritch words fell from his lips as he invoked his magic. The torch flared to unnatural brilliance and shot a bundle of flames into the darkness. By the flickering greenish light, grotesque shapes were revealed.

'Ghouls,' Kvetka gasped as she recognised the crooked figures with their wide, fang-ridden mouths and long clawed hands.

'Get Omid!' Gajevic shouted, focusing his power to send a second flare from the torch. The ghouls covered their faces with their claws and whined like curs as they were blinded by the dazzling light.

Kvetka dashed over to the soldier. Omid had been hit from behind by the ghouls, his coat slashed to tatters by their claws. He rallied when she reached him, stumbling back to his feet and following her as she led him away from the incapacitated cannibals.

'Run! Hurry!' Venteslav shouted to them. He was already ordering the others to dash off farther into the tunnel and away from the ghouls.

'They'll catch us,' Kvetka shouted back, but the captain refused to be swayed. He waved his arm and hurried after the Veiled Oracle.

'Go!' Gajevic yelled. 'I'll hold them off for as long as I can.'

'And what happens when you can't conjure another spell?' Kvetka glared at him.

Omid pulled at her arm, urging Kvetka to flee. 'He knows what he's doing. Let's go.'

Kvetka shook free of the soldier's grip. 'I'm not leaving him. Go ahead with the others,' she said. Omid didn't linger but hurried to follow Venteslav.

Another flare leapt from the torch as the ghouls started to creep forwards. Again, they jumped back and covered their faces with their hands. Their eyes reflected the light, reminding Kvetka of jackals prowling around a campfire. There were at least a score of the creatures. It was suicide for Gajevic to try to hold them off on his own.

'You can't stay here,' Kvetka said, trying to reason with the wizard. 'They'll be all over you in a heartbeat when they see a chance.'

'My magic can last longer if I limit the strength of my conjurations,' Gajevic said. 'Just a light to blind rather than a fire to destroy.' He spoke another incantation and hurled a blob of green flame at the ghouls as they started to creep forwards again.

'This won't work,' Kvetka warned him. 'They're not dumb animals...'

The warning was late. While the ghouls in front kept up the

pretence of mindless aggression, those behind them ripped rocks from the rough walls. They sprang forwards, shielding their eyes with one arm while throwing their crude missiles with the other. A rain of stones pelted the wizard and knocked the torch from his hands.

'Move!' Kvetka shouted at Gajevic as she swung him around and sent him stumbling off down the tunnel. She turned just as the first ghoul got close to her and jammed the blazing end of her torch full in its face. The cannibal screamed and fell back, its agonised spasms blocking the ones following behind it. Kvetka didn't linger over the scene, but turned and ran.

She knew the pack would be on her heels. Kvetka's only prayer was that the Veiled Oracle was right and that the place beyond which the ghouls wouldn't enter was near.

Venteslav hurried the others through the tunnel. There was no knowing how many ghouls were on their trail. There could be anything between a dozen and several hundred. If he could only get their group out ahead of the monsters, into the region they were afraid to enter, then it wouldn't matter. If he ordered everyone to stop, had them stand and fight, then they could easily be overwhelmed.

'How much farther?' he gasped as he ran.

'It is difficult to judge,' the Veiled Oracle answered. Despite her long isolation within her citadel, she was the least fazed of any of them by the frantic retreat, keeping pace with them yet not seeming to put any more effort into her gliding step than she had before. 'I have seen this place only through my pool. The glass can distort distances.'

'It better not have distorted them too much,' Mahyar growled. The priest threw a look back over his shoulder at Venteslav. 'I could stay behind and try to delay them.'

Venteslav rejected Mahyar's offer. He could see Omid running behind him and farther back there was the light of a torch, so he knew at least somebody else was following them. That could still mean they'd lost either Kvetka or Gajevic. 'I don't want to lose anyone else,' he said. 'If the pack closes in, then we stand and fight. Otherwise we keep moving. The more of us who reach the crypt-fortress, the better our chances are.'

At the forefront of their little group, Soraya suddenly cried out. Venteslav couldn't distinguish any words, but he could see from the flicker of her torch that the tunnel was different ahead of them. The walls weren't jagged and uneven. They had a semblance of regularity to them and a curious bubbly contour that disturbed him for no discernible reason.

When he reached Soraya, Venteslav saw what his subconscious had noted. The walls were layered with old bones, columns of skulls and femurs, and rows of ribs and pelvises. The raw unworked tunnel proceeded as a catacomb. It stretched onwards as far as the light revealed. Scores of human skeletons were set into the walls with grey mortar. There might be hundreds, thousands more lining the farther passage, allowing it didn't branch off into a mortuary maze like those found under the mansions and temples of Belvegrod.

Soraya was a veteran of the Tombwatch, and for an instant Venteslav was puzzled as to why she'd cry out. Then he saw them. Slithering among the bones were translucent worms the size of his finger. The creatures weren't completely solid, phasing in and out of the skeletons as they undulated along the walls. Venteslav brought his torch close to the things, but though the fire blackened the bones on which they crawled, it wrought no harm to the worms themselves. Instead, the things were attracted to the heat, creeping out and waving their trunks at his torch.

'Keep back,' Venteslav hissed at the others. He could feel that the worms were much more than simply revolting. There was danger here, even if he wasn't sure what it was.

'The ghouls!' Omid shouted as he reached the group. 'They're in the tunnels! They're right behind me!' His eyes gaped wide when he noticed the masses of worms crawling on the walls.

'The way to the crypt-fortress is ahead,' the Veiled Oracle reminded Venteslav. 'The longer you tarry here, the more you court disaster.'

'Stay clear of the walls,' Venteslav cautioned the group. 'Keep moving. Whatever happens, keep going.'

Venteslav didn't follow his own orders. The torchlight cast by whoever was behind Omid was drawing closer now. He could see the gleam of hungry eyes chasing after it. His fingers closed tight about the sword he held. He glanced over at the Veiled Oracle who was lingering beside him.

'Go ahead with the others,' Venteslav told her. 'I can't leave.'

The Veiled Oracle pointed at the walls around them. 'There's need for haste, but not because of the ghouls.'

Venteslav didn't have time to consider the meaning of her words. The light was near enough now that he could see two people approaching. Kvetka and Gajevic! Both of them had escaped the cannibal horde. 'Hurry! This way!' he shouted. His cry seemed to bolster them, for they put on a final spurt of speed that allowed them to gain some slight distance on the slavering mob chasing them.

'Can't you do something?' Venteslav pressed the mystic beside him.

'This near to the Lady of Sorrows, I do not dare invoke my magic,' the Veiled Oracle replied, shaking her head. 'She would sense my presence and then all you have worked towards would be undone.' Her voice fell to a solemn pitch. 'Your friends must prevail on their own.'

Venteslav curled his fingers together to catch whatever luck had seeped down into these catacombs. There was no mistake now. The ghouls were gaining on the pair. Some of the monsters were hurling rocks at the humans, trying to bring them down and end the chase. He saw stones hit each of them, but none struck hard enough to make them fall.

The same couldn't be said for the ghoul that was closest to its quarry. The flesh-eater reached out with a clawed hand to snatch at Kvetka, but before its noxious talons could grab her robe the creature was struck by one of the rocks. The missile cracked squarely in the back of its skull. It tumbled across the floor, tripping up those running close behind it. A gap formed between pursuers and pursued, a gap that widened when several of the frenzied monsters fell on their stricken comrade and tore into its flesh with cannibalistic savagery.

Most of the ghouls weren't distracted by the fratricidal scene. They remained intent on their human quarry. Sight of Venteslav and the Veiled Oracle waiting ahead, the prospect of a still greater feast, only goaded them to greater effort.

'Down the tunnel! This way! This way!' Venteslav yelled. Kvetka and Gajevic reached the bone-walled catacombs. They ran onwards for a few yards, but no farther. They were spent by their exertions. Without a rest, they couldn't go on.

'Take them back,' Venteslav told the Veiled Oracle. 'Get them moving again.' Brandishing his sword he started forward to meet the oncoming ghouls.

'It is you who must come back,' the Veiled Oracle reprimanded him, 'away from the tunnel and back into the catacombs. Here you will be safe from the ghouls.'

Venteslav didn't hesitate. He did as the mystic told him. Her advice had brought them this far and he wasn't going to question her now. Even when the ghouls charged into the catacombs after them, he didn't lose his conviction that the Veiled Oracle knew what must be done to save them.

The ghouls faltered only a few feet into the bone-lined walls. Their grotesque faces peeled back in expressions of absolute horror. Shrieks, hideously too human considering the fang-ridden jaws that mouthed them, rang out through the passageway. Venteslav quickly saw the reason why.

The worms – those obscene translucent maggots slithering along the walls. They'd shown a menacing interest in him when Venteslav had struck at them with his torch. They took a far more active notice of the ghouls. From their perches among the skeletons, the worms leapt at the flesh-eaters. The first two ghouls fell, almost completely covered in the writhing mass. Others were struck by only a few of the creatures. These turned and fled, screaming back into the tunnels and throwing the rest of the cannibals into a panic. The gleam of their eyes vanished in the darkness as the horde retreated to the surface.

Venteslav watched in morbid fascination as the two ghouls left behind thrashed and flailed on the floor. More and more worms dropped onto them; indeed, the walls were now a squirming mass as legions of the creatures came crawling out from the depths to claim their portion of the prey. Beneath the translucent writhing heap, he could see the bodies of the ghouls dissolving as though immersed in acid.

'Grave grubs,' Kvetka said, supplying a name for the worms. She shook her head in disgust. 'They feed upon the flesh and spirit of the dead, leaving only bones behind.' She pointed at the engulfed ghouls. 'They were near enough to carrion themselves to provoke the worms' hunger.'

'Let us be grateful they didn't decide we'd make good eating,' Venteslav said, watching the squirming walls as still more of the worms descended upon the ghouls.

Kvetka's face was drawn, pale with horror. 'They will,' she warned. 'Long ago the priests of Belvegrod tried to cultivate grave grubs to dispose of such undead as haunted the old city. They soon discovered that the things were uncontrollable. Once their hunger was aroused, it wasn't easily sated. They would feed upon the living if there was nothing else to satiate them. The undead are their preferred prey, not their only one.'

'We've got to get out of here before they finish their meal,' Venteslav said.

'There might be miles of these catacombs before you gain the crypt-fortress,' the Veiled Oracle warned. 'Do you think you can elude every worm within these halls?'

'What else can we do?' Venteslav demanded.

'I think I have a solution,' Kvetka said. She reached into the satchel she still carried. Though the books had been destroyed by the Sea of Tears, other resources remained. She pulled out a bundle of herbs. 'Wolfbloom,' she explained. She took one of the stalks and bent it in upon itself, looping it until she had shaped it into a circle.

'A talisman against snakes.' The captain shook his head. 'I've used one before.' He tapped his forearm where a slight discolouration still marred his skin. 'Either it was made wrong or that is one tradition the Azyrites are right to call superstition.'

'I can't say why it didn't work against your snake,' Kvetka said, 'but the old priests used talismans like these to ward off the grave grubs when they were tending them.' Before anyone could stop her, she held the token towards the wall. The squirming mass of worms parted before her fingers, writhing away to avoid contact with the herb. 'See? It works.'

Venteslav bit back an angry rejoinder about what they should have done if it didn't work. Instead he took one of the stalks from Kvetka and bent it around to form a circle of his own. Gajevic did the same with the wolfbloom she offered to him.

The Veiled Oracle shook her head when Kvetka would have given her another of the stalks. 'I have my own protections,' she said. 'But you are forgetting the rest of your party. They are without protection.'

'The Azyrites!' Venteslav looked aside at the ghouls. They were reduced almost to skeletons now. Although the grave grubs continued to slither along the walls, drawn in their mindless way to partake in the dwindling feast, once the corpses were only bones they'd be prowling the catacombs looking for more prey. 'We've got to make talismans for them! We've got to get protection to them before...'

Kvetka held out her hand. Venteslav saw at once the reason for her sickened look. Mahyar, Soraya and Omid. Three Azyrites. In the scholar's hand there were only two stalks of wolfbloom.

Soraya ran her fingers across the little loop of wolfbloom Kvetka had given her. She shuddered to think about the way the ghouls had died, but at the same time it seemed to her nothing more than a Reclaimed superstition that the talisman would fend off the grave grubs. Mahyar was even more forceful in his doubt about the charms' efficacy. Only when Venteslav ordered him to take it did the priest grudgingly accept the token.

Omid, on the other hand, was in such a state of fright that he simply didn't believe the talismans would work; he was convinced the ones given to him and Soraya were faulty. 'The Reclaimed all carry loops made from a whole stalk of wolfbloom,' he whispered to her as they marched through the catacombs. 'So does Mahyar. But we, we've just got these.' He paused and held out the token he'd been given. 'Both of them made from half a stalk.'

'Careful,' she admonished Omid, 'you're starting to sound like the Reclaimed. Next you'll be saying that if you spit three times a banshee loses its scream.'

'I'm saying we need better protection than this,' Omid growled, thrusting the token back inside his tunic.

'And I'm saying that it isn't any protection at all,' Soraya said. She turned and looked at the skeleton-encrusted walls, watching the translucent worms slithering off down the passageway. 'If those things decide they're hungry, a loop of weeds and a dollop of superstition isn't going to stop them.'

They continued on deeper into the catacombs. Mahyar had taken the lead now, while close behind the priest the Veiled Oracle provided directions whenever they came to a crossroads. The farther into the tunnel they went, the more of these they encountered. Soraya had long ago lost track of all the branches and intersections they'd passed. If they were forced to go back the way they'd come, she doubted if she could pick the correct turns. Venteslav had cut marks into the floor at intervals, but they'd be easy to miss if they had to retrace their tracks in a hurry.

Venteslav kept at the rear of the group with Kvetka and Gajevic. Soraya knew what they were watching for. At some point the grave grubs would begin filtering back through the catacombs. Though he was Reclaimed, the captain's confidence in the old superstition wasn't complete. When the worms realised there wasn't anything left of the ghouls to consume he intended to use Gajevic's magic to fend them off. The talismans, as far as he was concerned, would act as a last resort.

'Something ahead,' Mahyar's gruff voice drifted back to the soldiers. Soraya turned and repeated the message to Venteslav, then she started forwards with Omid. Both of them had their swords drawn.

What Mahyar had found proved to be a wide chamber. Several passages branched away from it. In the middle of the room was a morbid shrine, a great fountain fashioned from the cemented bones of hundreds of people. A statue of a man stood at its centre.

Soraya was impressed by his physique. He was the most handsome man she'd ever seen, though there was an arrogance to his features that left no illusion about his character. His mouth was partly open and from it there spilled a torrent of dark liquid. Soraya was unsettled when she realised it was blood and that the basin in which the statue stood was likewise a sanguinary pool. She looked back at the statue's face and noted the long fangs that protruded from under his lips.

'Vampire,' the Veiled Oracle named the figure. One of her gloved hands tapped against the statue's leg. 'Baron Waldemar. He coveted Lady Olynder and demanded her as his bride. This was her answer. Her magic turned him to stone. She filled his mouth with blood so that his imprisoned essence might always be tormented by the sustenance he so desperately craves.' She turned and faced Soraya. 'That is what it means to challenge the Lady of Sorrows. Vengeance that reaches beyond the mortal world.'

'You risk much to accompany us,' Soraya said. 'You could have stayed beyond her power in your citadel.'

The Veiled Oracle was pensive for a moment. 'She has brought so much grief to others,' the mystic said. 'It is long past the time for her enemies to strike back.' The mystic looked around at the many branches leading away from the sinister shrine. 'I must concentrate and decipher which path we must take now,' she told Soraya, bowing her head in apology. The Veiled Oracle withdrew, pacing around the periphery of the chamber, trying to match their surroundings with her knowledge of the catacombs.

Mahyar and Venteslav were engaged in a hurried conference while Gajevic sat on the floor, obviously still fatigued from escaping the ghouls. Soraya turned around to find Kvetka and Omid discussing something. It struck her as peculiar that the soldier would have anything to say to the Reclaimed scholar. As she came close, the situation seemed to explain itself.

'I owe my life to you,' Omid told Kvetka. 'If you hadn't turned back to help me, I'd have been eaten by the ghouls.'

Kvetka was obviously embarrassed by his gratitude. 'You'd have done the same for me,' she commented. Soraya thought that unlikely. Omid was a dependable fighter, but he wasn't someone who'd risk his own neck as recklessly as the scholar and Gajevic had.

'You have my gratitude,' Omid said. 'I am beholden to you.' He embraced Kvetka in a quick hug, then, apparently uncomfortable with the gesture, he just as quickly withdrew. With a brief bow, he departed from the scholar.

Soraya was uncertain what to make of the scene. She knew Omid too well, knew his animosity towards the Eastdalers. Saving his life might have changed his attitude, or he might be playing some other game. She followed after him as he walked towards the grisly fountain.

'What was all that about?' she asked him.

Omid didn't look her in the eyes when he answered. 'The scholar saved my life. I was thanking her,' he said.

Soraya caught him by the chin and forced him to look at her. 'I asked you what you were doing,' she snarled. She was certain now that something was wrong.

'The worms are coming back!' Venteslav's shout rang through the chamber. Everyone turned to watch as a creeping wave of the creatures slithered along the walls into the shrine. They didn't just come from the passage they'd followed into the catacombs, but from all the others as well.

Mahyar held the wolfbloom talisman in his hand and boldly walked towards the closest wall, deaf to the calls to come back. 'Sigmar is my shield and my faith,' he prayed as he reached out with his hand and repeated the test Kvetka had used. The squirming mass recoiled away from him. He turned, a mix of surprise and relief on his face. 'By the Hammer, it works!' he exclaimed.

Soraya looked at her own token, cut from half of a wolfbloom stalk. Would it be enough to keep her safe? She felt the sweat dripping down her face as she watched the grave grubs crawling ever closer. From the corner of her eye, she could see Omid. He wasn't sweating. In fact, given his earlier panic, he was strangely calm.

Soraya knew at once what had happened. Before she could shout a warning, an agonised scream echoed through the chamber. She turned her head and saw Kvetka collapse to the floor, a transparent mass of worms engulfing her, lunging at her from the skeletal walls. The scholar's face was a mask of agony, but after that first shriek, all other sound was muffled by the squirming horde.

'Kvetka!' Gajevic was on his feet in an instant. He rushed towards the fallen scholar, the words of a spell flying off his tongue. His fingers curled and cracked as he hurriedly wove them in arcane gestures. Then his whole body was enveloped in fire, a crackling flame that burned green in the darkness. He threw himself at the spectral worms, his magic immolating them, bursting them into vapour. He drove his hands into the writhing mass and tried to free Kvetka from its consuming embrace.

Venteslav and Mahyar rushed to help the wizard. They used the talismans they bore to ward off the new streams of grave grubs seeking to join the ghastly feast. Slowly, much too slowly, the worms were beaten back. As the tide ebbed, Gajevic's fire was able to burn through the mass that yet engulfed Kvetka. The wizard's cry when he saw what remained was the most piteous sound Soraya had ever heard.

The Veiled Oracle had joined the horrified group gathered around Kvetka. She shook her head sadly as she stared down at the partly consumed woman. 'There is no magic I know that could heal such wounds or ease her suffering,' she said.

Gajevic looked up, tears streaming down his face. 'There's magic I know that can.' He looked back into the corroded mush that had moments before been the woman he loved. There was just enough left of her face to express the agony she was in. Grimly, the wizard drew his knife and put an end to her pain. Then he hugged the lifeless body and began to cry.

'I don't understand,' Venteslav said. 'Kvetka made the talismans. We know they worked. I saw her repulse the worms with my own eyes.'

Soraya chose that moment to act. Her dagger stabbed deep into Omid's chest and pierced his heart. The soldier gave her an incredulous look before his eyes glazed over and he fell dead at her feet. Venteslav and Mahyar stared at her in shock.

'It was Omid,' Soraya told them. 'He was afraid of the worms. Afraid that a talisman made from only part of a stalk wouldn't protect him.' She kicked over his body, then reached down and drew two of the charms out from beneath his tunic: the smaller one he'd been given and the larger one he'd stolen.

'The coward,' Mahyar spat. 'The damned coward.'

'Traitor,' Venteslav muttered, a haunted look in his eyes.

'He betrayed Kvetka because he was afraid,' Soraya said. She wiped away the tears that were in her own eyes. Omid had been the last of her comrades from the Tombwatch. The last link to a happier past.

'I couldn't take the chance he'd do it again,' Soraya told Venteslav. 'I couldn't take the chance he'd get someone else killed.'

CHAPTER THIRTEEN

The bone-lined catacombs stretched on for miles, a grisly labyrinth that burrowed its way deep beneath the mountains. Only the
guidance of the Veiled Oracle kept the small group from becoming hopelessly lost. At each turn, the mystic would pause and
contemplate the path ahead. Soraya took a close interest in these
moments, feeling as if a hand of ice were squeezing her heart. If
the Veiled Oracle got lost there was no chance any of them would
be able to find their way back out. They would wander the catacombs until death at last came for them. Their bodies lost in the
darkness.

Soraya glanced at the bone-lined walls. The spectral worms were
there, weaving their way between the skeletons. Her hand fell to
the talisman she now wore, the one that Omid had stolen from
Kvetka. In the aftermath of their deaths, Venteslav had given her
the loop of wolfbloom – just in case Omid's fears hadn't been baseless and the worms would not be repelled by the lesser charms.

Soraya's attention shifted back to Gajevic. The wizard hadn't said a single word since he'd been compelled to end Kvetka's suffering. Venteslav kept close to him, steering him through the catacombs for fear that, in his morose daze, the wizard would wander away and become lost in the passageways.

'He might've been more fortunate if he hadn't recovered his wits,' Mahyar said, following the turn of Soraya's gaze. The warrior priest walked with her at the front of their diminished group, the Veiled Oracle a yard or so behind them and the two Eastdalers bringing up the rear.

'I think he must've truly loved her,' Soraya commented. She was puzzled by the incredulity she saw in Mahyar's expression. 'You don't think so?'

'Wizards are a different breed,' Mahyar replied. 'They aren't the same as normal people. The magic they study warps them, turns their minds down strange paths it is better not to contemplate. They gain strange powers, but at the same time they lose many of the things that should be a commonality among all people.' He shook his head. 'What he felt for Kvetka was obsession. He was devoted to an ideal, an illusion conjured in his own mind to ease the emptiness around him. The dream that there could be something better ahead of him and the delusion that he could still claim happiness like other men.'

'You think his sorrow is a pretext?' Soraya looked again at the wizard as Venteslav helped him through the catacombs. To her, it looked like Gajevic had aged ten years since they'd left Kvetka's body behind at the shrine.

'No, his grief is real,' Mahyar said, 'but we can mourn things that aren't real. His sorrow is not just for Kvetka, but the dream he'd woven around her. The scholar and his ideal of the scholar, blended together until there was no distinction between them in his mind.' His hand reached to the spot where the Hammer would have hung around his neck. The fingers fumbled there for a moment before dropping away, belatedly remembering that the symbol was gone. 'There are many who do that. They delude themselves into rejecting what *is* and instead see only what they *want* things to be. It is worse for wizards though. Their art is a thing that seeks to make the unreal into the real. They use magic to transform the world around them to match their own vision. Even those who understand the limitations of their power usually adopt a skewed perception. That anything *is* possible if only the magic is strong enough to make it happen. It is that hubris that makes it so hard for a wizard to truly put faith in the gods. They resist relying upon the divine because they think they can accomplish anything they desire if only they can expand the scope of their own magic.'

The priest's words had a profound impact on Soraya. She saw Gajevic from a different angle now. 'When he tried to commune with the remnant of the green-folk,' Soraya said, 'did he expect danger or did he simply think it was something else he could mould with his magic?' The thought brought another one. 'How certain can we be that the Veiled Oracle brought him back to his senses? We saw in the Hanging Glade that her magic has its own limitations.'

'We must have faith,' Mahyar replied. 'Remember that we are Sigmar's people.'

Soraya nodded her head. She didn't know how she could confess that her faith had its limits. The strength of Sigmar was mighty, but so too was the reach of Nagash. Especially here in Shyish. Trusting too much in the God-King's protection and the certitude of destiny was what had brought Jahangir to ruin.

The group pressed on through the catacombs. Soraya couldn't easily judge how far they'd gone since the shrine, but it felt as though it must've been hours. She despaired of ever seeing an end to the skeletal walls and the translucent worms that squirmed among the bones. Then, with an abruptness that was shocking, the morbid walls gave way to slabs of white marble veined with black: regular walls that had been polished down to a glassy smoothness.

'We are through the catacombs,' the Veiled Oracle announced, sweeping past Soraya and Mahyar to stroke the walls with her gloved hands. 'Here begins the crypt-fortress of Lady Olynder.' She turned around and nodded to Venteslav. 'This is the way to the tombs beneath her mausoleum. To the hidden vaults and forbidden sepulchres where she keeps her treasures.'

'We didn't come here to steal treasure,' Mahyar reminded the mystic. 'We care only about the curse that threatens our people.'

The Veiled Oracle's laugh echoed through the gloom. 'To the Lady of Sorrows, the misery she inflicts upon the living is her treasure. What is more precious to the Mortarch of Grief than the tears of her victims?' She wagged a black-clad finger at Mahyar. 'Make no mistake, the curse she has cast upon your towns is more valuable to her than hoarded gold and precious gems.'

Soraya gave the marble walls a closer look. There was motion there. For an instant she thought it was the grave grubs from the catacombs, for this was movement without substance. Shape without mass. When she peered closer, she saw a face staring back at her. Drawn, gaunt and pale, it was a grisly visage devoid of colour or warmth. She started back, her hand closing about the grip of her sword.

'There's something here!' she gasped. 'A figure behind the wall!'

'Not behind, but within,' the Veiled Oracle corrected her. She nodded. 'Victims of Lady Olynder. Though their bodies have long collapsed into dust, their spirits remain, imprisoned in these vaults until the grim day when Great Nagash summons all the dead to rise for the final conquest.' She tapped her finger against the marble. 'There is nothing to fear from such as these. They are naught but echoes, reflections lost in the night. They neither see nor hear us.'

'The undead have other senses by which they hunt the living,' Mahyar said.

'Just so,' the mystic replied. 'But these spirits can do no more than sense. They have no freedom to act. It is not these wretches you must fear, but the things which are their gaolers – the spirits so foul and wicked that they were chosen to serve the Lady of Sorrows.'

Soraya managed to look away from the spectre trying to claw its way out from inside the wall. 'Are there many such gaolers?' she asked, unable to quite restrain her dread.

'Lady Olynder has had a very long time to gather her forces,' the Veiled Oracle said. 'She has drawn gheists and wraiths from across Shyish and even from realms beyond to serve her. You must be swift and you must be wary. Each moment spent within these vaults is to tempt fate.'

'What do you mean?' Venteslav led Gajevic closer to the mystic.

'Despite the ghouls and the grave grubs and even these wretched spirits locked within the walls, you have not drawn the Mortarch's notice,' the Veiled Oracle said. 'While that holds true, you still have a chance to break the curse laid upon your people.'

Soraya shivered at the unspoken menace in the Veiled Oracle's declaration. 'If we should draw her notice? If the Lady of Sorrows should learn we are here?'

The Veiled Oracle bowed her head and clasped her fingers together. 'All you have endured would be for naught. Your quest would end in disaster and death. Doom would still cast its shadow over your people.'

'We will not fail,' Mahyar vowed. 'By Sigmar, we will not fail.'

Soraya was emboldened by the conviction in the priest's voice. She just wished she could share his sense of surety.

Venteslav tried to keep from looking at the marble walls as the Veiled Oracle led them deeper into the vaults. It was too much for him to resist, however, and he found his eyes continually straying to stare at the spectral figures that peered from within the polished stone. Their gaze was empty and unfocused. As the mystic had said, the spirits couldn't see them, but it was clear they had some nebulous sense that there were living bodies nearby.

The captain kept the fingers holding his torch crossed, trying to hold such luck as might have seeped its way down into such a blighted place. Venteslav was also reminded of the custom that whistling fended away ghosts, but his lips were too dry to put that to the test.

The spirits within the walls were both piteous and horrible, provoking melancholy paired with disgust when Venteslav looked at them. He saw long-dead mothers holding long-dead infants, their arms outstretched, imploring for help he was powerless to give. He watched soldiers brandishing phantom swords in salute, but always with a suggestion of mockery in the gesture. There were depraved spectres that clawed at the walls, eager to strike at the living they could sense but not see. There were lascivious wraiths, gesticulating wildly as though to tempt others to join them in their ghastly existence.

Venteslav could almost envy Gajevic. The wizard was immune to the apparitions around them. Bound by his melancholy, he gave them only the most diffident regard. Even that detached awareness was a good sign. Venteslav had feared his mind had collapsed back into dazed oblivion.

'We will succeed,' Venteslav assured the wizard, still keeping one hand on Gajevic's shoulder so he didn't wander away. 'We'll succeed and save Eastdale from the Lady of Sorrows.' He turned from the wall when a particularly pathetic spirit became too distinct for his comfort. 'We'll save everyone from the Mortarch. Everything will be worth it then. Everything we've sacrificed and lost will be worth it.'

It wasn't clear that his words made any impact on Gajevic. Venteslav thought nothing could stir the wizard from his walking stupor. Then, with a suddenness that caught him completely by surprise, Gajevic threw off his hand and jolted forwards a few steps without the captain's guidance.

'They're coming,' Gajevic hissed, an intense expression on his face. He waved his hands in a series of arcane passes. 'We are discovered and they're coming!'

'What's wrong?' Soraya called out, turning back towards the two Reclaimed. Her gaze narrowed as she looked at Gajevic. 'What's wrong?' she asked again, but this time there was a sharp edge to the question.

Before Venteslav could give her an answer or see to Gajevic, the temperature around them dropped to an icy chill. He saw his breath turn to frost and felt the hairs prickle along the back of his neck. There was a palpable tension in the atmosphere and again the wizard's voice rang out. 'They're coming.'

Across the marble walls, dark shapes now sped forwards, swelling in size as they boiled up from the spectral prison's depths. The apparitions that had previously haunted the survivors now vanished, whisked away in the blink of an eye. In their stead came figures draped in black, grisly images that grew larger and more distinct as they surged towards the polished marble surface. Venteslav felt disgust when he saw the fleshless skulls protruding from beneath black cowls. They were inhuman in their contours, long and narrow with chisel-like fangs. These weren't the wraiths of even the most debased human form, but rather the slinking spectres of ratkin.

'They're coming.' The words echoed through the vault. It took Venteslav a moment to understand they'd issued from his own mouth. He whipped his sword free and clenched it in a shaking hand as the rat-like phantoms drew to what he knew must be the barrier that divided the physical world from the ghostly prison within the walls. The spectres reached that barrier, but unlike the wretched spirits they guarded, it did not restrain them. Out from the polished marble surface the wraiths emerged, rusty glaives clenched in their skeletal paws.

'No!' The defiant shout sprang from Gajevic. The wizard stretched forth his hand and a sphere of greenish flame billowed away from his palm. The fire struck the wall beside him just as two of the rat-wraiths erupted from its surface. The apparitions exploded in a swirl of smoke and shadows, shrill wails scratching across the passageway.

Venteslav was emboldened by the wizard's display. He rounded upon the spectres spilling from the wall closest to him. His sword licked out, shearing through one of the wraiths, working no harm upon it until the blade connected with the glaive it bore. Unlike the phantom, the weapon possessed at least a pretence of physicality. The sword chopped through its haft and sent the spirit flying back into the wall. The detached pieces of the glaive rattled against the floor as the rat-skulled thing filtered back through the polished surface.

A second wraith lunged at Venteslav. He saw the glaive strike sparks as it raked down against the floor. The captain spun around, lashing out at the wraith. Again his attack met no resistance until the blade cracked against the assumed solidity of the glaive. His steel bit down. Twisting around still further, he was able to push his adversary back against the wall. As with its companion, the spectre met no resistance against the polished surface and Venteslav found himself forcing it through the marble itself.

'We're surrounded!' Soraya cried out.

From the corner of his eye, Venteslav could see her trying to stave off more of the spectres as they oozed out from the walls. Nearby he could see the Veiled Oracle making arcane gestures with her hands and hurling spheres of grey mist into the wraiths, dispersing them back into the marble. For each that she banished, three more spilled out and flew at her with gnashing fangs and gleaming blades.

'There are too many,' the Veiled Oracle declared. Venteslav could hear the strain in her voice. For the first time he detected a note of weakness behind her words. Gajevic and Soraya too were sorely pressed, surrounded by the inhuman spectres. Yet when he looked towards Mahyar, he found that the warrior priest was unchallenged. The phantoms shunned him. When he moved towards them, they recoiled, whipping away before his heavy blade could come cleaving through their vaporous essence.

Venteslav had only a moment to notice the peculiarity before he was again fighting for his life. Converged upon from either side, he struggled to fend off a pair of the wraiths as they boiled out from the walls. The spectres bared their sharp fangs as they brought their glaives slashing around, the wicked blades whispering only inches from him as he twisted away. He countered with a slash that licked through the arm of one apparition and severed the butt from its weapon. The spirit pulled back as it readjusted its grip and glared at him from the vacant hollows of its skull. While he was distracted, the other foe whipped its blade around, missing his neck by a matter of inches. Venteslav dived away, rolling across the floor in an effort to put both enemies at his front. His attempt only brought a third rushing at him from his right flank.

The situation seemed hopeless to Venteslav, but then a pulse of green flames rippled through the corridor. He felt an eerie sensation crackle through his flesh as the wave hit him, as though the circulation had been numbed throughout his body for a few heartbeats. Against the wraiths, however, the effect of the arcane energy was much more profound. The apparitions seemed like leaves caught in a roaring fire. Their shadowy essence curled in upon itself, at the same time cracking away in charred flakes. The magical fire spared neither wraith nor glaive, but immolated them all with the same rapacious ardour. The destruction spilled onwards, crashing against the walls themselves. Where there had been a bright sheen there was now only a scorched crust from which no spectral reflection now loomed.

'It... is... done...' Gajevic muttered the words. The wizard swayed and fell to his knees, an aura of arcane power shining around his entire body. The annihilating flame had been his conjuration and the effort had taken its grim toll. Weak as he was, he made a warning motion with his hand when Venteslav would have helped him. 'No... I must recover... on my own...'

Venteslav turned away to look at the rest of their diminished group. They'd suffered no more losses, but both Soraya and the Veiled Oracle looked exhausted by the vicious fray. Only Mahyar seemed hale, reinforcing the impression that had struck Venteslav during the fight. The wraiths had been avoiding the warrior priest.

Pushing that thought to the back of his mind, Venteslav walked to where he'd dropped his torch during the fighting. He raised it from the ground and approached the others. 'Is everyone all right?'

'I was unprepared for such ferocity,' the Veiled Oracle admitted, shaking her head. 'I did not expect your presence to provoke such a retaliation so soon.'

'If you had been prepared?' Venteslav posed the question.

'Things might have been less perilous,' the mystic said. 'There are wards I could have cast upon each of us that would have spared us the worst of their attentions. Such magic is not easily invoked, however, and is of limited duration.'

Venteslav turned again to Mahyar. The suspicion lurking in his mind was now taking definite shape. 'What about you, priest?'

'I suffered no hurt in the fighting,' Mahyar said. He shook his head and told Venteslav something he already knew. 'The wraiths avoided coming close to me. I had to bring battle to them.'

'You were more fortunate than the rest of us,' Soraya stated while tending a cut that ran down the length of her leg. 'We had enemies enough to spare.'

'How do you account for that?' Venteslav pressed, his eyes narrowing.

Mahyar reached to his neck and the Hammer icon which was no longer there. 'It can only be the grace of Sigmar. They must have sensed the God-King's blessing flowing through me and were repulsed by its power. There can be no other explanation why the rest of you were sorely beset while they fled before me.'

Venteslav could think of another reason, but it wasn't one he cared to put into words. At least not yet. 'Since you're the least hurt among us, I need you to take the lead.'

'Which way do we go? Ahead or back?' Gajevic asked.

'If the Lady of Sorrows knows we're here, what chance do we have of accomplishing anything?' Soraya wondered. 'Surely she'll seek to stop us.'

'It may be that she's as yet still unaware of you,' the Veiled Oracle offered. 'The spirits that attacked were of a lowly nature. Gaolers set to a specific task. Warning their mistress about intruders may be beyond their capacity.' She nodded. 'Yes, the undead do not enjoy the same independence of action afforded to the living.'

'Can we afford to proceed on such a theory without knowing for certain?' Mahyar asked. 'We might be overwhelmed by Lady Olynder's forces...'

'We could just as easily be overwhelmed trying to retreat as advance,' Venteslav interjected. With suspicion now gnawing at him, he felt compelled to reject any suggestion the priest made. 'If we are fated to be dragged down by the nighthaunts, I would prefer it happen while trying to achieve something rather than escape. That way, at least, we would be striving to help our people when we met our doom.'

The Veiled Oracle took up Venteslav's words. 'The crypt I showed you in my citadel is not far now. Certainly nearer than the cave above the Hanging Glade. I agree with Venteslav. It is better to try. Even if you made good your escape, you should never claim such an opportunity again.'

'It is decided,' Venteslav said. 'Mahyar, lead the way.' He turned to the Veiled Oracle and bowed. 'If you would guide his steps with your wisdom.' The mystic nodded in reply and fell into step behind the priest as he started down the passageway. Soraya made to join her, but Venteslav held her back, letting Gajevic draw ahead. They waited a moment so the others would be out of earshot.

'Be mindful of the priest,' Venteslav whispered. 'Keep a close eye on him and be ready.'

Soraya had a stunned look on her face when she heard his words. 'Mahyar?'

'When we were fighting, the wraiths avoided him,' Venteslav explained. 'He says it is because they sensed Sigmar's power. I think it's because they were commanded not to harm him.'

'Why?' Soraya's voice was incredulous.

'The Veiled Oracle warned me in her citadel that she sensed a traitor among us,' Venteslav explained. 'I had believed it was Zorgrath… or maybe Omid. Now I wonder if neither was the wolf in the fold.'

'And you suspect Mahyar?' Soraya retorted. 'A priest of Sigmar?' She nodded at Gajevic's back as the wizard preceded them down the corridor. 'Your attention should be on him,' she said. 'Ever since the Dreadwood he's changed. There's a jade light that shines from his eyes and a green cast to the magic he evokes.' She hesitated, trying to put her suspicion into words. 'He isn't Gajevic any more. Not completely. There's something else, something that's infected him. Something inhuman.'

Venteslav shook his head. 'Mahyar makes more sense,' he stated. 'He isn't the pious holy man he pretends to be. He let Ratimir die in the citadel's traps rather than confess his own sins. It may be that he'd allow all of us to die if it meant preserving his own life.'

'I don't accept that,' Soraya replied. 'You'd be better turning your doubts towards Gajevic. Or do you consider him above suspicion merely because he's Reclaimed rather than an Azyrite?'

'Even if he's been *contaminated* as you suggest, any influence the green-folk or their spirits have wouldn't make him a friend to the undead,' Venteslav pointed out.

'Perhaps not,' Soraya conceded, 'but would *we* be any less an enemy to the green-folk? It was the refugees of Belvegrod who destroyed Shiverbloom.'

Venteslav paused, giving her words careful thought. 'Keep watching Gajevic,' he said. 'I will watch after Mahyar. Pray neither of us is right to suspect them, but stand ready to act if either proves to be a traitor.'

There was a brooding intensity about the darkened vaults as Mahyar marched ever deeper into the deathly gloom. His footfalls sounded as loud as kettle drums in the watchful silence. Though they'd left the region scorched by Gajevic's magic and the marble walls again displayed their polished sheen, no phantoms rose up to stare at him from inside the reflections. All was sombre and quiet. Dead and desolate. Almost he could have wished for the ghastly attentions of the doomed spirits. Anything to distract himself from the troubled thoughts swirling through his brain.

Mahyar could sense the animosity and suspicion with which Venteslav now regarded him. Though he had stopped short of levelling a direct accusation, he felt it just the same. His mind turned back to Zorgrath and the ruthlessness with which their captain had dispatched the cryptborn when he was believed to be a traitor. Perhaps there were similar ideas now running through Venteslav's mind. It might be necessary to strike first before the Reclaimed's superstitious paranoia won out.

'Sigmar grant me strength,' Mahyar prayed. He repented the flicker of doubt that beset him, that he could dare to wonder if his words could reach the God-King from this blighted place. Faith was an easy thing to proclaim from the pulpits of Westreach, but it was in forsaken places such as this where it was truly put to the test. The test he'd failed before, but which he was determined to never fail again. Without faith, he was nothing.

'To the left,' the Veiled Oracle instructed him. She waved her gloved hand in the indicated direction.

The corridor into which he turned was different from the one he left behind. Mahyar could see massive metal doors set into the walls, each portal etched with letters in a language unknown to him. They were spaced at regular intervals a dozen feet or so apart. As he reached one door, the light from his torch reached just far enough to show the dull gleam of the next. At intervals, reposing within little niches spaced between the doors, stone urns came into view. Like the doors, they too bore strange letters of an unknown script.

'Crypts for bodies, urns for ashes,' Mahyar muttered to himself as he continued down the silent hall. For a time he tried to count how many doors and niches he passed, but he soon abandoned the effort as the totals began to soar into the dozens. Sometimes the pattern was disrupted by a cadaverous statue, a leering bas-relief of Nagash cut into the marble wall. More sparingly there were intersections where another hall connected to the passageway. Mahyar hesitated at each juncture, but no call for a change of direction came to him. If he lingered too long, the Veiled Oracle simply waved him onwards with a flutter of her gloved hand.

For a time he could hear the voices of Venteslav and Soraya whispering to one another. He couldn't catch the flow of their conversation, but simply the sound of human voices became a source of comfort. A reminder that not everything around him was dead and desolate. Eventually their discussion fell away, smothered by the morbid atmosphere, leaving the echo of their footfalls and the occasional prayer Mahyar dared to whisper the only sounds.

'Follow the turn to the right,' the Veiled Oracle instructed him. Mahyar hadn't gone far this time before more directions came. They'd entered some new region of the vaults, an area not characterised by long stretches of wide halls, but short, sharp passageways that wound amongst each other, shaping themselves into a funereal labyrinth. Here the doors were more frequent, the urns and statues more sparse in their distribution. As the Veiled Oracle's directions came more frequently, Mahyar realised he would never be able to retrace his steps.

Finally, when the priest began to think there should never be an end to the mortuary maze, a massive bronze door loomed out of the darkness, throwing back at him the glow of his torch.

'Here,' the Veiled Oracle said. She turned back and gestured to Venteslav. 'This is the place you saw in my pool. This is where the curse laid upon your towns is entombed.'

The words had an electric effect on the weary band. Almost as one they approached the huge door. Soraya started to reach towards it, but Mahyar snatched her hand away before her fingers could touch the bronze. 'It may be trapped,' he cautioned her. He turned to regard Venteslav. 'If the maledictions she's laid on others are so precious to her, then it is certain Lady Olynder hasn't left this place unguarded.'

Venteslav's eyes roved across the panels, trying to find any hint of hidden mechanisms. Finally, he turned back to the Veiled Oracle. 'Did you see any traps when you looked into your pool?'

'I did not see any, but that does not mean they are not there,' the mystic answered. 'Never when I have looked upon this place did I see anything but phantoms prowling through these crypts. A barrier that would not thwart a wraith may be impassable to mortal flesh. Such can also be said of traps that do not recognise the whisper of an apparition but which are deadly to anything alive.'

'Allow me to try,' Mahyar said. He eased Soraya away from the door and motioned Venteslav back. To his annoyance, he found that Gajevic refused to withdraw.

'Your valour is commendable,' Gajevic said, 'but it is craft which is needed here.' He nodded, more to himself than any of his companions. 'Yes, there are spells that will thwart any mechanism or minor enchantment set to guard this door.' His expression faltered when he met Mahyar's stony gaze, turning from confidence to appeal. 'Please, let me try.'

'Magic might alert the Lady of Sorrows,' Mahyar cautioned, glancing to Venteslav.

'So too would disturbing any wards laid upon this door,' the wizard responded.

'Step away,' Venteslav ordered Mahyar. 'Let Gajevic do what he can.'

Mahyar moved away from the door and joined the others as they withdrew to the nearest corner and watched Gajevic work his magic. The wizard's body began to exude a green light, a glow that emerged from his eyes until it created an aura around his entire figure. He laid his hands against the bronze door, a shudder quaking through him as he made contact with it. Then the fiery light spread out, spilling away from his body to flare out across the door. For several heartbeats the door lost its solidity, becoming as phantasmal as any of the nighthaunts, burning with a green light. Then, as quickly as it had been evoked, the jade glow was gone. Now the shudder was that of the great door. With a grinding groan it shifted inwards, drawn back upon its ancient hinges.

Gajevic turned. Though his face was dripping with sweat, there was a flicker of triumph in his countenance. He gestured to the open door. 'The way is cleared.'

Mahyar was the first to enter the chamber. It was the same crypt they had seen reflected in the Veiled Oracle's pool, a morbid vault lined with stone sarcophagi. Though the course to find their way here through the catacombs had been a meandering confusion of corridors and passageways, he had no problem detecting the sepulchre revealed to them in the citadel. Tightening his grip upon the brutish sword he carried, Mahyar boldly strode to the sarcophagus.

'Here,' he bellowed in triumph. 'Glory to Sigmar, this is where the curse is laid!' Mahyar studied the tomb, looking for the best angle from which to pry it open and expose the secret within. The secret that would deliver the Twinned Towns from the malice of Lady Olynder.

CHAPTER FOURTEEN

'This is where the doom laid against your people is preserved,' the Veiled Oracle echoed Mahyar's words. Her black-clad finger pointed accusingly at the sarcophagus. 'Break that tomb and expose the magic of Lady Olynder.'

Mahyar didn't need to be told twice. Laying down the orruk choppa, he took the knife from his belt and tried to work its point under the lid to prise it upwards. Try as he might, he couldn't manage to wedge the blade into the gap. Frustrated, he circled to the other side to try a new angle. Again, he was thwarted in his effort. 'Bring the light closer,' he told Soraya.

Better illumination did nothing to help his labour. The knife simply refused to gain purchase, though Mahyar could see no reason for it. When he leaned down to inspect the lid there was a visible division between it and the body of the sarcophagus.

'Let me help,' Venteslav offered. He handed his torch to Gajevic and positioned himself on the side opposite Mahyar. His knife had as little success finding purchase as the priest's. The point simply refused to slide into the thin crack.

'There's witchery in this,' Mahyar said. He put his knife back under his belt.

Soraya handed her torch to Mahyar and crouched to the floor. The priest was puzzled as he watched her tug off her left boot. She reached into it and pulled out an old copper coin. It was then he recalled the superstition among the Reclaimed that the guardians of the underworlds had to be bribed to allow a spirit past them. Many Eastdalers persisted in the custom of carrying a coin hidden in their boot lest they die far from home without anything else to present to Nagash's sentinels, but Mahyar was shocked to see the custom followed by an Azyrite.

The soldier leaned over the sarcophagus and wedged her coin into the narrow crack. 'Now try,' she said.

Again, the knife refused to find purchase under the lid. It slipped against the stone, defying any effort Mahyar could make. Venteslav came around to the side of the sarcophagus, but he too was unable to work the blade into the gap, despite the evidence of Soraya's coin that it was possible.

'It is magic,' Gajevic declared. 'Old spells that watch over this tomb.' The wizard motioned to Venteslav and returned the captain's torch. 'For any spell, there's always a counterspell,' he said, more to himself than his companions. 'If one but has the wit and the luck to unravel it, any enchantment may be broken.'

Mahyar frowned at Gajevic's words. It was in keeping with the character of wizards that they would think of their own skills rather than asking for the aid of Sigmar. He kept his thoughts to himself, however, for he saw the flicker of hope Gajevic's statement brought to Soraya and Venteslav. Crushing a forlorn hope only provoked anger and resentment. Some illusions had to be shattered on their own.

Gajevic walked to the head of the sarcophagus. His hands wove in mystical patterns over the lid, describing a set of interlaced pentacles as they moved. 'Keep a careful watch,' the wizard advised them. 'I don't know how strong the enchantment laid upon this tomb is. It might demand great concentration and much power to break the wards. Such an aetheric focus, in a place such as this, might be *noticed*. Be on your guard.'

His warning given, Gajevic resumed his conjuring. Mahyar was unsettled to see a green light bristling about the man's hands, a thin sheen of illumination that caused his fingers to leave a faint glow behind them. Now the interlaced pentacles were not simply suggested by his movements. An after-image lingered behind, like the silhouette of a flame the instant after a candle is blown out. Faster and faster Gajevic's hands wove their mystical pattern above the sarcophagus, and by his gestures the after-image became more substantial. No longer did it flicker or fade from view between each pass. It hung in the air like a physical thing. Then, slowly, it began to sink down towards the lid. Mahyar couldn't decide if the wizard's hands directed that descent or were drawn down after it, caught like boats in a whirlpool.

Lower and lower the arcane sigil and the hands weaving it were drawn. The soft chant that had grown so gradually from the wizard's lips that it was impossible for Mahyar to say when it had started, now rose to a violent shout. Abruptly Gajevic's outspread fingers curled into fists. He drove them down through the double pentacle and slammed them against the sarcophagus. The pentacle exploded, sending a burst of magical energy surging through the tomb in a silent detonation. Mahyar could feel his skin crawl as the arcane reverberation swept through him.

Gajevic staggered back, sweat streaming down his face. His eyes smouldered with a jade light that only gradually diminished. 'Try... now...' he stammered, each word forced up by an effort of sheer will.

Mahyar took his knife and again tried to work its point into the gap. Again, the blade slipped away, repulsed by what could best be described as a magnetic force. Venteslav tried the other side of the sarcophagus, but his attempt to prise it open was likewise thwarted.

'Do you think you could try a stronger spell?' Soraya asked Gajevic.

The wizard shook his head. 'It would be certain to be noticed,' he said. He waved his hand at the lid. 'Something may have already noticed.'

'Then we've no time for subtlety,' Mahyar declared. He took up the orruk choppa from the floor. Lifting the cumbersome weapon in both hands, he brought it smashing down onto the lid.

The impact sent Mahyar staggering back, his arms quaking from the shudder that pulsed through them. The choppa's edge was dulled, a fragment of it glancing off the ceiling as it spun away from the weapon. The metallic clang of the impact continued to echo through the vault.

Upon the sarcophagus, not so much as a scratch showed.

'Jahangir.' Soraya spoke her former commander's name with reverence. A bitter laugh rolled through her as she spoke. 'He was the one named in the vision. The one fated to "break the curse". Or perhaps simply break into the place where the curse is kept.'

'All this way.' Venteslav shook his head. 'All this way… and for nothing.'

Mahyar slammed his fist against the defiant lid. 'By Sigmar, there has to be a way! We did not come so far, endure so much, only for it to come to nothing!'

Venteslav swung around and faced the Veiled Oracle. 'Your magic. Can your magic open it?'

Mahyar was unsettled by the desperation he heard in the captain's voice. Through all their journey, it had been Venteslav who had kept them going. Now even he was surrendering himself to despair.

Mahyar was even more unsettled by the Veiled Oracle's reply. 'In time, perhaps, you might find a magic to unlock that which protects this place.' She shook her head. 'But there is no time. I can sense darkness closing in all around. You've drawn the notice of more than simple guardians now. The crypt-fortress is aware of your presence... and your purpose.'

The air in the vault grew colder, a chill more pronounced than even Gajevic's conjuring produced. Mahyar could feel the supernatural aura that tainted the air, seeping through his skin to curdle his blood. There was no need to warn the others. All of them felt it and all of them knew of what it was the harbinger.

The shadows in the tomb grew darker, thickening into stretches of blackness that oozed towards the torchlight. Within them were faint suggestions of shape and form, the outlines of shoulders and heads, bony hands and skeletal arms. Mahyar invoked the name of Sigmar and reached once more for the symbol he'd worn. He felt a swelling of psychic mockery cackle inside his head. The God-King's symbol was lost, vanished in the Barrowbogs. Mahyar's god wouldn't help him now. Nothing would.

A surge of utter despair sapped Mahyar's strength. He slumped to his knees, his mind reeling with hopelessness. Who was he to think he could bear Sigmar's name into the crypt-fortress of a Mortarch? What presumption for a faithless man like himself to dare pit his convictions against the Lady of Sorrows! He was nothing and less than nothing, a priest who deluded himself into believing his god would forgive the unforgivable. Every breath he drew was an insult. Only in death could he atone for his lack of faith.

Mahyar's hand inched the choppa towards his own neck. One quick jerk of the brutish blade and he could open his veins. He could end the pain and horror. The dead were beyond all suffering when they entered the underworlds.

'Bollocks,' Mahyar growled. He shook free from the despair that sought to crush him down, recognised the thoughts storming his mind as things that were not his own. 'I've seen your victims locked away inside the walls,' he challenged the growing shadows. 'They're certainly dead and certainly not beyond suffering!' He lurched back onto his feet and laid his palm against his chest. 'I don't need a pendant of gold to carry the God-King's faith and I don't need a fiend that hides in darkness to remind me that I must atone for my past weaknesses.'

Mahyar looked aside at his companions. Soraya, Venteslav and Gajevic had been beaten down to their knees, crushed by what he imagined had to be a similar psychic attack. He could feel their eyes on him and the faint ember of hope they clung to. Hope they'd invested in the warrior priest.

'The way one chooses to die can bring more honour in the final reckoning than how one has lived,' Mahyar told his companions. He turned and waved his chipped blade at the gathering shadows. 'The final measure of life is not reckoned until the last breath has been spent.'

A crackle of bitter laughter hissed through the vault. The shadowy mass of spectres rolled away like a tide of darkness. In their midst there now loomed a figure clad in white, her face hidden beneath the skein of a long veil. None who'd been there when Jahangir's expedition was brought to destruction could forget that sight. They gazed upon the Mortarch of Grief herself. Lady Olynder.

'She can only kill us,' Mahyar growled through clenched teeth as he forced himself to gaze upon the ghastly apparition. 'The worthiness of our souls is for Sigmar to judge! The valour of our lives is for the God-King to decree!'

The priest's words were valiant. Defiant. His companions were inspired by his bravery. They struggled to their feet and made ready to meet the nighthaunts and their spectral mistress.

'You will have to fight us,' Mahyar declared. 'We will not cower in terror. We will not plead for mercy. We are ready to die if such is the will of Sigmar!'

Mahyar could feel the withering glower of Lady Olynder's veiled eyes fixed upon him. Slowly the Mortarch gestured with her pallid hand, the bony fingers curling back, beckoning to something in the darkness. Out from among the shadows an apparition swept into view. At first it was nothing more than a shrouded figure, a skeletal shape of death and decay. As it drew closer to the Lady of Sorrows, it took on greater distinction. The shroud dissipated into armour and uniform; the bones evaporated and became flesh. Eyes grew into the empty sockets. Though still translucent and spectral, what stood beside Lady Olynder was more than a faceless wraith. It was the echo of a man... a man all the survivors recognised.

'Jahangir!' Mahyar gasped, feeling as though icy fingers closed around his heart to crush the last ember of hope that burned there.

Jahangir, the hero chosen by the great and wise of the Twinned Towns to deliver them all from the curse. The champion who had fought bravely above the Sea of Tears, defying to the last the legions of the dead. The leader who had perished for the sake of his people. Now he had arisen, not as one of Sigmar's champions, but as one of Lady Olynder's creatures. Mahyar could sense this was no trick, no illusion woven by the Lady of Sorrows. There was too much for her to savour in revealing to them that their hero was now nothing but another of her eternal slaves.

'You've seen enough to know better, priest.' Lady Olynder's words sliced through the vault like icy knives. 'Here, the will of Sigmar counts for less than the might of Nagash. Perhaps you made a poor choice when you picked which god to serve.'

As the Mortarch spoke, the shadows crept forwards, becoming more distinct as they advanced – a spectral host of tormented souls with only one desire: to torment the living.

Mahyar saw Lady Olynder wave her procession of the damned forward to indulge their vengeful yearning.

Soraya gazed in horror as the ghost of Jahangir advanced towards them. Behind him came the grim procession of nighthaunts, their skeletal visages grinning in silent mockery. Her heart felt like a lump of lead inside her chest, all vestige of hope gone. Jahangir! The leader who she'd followed through the haunted hinterlands of Westreach for so many years! The hero who the Belvegrod lighthouse declared would break the curse laid upon the Twinned Towns. Yet here he was, not a champion fighting against the evil of Lady Olynder, but simply another of her undead slaves.

The sword felt heavy in her hand, a useless weight that could do nothing to oppose the Lady of Sorrows. Every memory of the trials and ordeals she'd endured since leaving the Twinned Towns now resonated with cruel mockery. Of what use was it to oppose the inevitable? Soraya knew there was nothing more that could be done. They'd lost the very moment Lady Olynder attacked them as they crossed the Sea of Tears.

Soraya's sword dipped towards the floor. To fight now was pointless. It was better to accept the inevitable.

A bright flash surged through the vault, a jade light that dazzled Soraya's eyes. Instinctively her fingers tightened about her sword before it could slip from her hand. The shadowy procession of spectres recoiled from the brilliant light, the foremost of the horde transformed into blazing wisps of green fire as their ectoplasm was consumed.

'That was for Kvetka!' Gajevic roared. The wizard's jade eyes burned as he strode towards the ghostly mob. He held his hands out and from each fingertip a new crackle of fire emerged. The flames leapt towards the nighthaunts, searing into their shrouded forms. Wails of anguish rose from the undead as their essence was pierced and they writhed upon the aetheric spears. Smoke billowed from them as their spirits burned.

'You'll pay for what you've done!' Gajevic shouted at Lady Olynder. There was neither grief nor despair in the wizard's tone, only an unbridled fury. The rage of one who has lost everything and stands before the culprit responsible. The jade glow, that eerie legacy from his contact with the spirits of the green-folk, was even more prominent now, colouring his magic with the echoes of Shiverbloom. Orbs of searing flame sped from his hands to immolate clutches of wraiths, consuming the apparitions in searing flashes. He gestured towards the Mortarch herself, hurling at her a lance of fire that crackled through the spectres that surged into its path. The arcane spear exploded against an invisible shell surrounding his enemy, but such was the attack's force that the Mortarch was blown back by the impact, her illusion of invulnerability pierced.

'I'll send you crawling back to your foul master!' The wizard marched towards the reeling Mortarch, his spells evaporating any wraith that got in his way.

Soraya repented her earlier suspicion of Gajevic. By himself he was trying to seize victory from disaster, challenging alone the terrifying Lady of Sorrows. Yet in his wrath he was sparing no thought to his own defence. 'Come back!' Soraya shouted at the wizard. She started forwards, but it was already too late. Disaster was reaching out to claim the vengeful conjurer.

The attack came from a quarter none had anticipated. A lance of ghostly light pierced Gajevic's breast, skewering him from behind. Gajevic screamed as his skin came away in flecks of dust and his hair drifted to the floor like strands of cobweb. The wizard's body withered upon that transfixing spear, his flesh shrivelling until the bones broke through the desiccated skin. The jade glow evaporated from around his hands as it too wilted before the spell. The last ember of animation faded from his eyes and he collapsed to the floor, his brittle bones shattering into fragments.

The wizard's killer stood triumphant. Smouldering bits of black glove drifted away from the Veiled Oracle's outstretched hand.

'Witch! Traitor!' Soraya shouted. She started towards the mystic, but already it was too late. The black veil and gown were now crumbling away. Beneath was a pale figure arrayed in spectral white: the image of Lady Olynder. Treacherous and triumphant.

'Translocation,' Mahyar gasped. He had been rushing towards the betrayer, but now his charge faltered as the full magnitude of the treason was exposed.

Soraya's mind reeled. From the moment they'd entered the citadel they'd travelled with their enemy, an enemy whose magic was great enough to allow her to be in two places simultaneously.

As though reading her thoughts, the apparition that had been the Veiled Oracle turned to Soraya. 'It was a fool's hope from the start,' she mocked. 'A forlorn prayer from a doomed people.'

While she spoke, the phantom diminished in clarity. Wisps of her essence drifted away, drawn back into the greater shape that was the Lady of Sorrows. Laughter rang out as the last of what had called itself the Veiled Oracle was absorbed into Lady Olynder.

'Now you can appreciate the magnitude of your failure,' the Mortarch declared.

A gesture from Lady Olynder set the nighthaunts surging forwards once more. Soraya tightened her hold on the hilt of her sword. If she couldn't stave off the doom that now threatened her then she could at least meet it bravely. As defiantly as Gajevic had before he was betrayed.

'The judgement of Sigmar take you!' Mahyar shouted. The priest rushed ahead of Soraya and plunged into the mass of shrouded phantoms. There was something more than mere metal and flesh that opposed the spectres. The crude weapon burned into the wraiths, searing their undead essence and spattering blobs of their ectoplasm upon the floor.

'For Westreach!' Venteslav yelled before he too gave battle to the undead. The edge of his blade ripped into the creatures trying to circle around Mahyar and flank him from the right. Though they weren't destroyed by the captain's attacks, the wraiths were forced to withdraw while they recovered their spectral shapes.

'For Eastdale!' Soraya added her cry to the din of battle. She closed with the apparitions moving towards Mahyar's left. Like Venteslav, the slashes of her sword dealt the undead no lasting wounds but they were enough to drive the entities back while they struggled to reform.

It was Mahyar who inflicted true hurt upon the nighthaunts. The spectres that were struck by his heavy blade were rent asunder. Divine wrath coursed through him, empowering his assault with a holy energy that was anathema to the undead. As he drove his advance deeper into the midst of their enemies, Soraya began to hope that some miraculous victory was still possible.

Then Mahyar was through the procession of wraiths. Ahead of him was Lady Olynder. Only a dozen feet separated the priest and the Mortarch. He made ready to charge her, to pit his faith in Sigmar against her necromantic power, but just as he started his rush, he faltered. Into his path a lone wraith stepped.

'Jahangir!' Soraya cried. The spirit of the hero had risen to protect the Lady of Sorrows.

Mahyar hesitated, his determination shaken by the sudden appearance of Jahangir before him. Perhaps in another heartbeat he would have recovered from his shock and struck the wraith, but it was an opportunity he would never have. While the priest faltered, the phantom didn't. Jahangir stabbed his ghostly blade through Mahyar's heart.

'No!' Soraya beat back the phantoms around her and rushed to aid Mahyar, though she knew it was already too late. Before she could reach the priest, his lifeless bulk fell free of Jahangir's sword and collapsed to the floor. The wraith that had once been her commander shifted his attention towards her. The expression on his ghostly visage was devoid of emotion, but in his smouldering gaze there was a pitiless envy. The envy of the dead towards the living.

An instant before, Soraya had been rushing to help Mahyar. Now she recoiled from the priest's killer. It demanded a stout heart to stand against the faceless undead. To defy the shade of her former commander was a thing of still greater horror.

'Jahangir! Remember who you are!' she pleaded with the wraith. 'Remember the quest!' She backed away as the spectre came towards her.

'Soraya!' Venteslav shouted as he tried to fend off the nighthaunts around him. 'It's no good! Save yourself!'

Soraya continued to back away and plead with the spirit that had been her former commander. 'Jahangir, think of the people depending on you! The Lady of Sorrows is your enemy – their enemy! Fight her, Jahangir! Fight her!'

Her words only served to provoke the wraith. Jahangir's spectre surged forwards, his sword slashing out. Soraya retreated from his advance. As she did, her leg struck the unyielding edge of a sarcophagus. The impact spun her around just as Jahangir came at her once more.

Soraya raised her blade. Jahangir was upon her now. She could see the sarcophagus beneath him, through the translucent essence of his ethereal form. As he raised his sword to slash at her, she brought her own blade sweeping forwards.

A thunderous reverberation boomed through the vault. Soraya

was staggered by the bright flash. Her blade had passed completely through Jahangir's wraith and struck the sarcophagus below him. The contact caused the lid to shatter, to explode in a burst of energy that sent stony fragments clattering across the vault.

Soraya stared in wonder at the destruction. Her amazement swelled with the realisation that this tomb was the same one they'd tried to open before. The one the prophecy said only Jahangir could open. The one that had burst open when her blade swept through the hero's phantom before striking it!

'Venteslav! The sarcophagus!' Soraya shouted. She started towards the now open tomb, eager to break the curse and save the Twinned Towns.

Before she could see what was inside, Soraya felt a chill rush through her body. She looked down to see a spectral blade thrust through her heart. She turned her head to meet the deathly visage of her killer. Her sword had broken the sarcophagus, but it hadn't vanquished Jahangir. The wraith still had enough power in its fading essence to strike back at the soldier.

As darkness filled Soraya's eyes, her last sight was of Jahangir's face. For just an instant she thought she saw a flicker of regret in that ghostly countenance.

Venteslav heard Soraya's shout of triumph. An instant later came her death scream. He turned in time to see her body crumple to the floor and watch as the shade of Jahangir faded into nothingness. Dread closed in upon him. He was alone now, the only living thing within the crypt-fortress.

Venteslav turned his dread into action, harnessing the fear that roared through his veins. The disaster of his first command, the shame of that memory had taught him how to use his fear. He used it now. Used it to break away from the phantoms that were closing in around him. He dashed across the vault to Soraya's body. A single glance was enough to tell him that she was dead. No living body could be afflicted by such a pallor.

The sarcophagus beside the fallen soldier had been broken open, the rubble of its lid strewn all around it. Venteslav realised with a start that it was the same tomb they'd tried so desperately to open. Now its contents stood exposed. Unless this was but another of the Veiled Oracle's lies, here was entombed the curse laid upon the Twinned Towns by Lady Olynder.

'Yes. There is what you have come so far to seek.' Lady Olynder's voice echoed through the vault.

Venteslav turned about. All around him were the shadowy shapes of nighthaunts. The apparitions made no move to close upon him. Instead they parted to clear a path for the Lady of Sorrows. Her ghastly figure glided past the bodies of Gajevic and Mahyar. The chill of the Mortarch's approach made Venteslav's blood curdle.

'You won't stop me,' he vowed, knowing as he spoke how absurd the assertion was.

A crackle of laughter rippled through the vault, amusement that was like a cruel echo of crushed hopes and shattered dreams. Lady Olynder pointed at Venteslav. 'Did you think I brought you this far only to stop you now? Behold the prize for which you have risked so much. Turn and claim the treasure that will deliver your people.'

A compulsion that was not entirely his own seized Venteslav. Slowly he turned and stared into the open sarcophagus. If ever a body had lain within, time had reduced it to dust. The only thing of any substance that remained was a marble slab. Etched upon the tablet were words, words that were strangely familiar to him.

'Your friends risked everything to find this secret.' Lady Olynder's words were tinged with mockery. 'A secret already known to them.'

Venteslav stared in horror at the words. 'The curse,' he muttered. 'The curse is broken.'

'The curse is broken,' Lady Olynder agreed, 'the curse that has so long hung over your people. The legacy they inherited from Belvegrod of old.'

'The curse is broken,' Venteslav said. He lifted the tablet out from the tomb, eyes locked upon its damning words.

'Not what your wise and learned believed it to be. What you thought a curse upon your towns is in truth a blessing to you,' Lady Olynder mocked. 'Every generation my armies attack you. Almost I am able to overwhelm all, but never can I achieve my victory. Always at the last moment I am thrown back... by the curse. The curse laid against *me*. No matter how great the host set against you, in the final hour I would be thrown back and cheated of my triumph.'

The Mortarch threw back her head and a ghastly peal of laughter echoed through the tomb. 'That was the curse. The curse which is now broken!'

Venteslav dropped to his knees, the marble tablet clutched to his chest. In breaking the curse they had doomed everyone.

The procession of spectres that filled the vault dispersed, fading away into the shadows. Only Lady Olynder remained, savouring Venteslav's despair. 'Now you know the magnitude of sorrow. The grief of a cause that was lost before it was chosen.' She drifted closer to him, the nearness of her presence causing frost to form against his skin.

'For a time you shall bide here with me,' Lady Olynder told him. 'You will be my guest until the hour is right to send you back to your people. They will not understand when you tell them the curse is broken, but perhaps it will provide them with a few pleasant hours before the end.'

The Mortarch pointed at Venteslav. The next moment he felt

cold, skeletal hands gripping his arms. On both sides he found himself held by a hideous apparition, a fleshless manifestation arrayed in a tattered white gown.

'See to my guest,' Lady Olynder ordered the banshees. 'Keep him safe until I decide to send him back to his people.'

As the spectral handmaidens carried him away, Venteslav heard the Mortarch's final, mocking words.

'They will be so happy to see him again.'

EPILOGUE

'The curse is broken.'

The words were uttered by a pale, withered figure lying on a bed. Leather straps bound him to the frame and double locks sealed the chamber door. The chamber itself was hidden behind a bookcase deep within the vastness of the Belvegrod lighthouse. Until today, only a few people had been allowed to know this man was even here. Now a large group representing the leaders of Westreach and Eastdale was gathered in the secret room.

Hierophant Ivor frowned when he heard the words. Despite the attentions of the best healers and wizards in the Twinned Towns, they remained the only words Venteslav had spoken since he was brought back to the Belvegrod lighthouse by a band of Shadoom traders. Perhaps it was fortunate that the man's mind was unhinged, otherwise the Shadoom might have taken him for a slave, but right now Venteslav's condition was anything but fortuitous.

'It *is* Captain Venteslav of the Tombwatch?' Lord Heshmat asked for what felt like the hundredth time since he'd been summoned to the lighthouse.

'There is no question of that,' Ivor answered.

'But he's been gone almost two years now,' Tihomir objected. 'Prayers were said for him along with all the others who were lost in the Sea of Tears when Lady Olynder attacked.'

Ivor scowled at the Eastdaler. 'You can see for yourself that he survived. He has been somewhere these many seasons.'

Heshmat leaned closer, inspecting the man lying strapped to the bed. 'He certainly appears to have undergone a significant ordeal.' He turned back towards Ivor. 'Do you think it's possible? That some of our warriors survived the attack and were able to reach the Veiled Oracle?'

'It is more than possible,' Ivor told the leaders assembled in the chamber. 'Auguries and divinations have been made by both priests and wizards. The gravesands at the edge of Shyish have been studied. There can be no mistaking the signs. The curse *has* been broken.'

'Then everything that has been sacrificed was not in vain,' Bairam stated. He turned his blind eyes to the ceiling. 'Praise be, Mighty Sigmar, we are delivered from the menace of Lady Olynder.'

Venteslav thrashed about on his bed. 'The curse is broken,' he snarled. 'The curse is broken.'

'Praise Sigmar indeed,' Heshmat said. 'It has cost our towns much. We've lost many brave heroes, but their sacrifice will never be forgotten. No longer will we need fear the Lady of Sorrows.'

On his bed, the crazed husk of Venteslav struggled against his bindings. 'The curse is broken,' he raged, but even the wisest had become deaf to his ravings.

ABOUT THE AUTHOR

C L Werner's Black Library credits include the Age of Sigmar novels *Overlords of the Iron Dragon*, *Profit's Ruin*, *The Tainted Heart*, *Beastgrave* and *Cursed City*, the novella *Scion of the Storm* in *Hammers of Sigmar*, and the Warhammer Horror novel *Castle of Blood*. For Warhammer he has written the novels *Deathblade*, *Mathias Thulmann: Witch Hunter*, *Runefang* and *Brunner the Bounty Hunter*, the Thanquol and Boneripper series and Warhammer Chronicles: The Black Plague series. For Warhammer 40,000 he has written the Space Marine Battles novel *The Siege of Castellax*. Currently living in the American south-west, he continues to write stories of mayhem and madness set in the Warhammer worlds.

YOUR
NEXT READ

CURSED CITY
by C L Werner

When a series of vicious murders rock the vampire-ruled city of Ulfenkarn, an unlikely group of heroes – a vampire hunter, a vigilante, a wizard and a soldier – must discover the truth, even as the city's dread ruler takes to the streets and the bloodletting increases.

For these stories and more, go to blacklibrary.com, games-workshop.com, Games Workshop and Warhammer stores, all good book stores or visit one of the thousands of independent retailers worldwide, which can be found at games-workshop.com/storefinder

An extract from
Cursed City
by C L Werner

Though the shutters were barred, and the doors bolted, the Black
Ship was more alive in the long hours of the night than it had
been during the dreary grey day. The tavern was ablaze with the
light of whale-oil lamps and its common room rumbled with the
clamour of a hundred raucous conversations, people huddling
together in the warmth that was absent in the cold streets. Flag-
ons of ale, steins of beer, bottles of pungent vodka and glasses of
dark wine were carried to patrons throughout the building's three
levels, borne upon wide copper trays by the buxom, strong-armed
beer maidens employed by Effrim Karzah, the establishment's
roguish proprietor. Notes of music crawled through the rooms
as a rotund performer worked a hurdy-gurdy and bellowed sala-
cious sea shanties.

A long casketwood bar dominated one side of the common
room. Patrons flocked to the counter, loudly shouting for more
drink. Whalers with salt-encrusted slickers would brush shoulders

with crookbacked lobstermen, their fingers and hands scarred from the claws of their catch. Stokers who worked the immense try pots to render blubber into oil sought to cool their hot work with cold ales. Drovers and stevedores propped their boots on the copper rail that ran along the base of the bar and swapped lies about the day's custom. Among those seeking to retreat from their labours mixed those whose vocation catered to such relaxation. Gamblers and panderers, sellers of wares and seekers of services all ventured to the counter to engage those gathered there.

Only at one spot was the bar not crowded. Towards the back of the common room, for a radius of a dozen feet, there was an open space. Within that space only two people stood. The two men had been there for some time now, yet none of the carousing inmates of the tavern intruded on their privacy. From the guarded looks that sometimes were directed their way, it wasn't courtesy that provoked such distance, but fear.

One was tall with a light complexion and locks of fair hair spilling out from beneath his wide-brimmed hat. His features had a rugged handsomeness about them, with a hawkish nose and piercing blue eyes. A long coat encompassed his figure, but around the waist it was bound by a wide belt from which hung a rakish sword and a big horse pistol. It was not the open display of weapons that so unsettled the occupants of the Black Ship, however. Hanging about the man's neck was a pendant, a little silver talisman cast in a symbol long taboo in Ulfenkarn. The hammer of Sigmar. To openly display veneration of the God-King in the city was to invite swift and terrible destruction. Had night not already fallen, were the doors not already barred, there were many who would have slunk back to their slovenly hovels. As things stood, they tried their best to keep apart from the stranger. When doom came for him, nobody wanted to share in it.

Except perhaps the man who was with him. He was thin with

short black hair and a trim moustache beneath his knife-sharp nose. Though he wore clothes that were rich by the standards of Ulfenkarn, his skin had the grey pallor of those who toiled away in the mushroom plantations beneath the streets. His eyes looked as though they were caught in a perpetual scowl, disdainfully appraising everything and everyone they gazed on. From his haughty demeanour and sinister appearance, there were many in the Black Ship who marked him as an agent of Ulfenkarn's rulers, one who'd been promised the Blood Kiss by his masters. Why a spy for the vampires was sharing a drink with a Sigmarite was a mystery none felt inclined to explore.

Gustaf Voss pushed back the brim of his hat so he could better see the bottles arrayed on the rack behind the bar. 'They've a nice vintage from Carstinia there,' he commented to his companion. 'That is if you don't think it would be too strong for you?'

The other man gave him a stern look. 'That's an old Belvegrodian fable, you know. That *they* don't drink wine.' He frowned at his glass and tapped a finger against its stem. 'I don't like drinking in public. It dulls the senses and you never know what might be watching, waiting to exploit the first hint of weakness. If you're going to have libations, it's better to indulge when you're alone.'

Gustaf cast his eyes at the empty space around them. 'We're as good as alone right now, Vladrik,' he said.

'All it takes is wealth to be popular in places like this,' he replied. 'Though I don't know if there's enough money to make them friendly while you're wearing that.' He gestured to the hammer around Gustaf's neck.

Gustaf took a pull from his beer stein and wiped away the residue of foam from his mouth. 'There was a saying, something along the lines of "Let them hate as long as they also fear." That wisdom has served me well until now.' He gave Vladrik a more serious look. 'If I make myself conspicuous then the man I'm looking for might find me, instead of making me find him.'

'Or you might draw attention from those you don't want to see,' Vladrik cautioned. 'I've told you I'll find Jelsen Darrock for you.'

'It's been two weeks that I've been hearing that,' Gustaf said. 'You haven't given me any results.'

Vladrik swallowed some of his wine and dabbed a mono-grammed handkerchief against his lips. 'Better than anyone, you should know that those who serve the Order of Azyr can be very hard to find when they want to be. I think Darrock has been keeping himself under cover right now. He's been busy. Only two days ago someone broken into Count Vorkov's coffin and put a stake through his heart. Aqshian fyrewood. Very rare. Very dangerous. The kind of thing even a vampire doesn't recover from.'

Vladrik leaned closer and laid his hand on Gustaf's arm.

'That's one thing I'm still unsure of. Did the Order of Azyr send you to Ulfenkarn to help Darrock or to stop him? You've never told me which.'

'No, I didn't,' Gustaf said. 'If you expect an answer, find Darrock for me.'

Gustaf spun around suddenly, one hand dropping to the big horse pistol on his belt. Someone had entered the circle of privacy that surrounded them. A haggard stevedore, the quality of his tunic and the polish of his boots indicating him to be a mark above the labourers who crowded behind him, marched towards the shunned pair. He threw back his head and gave Gustaf a sneering study.

'You make sport of us, do you, outlander?' He gestured at the talisman hanging from Gustaf's neck. 'Even a fool fresh off the boat knows better than to wear that openly. So, if you aren't a fool, you must be an idiot.'

Drink slurred the man's words, but Gustaf wasn't one to allow even a tipsy antagonist to challenge him.

'Where I come from, men are still men. They don't hide their faith and cower in the shadows like vermin. They don't bow and scrape to the monsters that prey on them.'

The stevedore's face turned red. His hands curled into fists at his sides.

'He's got a gun, Loew,' one of the other labourers warned.

Gustaf fixed his steely gaze on Loew. 'I don't need gun or sword to settle accounts with cowards,' he said, moving his hands away from the weapons hanging from his belt. For a moment, the tableau held, the two men glaring into one another's eyes, each ready for his foe to make the first move.

Loud pounding against the Black Ship's door interrupted the brewing fight. Silence descended on the tavern. Most of the patrons turned to look towards the barred entrance while others retreated into the nearest shadow. From outside, an imperious voice demanded entry.

'The Volkshaufen,' Vladrik hissed. He quickly bolted what was left of his wine.

'Maybe,' Gustaf said. It was rare for the watchmen to be abroad at night. Ulfenkarn had other guards who patrolled the city when the sun set... but not the sort to ask admittance.

'Make yourself scarce until we know who it is,' Gustaf told Vladrik. He didn't watch his companion withdraw and climb the back stairs to the Black Ship's upper floor. His attention was fixed on the barred door and whoever was demanding entry.

Perched on a stool near the entrance was a short, scrawny creature with long ears and scabby green skin. The grot looked across the room to where Karzah sat at one of the gambling tables. The Black Ship's proprietor nodded reluctantly. The grot jabbed the hulking brute that stood beside it with a sharp stick. The square-jawed orruk roused itself from its fungus-addled lethargy and drew back the bar on the door. Karzah preferred to use the greenskins as his establishment's first line of defence because their blood wasn't appetising to the things that prowled the city.

Instead of the Volkshaufen, it was a trio of men in finely cut sealskin coats who sauntered past the orruk. Gustaf noticed the mirror discreetly placed on the ceiling above the door. All three men were reflected in it, but that meant nothing. If one of them was a vampire and was aware of the mirror's presence, he could project an image into the glass and thereby conceal his nature.

Of course, in Ulfenkarn, a vampire had little reason to hide what he was. At least from people who weren't Jelsen Darrock. Or Gustaf Voss.

'Looks like it's already too late to teach you anything,' Loew told Gustaf, a trace of regret in his voice. 'May the soil rest easy on your grave.'